UNTETHERED:
A CAREGIVER'S TALE

∞

a novel
by Phyllis Peters

This story is a work of fiction. Any resemblance to real life is purely intentional; actual events, names, places, or representations of persons living or non, however, are not included.

"Star Baby" lyrics gratefully used by permission.

Star Baby
Words and Music by Burton Cummings
Copyright (c) 1974 Shillelagh Music (SOCAN/BMI)
Administered by Bug Music, Inc., a BMG Chrysalis company
International Copyright Secured All Rights Reserved
Reprinted by Permission of Hal Leonard Corporation

For Edmund W. Peters, who passed a torch

— and —

For Michael H. Sommer, who insisted that it burns yet.

CHAPTERS

Part One | *Page 1*

CHAPTERS

Part Two | *Page 103*

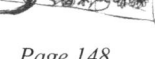

CHAPTERS

Part Two | *Cont'd.*

CHAPTERS

UNTETHERED:
A CAREGIVER'S TALE

PART ONE

Mel came out of the bathroom with one of those little plastic sticks.

"So? So?" I asked.

She held it in the air, her long, graceful fingers extended as if ready to drop it.

"Negative," she barely said.

She approached the kitchen where I was standing. As she released the stick into the trash can, I recalled the "f" word, "fecund." Originally, it was Marla's word. Marla—perky, fecund, ex. She used to say the f-word with gusto. I'd always thought there was too much of the animal kingdom in it, but she would say it when imagining that entire brood of kids she craved. Ours hardly constituted a brood—we'd managed just one before the long march of busy life took over. Then one day the march halted in front of my colleague, Mel. That inspired a long, busy divorce.

Remembering the Marla-word made me want to divert Mel's attention away from our negative pregnancy test to comfort her. I put my arms around her.

"You know, honey," I said as I kissed her, "everyone thinks it's a hoot that all the women in your family have men's names." I'd recently shown off her list of baby names, and mentioning it usually distracted her. My wife comes from a large, close-knit, French family that likes recycling its names for tradition's sake, and the list was rife with masculinity.

"Did you tell zem zat 'Nick' is my sister's name,'Nicole'?" she asked.

"I told them that 'Mel' is short for 'Melanie.'"

"Did you say zat 'Jo,' without 'e,' is French?" she asked.

I hadn't. Our plan was to name our first child after her great-grandmother. A male child would be "Joseph," and a female would sport Great Grandma's French name. They've dubbed Mel's great-grandmother "Jo" because her real French name starts with a "J" and is hard to pronounce, but what French isn't hard to pronounce? I wanted to stick with something simple when basing our kid's name on something foreign. I read once that the name of the pop group ABBA was an acronym made up of the first letters of the singers' names. I liked that about ABBA, but that was the only thing I liked about them. Mel wiggled out of my arms and walked over to the counter.

"Great *Grand-mère* will help with everything," she added as she spooned her dark roast into the coffee maker. It was such a casual remark—the idea of having Jo move in to help with a baby not yet conceived. It made our failure to conjoin seem like a tiny misstep and not some unmanly and possibly irreversible affliction I didn't want to know about. The word "motility" kept echoing in my mind. So did the thought of my next birthday: The Big FIVE-O.

Mel filled the coffee pot with water for her afternoon cup and flipped the little switch. I decided to join her. I had missed lunch, so I hoped to prepare a quick salt bagel with cream cheese to go with it, but as I opened the refrigerator door, my phone rang. I closed the fridge and answered it. There was a woman's voice on the other end.

"Mr. Conklin?"

"Yes?" I said. The aroma of brewing French roast filled our kitchen. I couldn't concentrate.

"I'm Officer Vargas," she clarified.

"Yes?" I repeated. I had to reflect, quickly. The IRS doesn't call their people "officers," do they?

"Mr. Conklin, we picked up your father in an incident this afternoon and he's named you as the person able to provide transportation home. Are you able to come down and get him?"

I didn't answer her at first. Taking coffee mugs out of the cabinet for me and Mel seemed a more real task. I set them on the counter, realizing slowly that I was not talking to the IRS. Mel couldn't hear Officer Vargas's side of the conversation, so she blinked and cocked her head. Behind her, the clock on the stove said it was 2 o'clock in the afternoon—a Tuesday afternoon, an early autumn one. We had both taken the day off from our hectic jobs at the hospital to relax and see the beauty. I was just beginning to see, and as that song from my youth says, I was now on my way. To the police. To spring my 85-year-old dad.

Writing down and naming my father's episodes here helps me keep them straight. I call them "episodes" because that's how it's done on TV: "Episode #1," "Episode #2," etc., and that seems to work. TV episodes are usually titled with funny and pertinent names, and they have those short paragraphs that appear on-screen so you can read about the story before watching. If I had to write a little blurb like that about my dad's latest episode, I'd write something like, "Left alone one afternoon, Mr. Conklin, Sr., becomes unusually frustrated at the sound of a neighbor's car alarm. When he decides to take action with a weapon against the offender's vehicle—and possibly against the offender himself—the long arm of the law steps in." I like reading that out loud in a really low voice.

Apparently, Dad had wandered out of the house, telephone in hand—not just the receiver but the whole apparatus torn from the wall—wires dangling out the back like guts. He marched down the street and smashed, repeatedly and violently, the windshield of his neighbor's vehicle with his "weapon." Yes, Officer Vargas referred to the phone as a "weapon." She probably writes blurbs for police shows on the side. I guess Dad thought that pounding the windshield would make the blaring alarm stop. He probably thought it would make his anger stop as well.

Dad is a strong guy. He just "picked it up," he said. "It" being the phone. Lil and Dad still have one of those old dial phones that are mounted to the wall, not a cell phone, not even a sleek, silver and black little cordless number a son buys for them and puts on their counter as a surprise when they're out, then has to return unused. Those old mounted-to-the-wall phones are really mounted and you can't budge them.

The owner of the vehicle was actually inside the car at the time. Apparently, he got out and attempted to rough Dad up a bit, but that was after he had defended himself via such loud verbal abuse that another neighbor called the police. Since the cops were on their way, the owner of the car didn't get a chance to rough Dad up the way he wanted, and besides, no one roughs Dad up the way he wants. I know that because the police report said the owner of the vehicle "escaped." I really don't want to picture that scene, even though the neighbor who called 911 insisted on describing it to me in great detail as I tried to avoid her recently in the supermarket parking lot. I might title this episode "Alarmed."

Bursting urgently into a public service building on a Tuesday afternoon would not get my father released more easily or quickly, but I couldn't help it. I did burst a bit. Officer Vargas was a pretty straightforward lady and didn't have time for urgent flourishes. Drama wasn't her thing. Talking to her in person helped me focus, though.

"In cases like your father's, Mr. Conklin, we try to find a relative to release to, and if no one is pressing any charges, we strongly suggest a complete medical exam," she said, slowing down at the "strongly suggest" part. She meant that they arrest people sometimes and then realize that they need medical help, not a jail term. What they do not realize, however, is that even though Dad has spent his entire life presiding over a medical facility, he's rarely been to the doctor. He's probably not going to start now. I wanted to make that clear.

"I appreciate that, Officer, but my father feels fine," I said.

She didn't react.

"I mean, I remember my friend's dad getting prostate cancer a few years back and he had to see a doctor. My dad doesn't have the same symptoms at all. And he'd never allow any rubber-gloved fingers poking into places that insinuate things." Officer Vargas's silence made my mouth speed up when it should have slowed down. She didn't know that Dad calls doctor visits "getting poked."

"Lil can't even get him to go," I said. Vargas seemed like she wanted an explanation. "Lil's my mom," I added.

"Sign here, please," she said and put some papers in front of me. I signed.

"You're right—I should probably insist on a check-up for him, but when I do, all I get is 'I feel fine,'" I said. Vargas took the pen and papers from my hand. "I know, I know. You women have a harder time of it, yes, I'll admit that," I continued. "You're used to doctors poking around. Lil makes that clear every time Dad or I won't go to the doctor. She says things like 'We women lie on tables and open our legs for teams of doctors and interns who stare and poke and cut through to bring men into the world in the first place, and you men won't even drop your pants for two minutes?!'"

The attention of every admin, cop, supervisor, and delinquent in the place was on me. My mouth was finally finished. Officer Vargas remained as cool as freezer burn.

"We're not in the business of diagnosis, Mr. Conklin," is how she put it.

At that moment, another officer came around the corner with Dad. Dad looked raw and a bit stiff. I guess raw + stiff = embarrassed. I tried to stay neutral and not appear to be babying my own father. My manner was straightforward, as if I always pick him up from a place where he enjoys a police escort.

"Hey, Dad."

Silence.

"Are you OK? How are you feeling?"

More silence.

"Listen," I said, leaning in to him and lowering my voice as if I were telling a secret, "Lil isn't home right now, so we can get back and blend in with a beer and TV just as if nothing's happened. Whattya say?"

He glanced furtively around the bustling space. No one was paying any attention to him. His shoulders relaxed a bit.

"I was, uh, wanting to talk to someone," he said.

I leaned in closer, ignored his confession, and lowered my voice. "If we leave right now, Lil won't be, you know, upset," I suggested. Dad straightened up.

"We should go," he said.

I understand my dad. When I retire, I'll want someone to talk to all day. I can say now, at 49, that I'm going to travel and see the world, but when I'm 85, there will be plenty of times when I'll be home and my wife will be there and she won't feel like talking to me. Or she'll be out somewhere and I won't have anything to do. I can see myself sitting there, reminiscing about my career or some pretty girl I used to know, and a neighbor's car alarm will start blaring. I sure as hell will want to talk to someone about it, especially if I'm a big guy like Dad, who used to be a top administrator of an entire hospital complex.

Lil was out walking her two miles that day. It's funny how women are so busy. Moms and women never seem to rest, but at the end of all that motion, we men usually drop dead first. She had returned from her walk just before we returned from establishing Dad's criminal record. My plan was foiled.

"Here are my men!" she said as we walked in, full of her usual cheer. That's how Lil always greets us. She looked down at the clear plastic bag dangling from Dad's grip and easily saw the destroyed phone through the plastic. It looked like a pile of charred bones. Officer Vargas had bagged it, all ready to take home, just like when you get your belongings back after an unexpected hospital stay. Lil stared at it for a moment, then looked up across the room to the messy patch of wall it was torn from.

"My poor guy," she said. She took the evidence from his hands and put it off to the side. "You just wanted someone to talk to."

Mel has insisted lately that, when Dad's episodes heat up, we should get away to refuel. I've agreed, lately. After picking my father up from the police, I agreed again. She likes hiking around the Lake Kashetau area. So when Friday hit, we put everything we needed into the car, drove to work together as we frequently do, then left directly from the office. We ended up staying all weekend at that nice bed and breakfast on the hill. It's called The Buccaneer.

It was great to wake up early on Saturday at a B&B, have breakfast, then head out to catch an entire day of great fall hiking. We went east on the trail this time, then took the south fork to hike along the water. We wandered and got a little lost, winding up on the ridge overlooking the lake. The view was spectacular, so we kept going. At one point, we tripped into a clearing where we stumbled, and I do mean literally stumbled and fell, onto a small, windowless hovel. I disentangled the vines from my ankles and stood up. I tried the only door. It was locked. I thought it might be abandoned and said as much.

"Zis place *is* abandoned, Tom," was Mel's reply. I don't know what made her so sure.

"I guess the only way to know would be to get in and look around," I said. I wished I hadn't. My wife may be the beautiful, young, extremely well educated director of planned giving at the hospital, but sometimes she has just enough larceny in her to make me wonder about her procurement techniques. And she really procures. She's very successful. I used to think it was her sexy and alluring French accent. That doesn't hurt.

"Here, take zis," she said. She was breathing heavily. I turned around to see her lugging a large, thick log in her arms. I quickly grabbed the other end of it. Pretty soon, we were ramming it, medieval-warfare style, into that small castle's door.

"Hey, honey," I panted, "I like to think I'm a respected hospital administrator like Dad was, but now I've run off with a beautiful woman 15 years my junior," I grunted. I lost my wind when we rammed for the fifth time. "Now we're in the middle of the woods, breaking and—*oof!*—entering."

The door caved inward. Mel and I dropped our ram-rod and tumbled inside.

"What is this, some kind of storage space?" I said. I couldn't tell. We fumbled around, and Mel managed to open the wooden shutters at the back. Some light came in.

You would think that if someone went to the trouble of building a quaint little place on a ridge overlooking an amazing lake, he'd want to look out at the water since it's there and all. But once we had some light, I saw that the only openings besides the door we just mangled were the two small windows at the back. They faced the hills.

Despite the dust rising thickly into the shafts of light, I could see that we'd burst into an unusual space. Mel agreed. She immediately pointed out the fireplace and mantel, the stone kitchen counters, the location, and the admittedly intriguing, weird patterns in the mosaic stone-and-tile flooring. She fell in love with it, she said, and I fell further in love with her. I did like the place, too, even though it had a slightly creepy edge to its otherwise rustic but classy charm.

"Oh, Tom. *Tom* ..." she said as she walked around touching everything. I can't resist it when my wife says my name like that. She kept repeating it as she ran her hand over everything—the kitchen counter, every corner and cranny, an old mortar and pestle on the fireplace mantel. It had a dead spider in it. There were a few burn marks on the tile floor.

"We will change zee locks. We will bring in our own furniture and zings," she said, as nonchalantly as if she were saying, "I stopped at the store for bread." That's what French people do. They nonchalantly stop at corner bakeries for those long breads. Mel insists I call them by their name—baguettes.

"Honey, we can't just move into someone else's house," I said.

"But if zey are not here for such a long time?" she said. I didn't ask how she knew when the owners had gone missing.

"Maybe they just left yesterday."

"And left all zis dust?" She turned and blew over her shoulder at the fireplace mantel. The dense inch of dust settled there took flight. We both coughed and waved at the air.

"Zey have given up zeir rights," she declared. She also saw the terrified look in my eye and lowered her voice. "Zat makes you an American *squatteur*," she said. When I didn't react, she clarified in French, which is almost no clarification whatsoever—except for "hello," "goodbye," and a few phrases that would help a tourist find a restroom, I don't speak French. I think she said: "*Un squatter est une personne qui occupe un lieu d'habitation illégalement*." I had to translate that online to write it down here. Mel had emphasized the word *illégalement*, so I just filled in the rest.

Then she laughed quite heartily. She knows how to jab me, then wander away humming some little ditty, which she did as she inspected the rest of the cottage.

The French have actually stolen the English word "squatter" and have sheepishly added a "u." I remember when I did a semester abroad in London, some of the art students were staying in an abandoned house on the outskirts of campus. They had simply gone in, changed the locks, and it was theirs. Illegally, in my opinion, but legally according to British property code. Since I'm American, the idea of helping yourself to someone else's house just because he took an extended leave seemed like communism to me. I wasn't the kind of student who would infiltrate another person's private property. Dad had made clear to us kids the expectations and responsibilities of being an American. Being responsible. Being gainfully employed in order to have gain. He wanted us kids to follow in his footsteps.

On Christmas break from my first semester of college, Dad and I were sitting in the living room late at night with all the lights off except for the tree lights. We were drinking together, and I was only 18. All I could

12

think was, "Never thought I'd be sharing my dad's 12-year-old Scotch with him," and "Man, those lights look like little candies floating in the air," when suddenly, Dad got serious. He lowered his voice.

"Son, are ya gonna like graduating with a degree in business administration? I mean really like. Don't get me wrong, Thomas, business is an important thing. I deal with the business of the hospital all day long. People think hospital administrators are just a bunch of former doctors who get tired of looking at naked butts all day. Not so. Our background is purely business." Dad never wanted to look at anyone's behind, and he was man enough to know it. And his big, imposing frame kept everyone in line, especially us kids. "So are ya gonna be happy with that?" he asked.

Throughout my teen years, he would reiterate that kind of thing—that a good job is not just a source of income, that his position had made him a man and a citizen. "You need to find something to do with your life that you really like," he said, "and I mean really like because you're going to be doing it many hours a week, forever."

"Yeah, Dad," was all I said. I said it in a matter-of-fact tone that squealed in my head like the bloodiest hog of a lie I'd ever told. Then I persuaded myself that it was the Scotch that was making me want to run as far away from college as I could to become a merchant marine. I wanted to travel and see the world instead of spending his money on an education that was making Scotch make me lie. The farthest I got was London for one semester.

Then, years later, when my son went off to college, I went with him. In a manner of speaking, I mean. I felt suddenly younger and began designing my life not as a provider's, but as a merchant marine of the mind, so to say. I was living a freshman life on the open seas, delivering cargo, landing in exotic ports. It induced a real euphoria, an eternally open question, and with no answer in sight, our big, fat divorce.

I remember peering at Marla from the porthole of my newfound inner freedoms.

"Marla, you know ..."

I started out that way, as if I were asking about the shirts at the dry cleaner. "I don't know how to say this ... I, uh ... I think there might be a better way." My stammering was making me omit details. I tried to concentrate. "You've said you want to travel, see the world, maybe start a business," I was finally getting the details in there that I'd planned on, "and it would be awkward for me to stop you from doing those things," I added, impromptu. I liked that—it sounded as if my leaving would be her gain. At that point, I ditched the particulars and simply jumped to "I've found someone else."

There was a pause of such tension that I wondered if I would get tears, or pleading, or gave-you-the-best-years, or some other line from the soaps. Marla loves soaps and drama. I don't. Instead, she looked at me with the most commonsensical, reasonable expression, as if everything had already been decided and equitably escrowed.

"OK," she said. Then she gathered her purse and keys. "We're out of eggs." Then she left for the supermarket.

Later that evening, as I lay in Mel's arms, I reported the whole scene.

"Ah," said Mel, "a simple 'OK.' So natooral." I do love the way Mel's accent can pull vowels around like taffy, but sometimes it makes me miss her meaning. "Marla looks at you zrough her own porthole." I don't know that I'd actually said the word "porthole" to Mel. Her saying it distracted me.

"What do you mean?" I said. Mel sat up. Her pretty breasts sat up with her. That didn't help my comprehension, either.

"She takes her freedom, as you do, perhaps?" she asked.

"What do you mean?"

"Perhaps she does what you do."

"What do you mean?" I kept saying that.

"What we do." She paused, then shoved her body back and patted the space on the bed between us. "Here." Then she explained her position—that a simple "OK" shows such immediate acceptance. She said that Marla was already free of me.

Actually, "rid" is the word she used.

"If you feel zat way, Tom, Marla must also feel zat way, no? You are married for many years," she added.

"No, no, no," I kept saying, "it's different for men." But as soon as I said it, I felt a mad rush of total body irritation from an unknown source when all she did was not answer.

When Mel was done touching everything in the cottage, we started calling it a cave because of the lack of light. Despite its gloom, her mind was made up.

"We will come back next weekend with our zings?" she said. She wasn't really asking

"Yeah, well, before we leave today, we'll have to put the door back together and get a lock on it," I said,

15

"D'ya think the hardware store in town will still be open? We'll need hinges and—"

"Tom," interrupted my lovely wife, "no person will take zis place from us." I didn't know how she could be so sure again, but I let it go. I didn't have any tools with me anyway, and it was getting dark. We propped the door back up against the frame and hiked back.

.   .   .

All this setting up in someone else's cave-house reminds me of the day Mel and I moved in to our new home together. We had been trying to combine our belongings, including Mel's favorite antiques from home salvage stores. As I helped her ruin her favorite table on its way out of the rented van—rented, that is, to transport the things we didn't want the movers to ruin—we made quite a ruckus. Some people call it an "argument." We unloaded things and heaved them up our new porch stairs and into the house. As we did, it struck me that the elderly gentleman next door who was reading on his screened porch never glanced up once, despite all the trampling and noise happening just five feet from his magnolias.

Even though he looked older than my father, he reminded me of Dad in a could've-been-a-statesman kind of way. I watched him put his book down and walk to his screen door. He stood at it for a while before coming out to introduce himself. When I saw him coming, I put down the table leg and neighborly met him half way. I extended my hand.

"Tom Conklin. Nice to meet you," I said. The gentleman kept his hand to himself and bowed slightly forward.

"Phineas," was all he said.

When he straightened up, my attention was drawn to his immense nose. It dwarfed his small spectacles but not his regal, genteel manner. He was full of class, as if he had come from a long line of distinguished scholars. His hand finally extended to embrace mine firmly. I remember being transfixed by his blue, blue eyes.

Later that night, I picked up my phone from the bare floor next to the mattress to see the time. 11:21pm. Mel and I lay in our dirty moving clothes, both of us too tired to assemble the bed frame or bring in the nightstand. Before drifting off to sleep, I felt compelled to give my impressions of our new next-door neighbor. Mel screwed up her face as I spoke. As she drifted into an exhausted near-sleep, she said, "Blue, *blue*?"

I admit I deserved that. I'd never used an adjective twice in a row before. It sounded like someone trying to serenade, with bad poetry and guilt, the person whose table he had wrecked just a few hours prior by snapping one of the legs clean off. Mel had said that we should prop the van door open all the way. I had insisted, belligerently, that we shouldn't.

"His name is Phineas," I said, knowing she would get a kick out of that—such an old-fashioned name for such an old guy and all, but she didn't. She was asleep.

One day soon after that, when I was trying to clear a patch in the yard for the vegetable garden I'd been wanting to start, I couldn't decide whether to use the small shovel or the hoe. I know that I could have done it with a tiller, but as Mel always says, my age is prompting me to "return to zee land and be close with it." Under a hot sun, I dug and hoed. Then I got down on my hands and knees and pulled and yanked and realized why chiding my wife's gardening gloves is always met with not one word of rebuff but rather a knowing silence. When I stood back up with my nails black and bug smear on my knees—but with weeds defeated and a nice clearing—I was face-to-face with him.

The wooden fence separating our properties came right up to our necks—Phineas and I were two heads afloat in mid air, appearing to have no connection to the bodies underneath. His head nodded at the hoe in my left hand, then turned to nod at the shovel in my right. I found my head doing the same.

"Thersites's body is as good as Ajax's when neither are alive," he said. His words held my tongue captive like a kind of spell.

"Uh ..." I said. I only knew that Ajax was a strongman in Greek mythology. And thanks to my double major in business and English in college, I knew that Thersites was some other Greek guy.

"I'm planting corn," I said, finally. I was worried about eliciting another alien response.

"Corn," he repeated and stepped back a bit. He was wearing a wool suit, but I was the one sweating profusely.

"Yes," I said. "I've always planted it with eating in mind, but I like the way it looks, too. You know, the green and the big leaves and all. When it grows." I didn't mean to say *when it grows*. His large, pockmarked nose seemed to be drawing the hot sun to it like a metal rod does lightning, but he still wasn't sweating.

"Thou art not altogether a fool," he said and smiled neighborly.

This evening, when Mel and I were having drinks on the deck, I told her about my encounter with him.

"Zat is wonderful!" was her reaction. While Phineas had been busy keeping his distance, Mel had been countering by pointing a neighborly persona at his property like a floodlight every time he came outside. She was hoping we'd establish a friendly relationship with him despite his reticence.

"Yeah. Well, he's a man of few words," I said. "First off, he gave me some advice about clearing the patch."

"Zat makes sense. What did he say?" Mel loves Phineas's gardens and always comments on his green thumb.

"He said ..." Here I paused. I had to remember how he worded it. "He said something strange. He said, 'Thersites's body is as good as Ajax's when neither are alive.'"

"*C'est bon!*" she exclaimed. "He was a college professor of *littérature*, perhaps? He quotes from *Cymbeline*."

Now, I love my wife, and I love the way *Cymbeline* sounds coming out of her French lips—very sexy—but how did she know that was a line from Shakespeare?

"He is a gentleman *très charmant*," she added.

"I was sweating," I went on—I was trying to put it in context, "and he was watching me," I continued, "and when I stood up with the hoe and the shovel I was trying to use—"

"Ah," she interrupted. "*Oui, oui*. Of course. He is saying zat both zee hoe and zee shovel are wrong for zat job. He is clever, no?"

I should have recognized that Thersites comment. But then again, I'm always surprised if I remember anything from that first year of college—studying was not the reason I went on to higher education, initially anyway. Hearing Shakespeare at this point in my life always reminds me of all those literature classes I had to take, those thousand suns I kept coming across in all those stories and poems from World Lit 101. I finally dropped English completely. I figured I'd be happier making lots more money in business than I would have as an English teacher. I was right about the money part, but that happier part kept burning for years like those thousand suns.

But my phone is ringing. Gotta go.

I've now realized that I can sense when an episode is coming on. Like a migraine. I'm calling this one "The Chase." I was sitting here the other day writing about Phineas when my phone rang. That strange episode-alert feeling welled up in my gut, probably because I didn't recognize the caller ID. I answered it anyway.

"Mr. Conklin?"

"Yes?"

"This is Officer Logan."

I paused.

"*Yes?*" I repeated.

"First off, I wanna tell you that your dad is in one piece, even though the chase ended in a crash. We're just calling to ask if you can come down to the scene—he's refusing to go in an ambulance, so your mom requested that we call you. Like I said, though, one piece. Don't worry."

Someone was cursing loudly in the background. Officer Logan paused for a moment before concluding with "You might wanna come right now."

Here's the story as I got it: Lil took Dad out to the pharmacy to buy a new shaver. She said that as she waited there, parked in front, she started reading, and I can just picture that because she always has a book with her. But after a short while, she heard loud voices. A young man was yelling and cursing violently inside an idling car in the middle of the parking lot. And when she looked up, she saw that he was yelling and cursing at Dad, who was sitting in the car with him.

At that moment, another young man came racing out of the pharmacy. He had apparently just robbed the place. Lil watched him jump into the idling car as it took off with the two young men and Dad inside. I'm told that the pharmacy's security systems and customer cell phones had alerted police already, so they were hot on the car's trail before it got very far.

I can just see it. Lil sitting in the car with her book while Dad comes out of the store, his little pharmacy paper bag in hand. He wanders over to the wrong vehicle, gets in, closes the door, then is perfectly bewildered when the driver scowls and brandishes his weapon.

"You're not Lil," says Dad. I know that part is true because according to witnesses, as they pulled the young driver from the wreckage and arrested him, he was screaming, "*And I ain't no 'Lil,' you fuckin' ol' weirdo!*"

Meanwhile, the other young man tears out of the store with his pistol, shoves the cash and drugs into his leather jacket, leaps into the car and yells, "Get the fuck outta here, man!" OK, I admit that I'm now improvising. But after a few hundred yards or so, I can see him fixing his eyes on Dad's almost bald head and demanding, "Who the fuck is *this*?"

22

At this point my frightened imagination will go no further—that's when the guns may or may not have gotten cocked at Dad, or the thieves may have understood that adding murder to larceny would be worse for them and would simply shove Dad out the door at the first opportune moment and hope he lives. Or maybe they just hit the side of that poor woman's garage too early in the chase to decide. I really don't want to know.

Emergency took forever—well into the evening. Poor Nurse Cynthia was doing her best.

"Mr. Conklin, the doctor will be here in a moment, but we do have to get a urine sample."

"Like hell—I run this entire operation!" yelled my father. I kept throwing knowing nods to the nurses when he said things like that. We weren't even at his facility, not that it would matter—he's been retired for over two decades. Lil was also trying her best.

"Honey, no one can help you if you don't give a sample."

My father grabbed the small package from Nurse Cynthia's hands, tore off the wrapper, unscrewed the cap, spit into the plastic cup, and handed it back to her.

Dad's belligerence transported me back to the beach of one of our earliest family vacations. Daniel and Deb were hopping into the waves, and I wanted to fling myself in, too, just like my big brother and sister. It looked like so much fun. I defiantly approached the water's edge under Dad's watchful eye, not really grasping that the edge was fast approaching me. I heard Dad's voice raining down on me from above, like God's.

"Here it comes, Tommy!" He was referring to the wave that had broken far away from the dry sand where I was standing. Its residue was rushing at my 4-year-old ankles, and as I imagined, had plans to make off with them. But I was too terrified to run. When it hit, my feet sank into the sand and held me in place, forcing me to stay put through all that rush and consequence.

"*Daddy!*" I was pleading, afraid that even my voice was being drowned. I became hysterical. When the water reversed itself, there were my dad's immense feet sinking immensely into the sand next to my pint-sized prints.

"It's OK, Tom-Tom, it's just water. There it goes. See?" His words were again filtering down to me from on high. He squeezed my hand, which he had been holding for some moments already. "Just a little water," he comforted, but I had no intention of stopping my crying, no matter what he said. I just wanted someone to cry to.

There in the ER, I almost said out loud, "It's OK, Dad, it's just water, see?" but I knew that he had no intention of stopping his belligerence, even though Lil and I were right there to be belligerent to. It did soothe me, though, that Mel showed up. She rushed in as urgently as a wave. I loved that. I wanted her to break all over me.

"Hi honey," I said calmly. "Everything's gonna be OK. Thanks for coming, but you didn't have to."

"What's going on, Tom?" she said, alarmed. As she stuffed her keys and phone into her purse, I briefly spied a new box of home pregnancy test sticks in there before she closed it. That unhinged me for a second.

"Uh, well, Dad just got into a little, uh ..." I walked her past the curtain and away from his bed so I could focus, and so he wouldn't hear the "e" word.

"*Episode*."

"Is he OK?" She leaned around my shoulder to look. There was a sudden commotion going on.

24

"I'll call Larry!" yelled my father. Larry is our family's lawyer. I turned and pulled the curtain back. Two orderlies were prying my father off a young, stunned intern. Apparently all that poor kid did was pull on a rubber glove while asking Dad if he had any pain. Larry probably wouldn't even return a call about that.

Dad never did let anyone touch him. And he finally worked himself into such a fit that he gave up from exhaustion. The sedative didn't hurt, either. Turns out he was OK, just angry, shaken, and embarrassed about his joy ride with some fellow criminals. But what bothered me about today was Lil. I tried to talk to her as we sat in those plastic chairs next to Dad's wheel-able bed. While Dad snored comfortably, I waited for a moment.

"So, Ma," I started, uneasily, "I'm curious—why did you drive Dad to the pharmacy today? He usually likes to do the driving—" but she cut me off. I didn't even get to my main point, that Dad is not what you'd call a chauvinist, but he does live by some sticky particulars about what real men do. Having his wife in the driver's seat while he sits passively in the passenger's in a moving vehicle is not one of them.

"Tom, your father was a bit tired this afternoon."

"But you know how he is about driving. How did you get him to—"

"Will you get me a coffee, Tom? From the cafeteria. I can't drink coffee from vending machines. Two creams, please."

"I will go," said Mel. We both watched Mel grab her purse and leave. When she was out of sight, I turned to Lil. She turned away. I surrendered.

"So how did Dad get into that car with those boys in the first place?" I asked her. One time, when our son was small, I was waiting in the car for Marla to come out of the bank. I looked up just in time to see her almost get into a similar car parked nearby. Even young Stephen laughed when she finally realized and climbed into our car instead, laughing and joking. I have to say that about Marla—she has a great sense of humor.

Who hasn't found himself on occasion in large parking lots approaching the wrong car and then wondering why it won't unlock? But at least the cars that I've approached looked like mine and were parked near mine. According to Officer Logan, the car Dad got into was a beat-up, black Toyota. Nothing like my parents' cream-colored Lincoln. It wasn't parked close to Lil at all. It wasn't even parked. Officer Logan said it was idling in the middle of the lot.

"It could happen to anyone, dear," was all Lil would say.

.   .   .

I think it was the toilet flushing that woke me, but I'm not sure. Next thing I was aware of was Mel—she had nuzzled her way under my arm and was crying. She had a little plastic stick in her hand. I curled myself around her and took it from her gently.

In the morning, I shuffled us off to the cave. It was the right thing to do. All that hiking, heaving, and hauling things in was therapeutic. We had found vehicle access to our little hideaway via a dirt road that comes up a back route from town. I brought tools and put the door back together while Mel cleaned a bit. And as an added bonus,

I found a guy in the village who cleans and inspects chimneys for a fairly reasonable rate so we could be ready when the weather turns. He inspected, installed a new regulation flue liner, and declared the fireplace useable. I was surprised. I don't want to admit squatter status, but a working fireplace does feel like we should be here. I just wonder about taxes—do squatters pay property taxes? I've just used the word "squatter" twice in this paragraph.

Mel was right about bringing lawn chairs and a small table. I'm enjoying sitting here, facing the lake and typing as dusk approaches. The ridge juts out over the lake a bit, so the water below forms a sort of semicircle around us. The sunset will be spectacular. It's so quiet, and the air is cool and fresh. No neighbors, either. No one from the area even seems to care that we're here. Except for our visitor today.

His name is Gregory. From the village. Nice guy, off-kilter, older than stone. Mel had gone to get takeout while I was still wrestling the door back onto its hinges. I finally got it into place, opening it and closing it and making sure the new deadbolt worked. When I opened it for the last time to step outside, there he was. Standing right at the entrance, out of nowhere. I shouldn't have let out that little screech, but I didn't expect anyone to be standing right there, three feet from me.

"Heh," he said. He pronounced some of his vowels like "e's" and not like their real sounds. That bugged me.

"Hello," I said. "Can I help you?"

"Name's Gregory. Pleased to meet ye." He leaned his walking stick on the door frame to free up his hand, which he held out to shake mine. It was filthy. As we shook, I noticed that he was splattered from head to toe with dried earth, as if he'd escaped just an hour prior from a quicksand pit.

"Yes," I said, "Tom Conklin. Nice to meet you."

"I'm looking to pick up some o' your eucalyptus, friend. Got the aches, if ye don't mind," he explained.

"There's eucalyptus here?" I asked. He nodded and motioned outside, toward the back corner of the place. "Sure. No problem. Take whatever you want," I said. Mel was suddenly in sight, coming up the path with our food.

"*Allô*, Gregory!" she yelled.

"Ma'am." He tipped his mud-caked golfer's cap to her. At least it looked like a golfer's cap. Mel told me later that she'd met him earlier on her way out and invited him to join us. When she arrived at the door, I helped her bring the food in.

"So you will join us for dinner?" Mel offered again. "I have bought enough for zree people."

"Well, that's generous o' ye. I did come by to ask after your herbals," he started.

"Apparently, we've got a eucalyptus tree in the back here," I interrupted and motioned with my head toward the back. There was a lot of Styrofoam in my hands all of a sudden. Mel had found the only Chinese takeout place in town.

"Oh, zat is excellent," she said, then paused. "Does zis tree grow here?"

"Yes, ma'am. 'Snow Gum' they call it. A hardy piece o' tree. I use it for the aches," repeated Greg. "I make a tea. First, ye gotta steep it in water, 'specially at this time o' year, ye see, then I leave it in a dark room ...."

In this day and age, no one needs to be stirring up potions like a wizard. Some tea made from a rogue tree can't possibly compete with years of research by the medical profession. "If you're in pain, why don't you just take some ibuprofen?" I asked. "I've got a whole bottle here, and popping a pill is a helluva lot easier than cooking trees."

Greg looked at me as blankly as a reptile. He didn't seem to know what ibuprofen is. I wanted to introduce it to him, but Mel was looking at me as if she wanted me to explain myself.

"Pharmaceutical companies invest big money in combining the right amount of pain killer to make them work fast, Gregory. And easily. You should try it." He looked to Mel, bewildered, then back to me.

"Nature works real fine," he said. Mel changed the subject.

"So you will eat with us, zen, Gregory? I hope you like zee Chinese foods," she said.

"I'd be much obliged," he said. I haven't heard the phrase "much obliged" in about 40 years.

We set up the folding chairs we brought. As we ate, Ol' Gregory rambled. He can really put it away. He held the chopsticks in his right hand and scooped the food into his cupped left hand with them, then ate from there. I couldn't always make out what he was saying behind the mouthfuls. Interestingly, he didn't ask how we came to be here. He said he was "born 'round these parts" and has been living here all his life. He then seemed anxious to fill us in on the local lore, which, as far as I understood, is taken as factual history around here.

"Ye've come to a site where there used to be pirate marauding back when pirates ruled the sea, don't ye know," he said, rather proudly. Mel and I exchanged looks. Our little lake here is beautiful, but it's nowhere near the sea. No sea access, either.

"That's right. One ship, The Buccaneer, made it all the way here," he continued. The look on my face must have given me away. "Ye don't believe me now, but there was waterways all through these parts at one time, and the captain followed 'em, sure they were leading him to a El Dorado inland somewheres." Here Greg shoved in a whole spring roll, then spoke through it. "The captain was a brave man and made it all the way here to Kashetau, but what he didn't know is that inland waters got the devil in 'em, and pretty soon, his ship was ship*wrecked*. Dashed to pieces, they say, right here on this very ridge." He made a sweeping motion with his chopsticks across the entire edge of our ridge-front property.

"How do you know it happened here?" I asked. I should have asked him how he knew it happened at all.

"They was a seafaring people. What did they know about surviving inland?" His question didn't answer my question. "Oh, they were a sorry band. Fell into madness, they did, forming tribes and groups and almost wiping each other out in feuds and fighting, until, until ..."

I couldn't wait to hear how it ended. Mel and I both leaned forward toward him.

"The earthquake hit!" he declared. Now, I have never, ever heard of an earthquake in this area, but that didn't stop Ol' Greg. "The lake line receded real quick, like when Goddess Sue Nami rages." Gregory said the word "tsunami" as if it were someone's name. He was becoming hysterical. He opened his arms wide, curving them outward like a ship's hull. Then he started rocking them back and forth faster and faster while closing his eyes, as if he were in a trance. "And didn't that rushing back o' waters leave that pirate ship teetering back and forth on the ridge for quite a while 'till it tumbled backward, off this here ridge and direct into the receding waters to be sucked down into the deeps o' the lake forever!"

With that, he tumbled sideways off our rickety lawn chair. His mostly empty Styrofoam container and sticks scattered off his lap. Mel and I jumped up, collected him and the chair off the floor, and propped him back up. Mel steadied him while I picked up his dinner utensils. We had to remind him where he was in the story. He continued, still overly excited. I pulled my chair closer and sat ready to catch him if necessary. Mel looked relieved when I did that.

"The boat'd sunk, friends, into the deeps o' the lake," he moaned, "fulla the provisions, and some o' the pirates as well, huddled there in their madness. Ooh, it's hard just telling the tale." He showed such duress that Mel, in her kindness, tried to interact kindly. I tried to not interact at all.

"Zat is terrible, Gregory. I am sorry," she empathized. "What happened to zee others?"

"They were in awe o' the power o' nature, o' course. After the tragedy, they got real spiritual-like, formed a brotherhood o' sorts, stopped the infighting, and built a small house o' worship right here on this very spot where they lost everything." Our man Greg then glanced lovingly around the cave. "They're the ones that planted eucalyptus out back for practicing their own herbals and healings so they could survive indefinite ...."

Our new squatters' paradise was built by pirates-turned-hippie herbalists. I couldn't take it anymore.

"Now, Greg, when was this supposed sea access, because—"

"They put no openings, like windows, facing the water. D'ye wanna know why?" he diverted.

"Because it lowered their tax bracket?" I asked. Mel threw me a bad look.

"Because o' the mighty power o' that element, friends. Ye don't go *peering into the face o' God*."

He proclaimed this last sentence as if the rapture were already underway. And if that weren't enough, he went on to say that no one ever dared move in to our little cave here because, as he claimed with the most serious of expressions, "The ghosts is the brotherhood, friend, and they ain't leaving. Ain't going nowhere. They don't want no one going and changing the place."

So the locals are afraid to move in to our cottage or fix it up because of ghosts. Let's face it: water receding, sea access—that's ice-age stuff, so I'm not going to swallow the idea that some ancient seafaring people laid down Italianate mosaic floors in a little structure in the middle of nowhere right after a natural disaster of such geologic import that even sea access disappeared forever. I went online just now to find out when this supposed access existed. I couldn't find a single waterway on any available map from any time period that supports such a claim.

Ol' Gregory asked to take home our leftovers. Mel loved that. She scraped off what was still stuck to his Styrofoam container after his fall and mixed it with ours. Then she double-bagged it all with half a baguette and a couple of our extra bottles of water. We said goodbye as we watched him sling it over his shoulder. He disappeared into the woods, not even taking the path.

Living abroad during college was exciting, and I wasn't even squatting back then. But it could get lonely. Sometimes I would have strange experiences where I would think I saw people I knew from my hometown right there in the streets of London. Like Miss Gilling. Miss Gilling was my 5th grade teacher. She was my favorite of all my teachers, and I'm even counting college professors. One day, I was getting a little lost in the city and letting the crowd take me along. All of a sudden, coming toward me was Miss Gilling. She was walking right toward me, but she didn't see me. I thought, "What's Miss Gilling doing here?"

I started smiling and pacing myself and veering left through all the people as I walked so I could step right up to her when she got close enough. As soon as she did, I said, "Miss G, you were the best 5th-grade teacher I ever had." The way I said it, though, I guess it sounded like I had been to 5th grade on and off throughout my entire childhood. I would have if I could've had Miss G.

But then she answered something like, "An tanis scher, zadren." I immediately translated silently to myself, even though I had no idea what she really said. My translation said, "Thomas! I'm so glad to see you after all these years—you were the best student a teacher could ever have, no one was ever so unique or gifted as you were, and I've been looking for you all my life." But she was looking at me as if she'd never seen me before, so I said, "Miss Gilling, it's me, Thomas."

As I waited for her to say, "Of course—what wonders have you accomplished since you were in my class, brilliant young man?" I noticed the wall full of about 100 TVs in the display window of the storefront right there beside us. They were all playing the same classic picture—Toto was pulling back the curtain on the wizard. About 100 exposed wizards were moving their levers and saying, "Pay no attention to that man behind the curtain."

Even though the TVs were inside and we were outside, I heard those words and all that windy machinery as clearly as if I were wearing a wireless headset. But there wasn't any wireless technology back then. There probably was at NASA or in the military, but not for your college semester abroad. I thought I could hear the wizard because I heard my mouth saying the words with him, synced up perfectly, and by the time Dorothy and the others were on to him, I turned back to Miss Gilling for her response. All she said was "Za?"

Or that's what it sounded like. I'm just spelling what I remember hearing. It wasn't until I got back to my dorm room and thought about it for three days: That was not Miss Gilling.

I had told Mel the Miss Gilling story the other day at the cave after Ol' Gregory left. She listened as we packed up the tools and our selves to return home. When

I was done, she didn't comment. She just said it was time to go. It felt good to turn that deadbolt I'd just installed.

When we arrived home, the day was waning. Phineas was coming up our walkway. He was carrying a large screwdriver. Actually, it was sticking out of the bag he had on his shoulder, one of those that looks like a woman's purse but is meant for men. It was square, plain, and made of nice leather. It was a bit beat up, though, and worn at the edges. Mel wants me to carry one and offered to buy a nice one for me. I don't want one and told her so. She said I'd find it great to have a few useful things with me all the time, like a book or an energy bar, my flashlight pen or things for work. I could also have my phone and wallet and iPad in there, and my Starbucks hot mug, but all I could picture in there was lipstick. She said French men carry those leather bags. I'm not French.

I walked over to meet Phineas as he approached. "Hey, Phin," I said. I nodded first at the screwdriver sticking out of his man-purse, then at his house. "Doing a little work on the place?" He stopped, looked over at his house, then down at the screwdriver.

"This month I have been hammering," he said. I thought that was funny because he wasn't holding a hammer.

"You weren't screwing?" I asked. I realized what I'd said and laughed, but he didn't seem to notice. He invited me over instead.

It was the first time I'd ever been in his amazing home. The entire place seemed to serve as a library. There were books everywhere, as if he were an ex-librarian or a retired college professor, as Mel had guessed. He brought me into his study—it was devoted entirely to the work of

William Shakespeare. There were regal volumes next to paperbacks next to little statuettes of Will next to his biographies. A coffee mug sat on the desk that had crusted coffee on the inside and a quotation by The Bard on the outside.

"Time's the king of men," he stated, reading from the cup and holding it up proudly. It was a huge mug, more like one of those big beer mugs they probably used in the Elizabethan taverns.

"Can't argue with that," I said.

He directed me to the shelving on the wall. He had been working on the lowest shelf, which was drooping under the weight of so many books. He took the screwdriver out of his man-purse, turned it around, and began hammering a supporting nail with the non-screwing end. Each time, the weight of the books would force the nail back out and the shelf would sag even more.

"This falls out better than I could devise," he complained.

"Ya know, I don't think that's got a stud behind it, Phin," I pointed out to him. "If we move the supports to where the studs are, it'll hold better."

"Ah," he sighed. He looked resigned. "Anything that's mended is but patched."

I took that as a guarded "OK." I excused myself, went home for my stud finder, and when I returned, Phineas was making coffee. When he opened the cupboard, I saw that it was filled with those quotation mugs, packed with them. Nothing else in there, like plates or bowls—just mugs, each one carrying a different phrase. It was interesting that they weren't the more known ones like "Brevity is the soul of wit" or "To be or

36

not to be ...." Instead, printed on the cups were "*Was* is not *is*," and "Here we wander in illusions," and others that you'd have to be a real aficionado of the Bard to know.

"Hey, Phin, impressive collection ya got here," I said. "Were you a professor of literature or something? Because some of these sayings are kind of obscure, you know, the ones most people don't—"

"Stand not amazed," he said. I stood amazed anyway.

"Yeah," I said, "well, I guess I can't help it. You're a real aficionado."

"The damned use that word in hell," he muttered as he took out two mugs. "Howling attends it," he added.

"Yeah, no, I see," I said, signifying nothing. I guessed that if you're a professor, "aficionado" was too wimpy a word.

"I am a votary," he corrected, humbly. That's when I realized that Phin probably was a professor and doesn't want to brag. He's a very proper guy.

"Being a votary is important," I said.

"Ay. We work by wit and not by witchcraft," he said as he poured hot coffee. He handed me my mug. I read the quotation on it aloud.

"Lend me a garter," it said. I looked up. Phineas was beaming. "Was this one a gag gift or something?" I asked. I imagined him collecting these mugs from the many literary conferences he must have attended throughout his career. "Because it doesn't have that, you know, make-you-think-deeply quality to it like the others," I added. He smiled.

"What cannot be eschewed must be embraced," he said.

We saluted our health, sipped our coffee, and went back to the shelves. I showed him how to use the stud finder. We located a stud close to the original spot and secured the shelf there. Phineas was pleased and very appreciative.

"Thanks, Jupiter. All that is mine I leave at thy dispose," he offered.

I decided to take him up on that. Even though the sun had gone down, I invited him to my corn patch, hoping to get more good advice. I ran inside to get my Markum Triple-E camping light. The advertisement says that it's "a floodlight you hold in your hand." It is. We could see the whole yard.

Over our tasty steaming coffees, we debated the use of commercial fertilizer vs. compost. Mel came out to join us. She was wearing her fuzzy bathrobe. She had her phone in hand and was just hanging up with Nick.

"*Grand-mère* Jo cannot wait to come," she said. She looked down at the plain plot of ground. "Tom, *Grand-mère* can coax—'coax' you say in English?—any vegetable from zee earth." She looked up. "*Monsieur* Phineas!"

Phineas loves Mel. Who doesn't? She continued.

"So nice to see you. You are helping my gentleman here with zee brown zumb, I see." That hurt. I wouldn't say I had a brown thumb. It's beige. I didn't know Mel even had an opinion about it.

"He weeds the corn and still lets grow the weeding," said Phineas. Then he launched into a discussion with my wife on homegrown vegetables that deserved a spot on cable TV and a book tour.

"I did try that," I interjected when they mentioned aerating. "But the commercial fertilizer gives a great yield," I asserted when they both agreed on compost instead, but they didn't seem to hear me. As I watched them talk, I finally realized what it is about Phineas that reminds me of my father: the bow tie. It reminded me to call Dad. I reached into Mel's bathrobe pocket to take her phone out. When I did, I felt a small, unwrapped plastic stick. I looked at her hopefully. She looked away, hopeless. I wanted to throw my arms around her and comfort her, but their conversation was fast-paced, and interesting, and except for my intrusion, it was taking her mind off it. I stepped away to the driveway and made the call.

The phone rang. And rang. Their voicemail didn't even pick up. I didn't like that. I thought about how I should insist that my parents each get a cell phone, but modern technology doesn't inspire them. Last Christmas when I gave them a nice user-friendly Mac, I made sure everything was hooked up and ready to go. I showed them how to use it, how to open a word document and save it, but no one touched it. Dad regularly wants it removed, but Lil persuades him to leave it there "for the kids." She means the grandkids.

A phone, however, is a simpler thing—everyone understands telephones. I tried calling again. Dad finally picked up.

"Hello?"

"Hey, Dad."

"Hello, Tom, how are ya?" I like it when my father is in a good mood.

"Great. How's everything going? You know, I just tried calling and no one picked up."

"Oh. Well. We were upstairs."

"Doing what?" There was a silence. It suddenly occurred to me that there are only four rooms upstairs: a bathroom, Lil's "den," a guest bedroom—and my parents' bedroom. Dad's response chased away the uncomfortable image forming in my mind.

"Well, your mother is sitting at that computer-contraption looking at pictures of hotels." An uncomfortable confusion on my part replaced the uncomfortable image.

"Hotels? Like the kind you sleep in?" I asked.

"By God, Thomas, like the kind you go to Las Vegas in," he replied, vexed.

For a moment, I saw in my imagination a rickety old motel-on-wheels lumbering down Route 66, happily heading west. Painted across the side in big, sloppy letters was the phrase "Las Vegas or Bust." A smokestack billowed exhaust out the top. As I sped by in my Ford Escort, trying desperately to cut them off, Dad and Lil were leaning out the window, each with a martini in hand. They were smiling and waving.

But I knew what Dad meant. He meant that they were planning their annual trip to Vegas.

"Dad," I said. I think I yelled. "You're going again this year?"

"Why wouldn't we take our trip this year, Tom?" He stated that answer calmly, as if he believed that episode-prone seniors should be turned loose on a comparatively sedate and unsuspecting place like Las Vegas.

I had no answer. The next thing I remember is Mel and Phineas standing in front of me. Mel had her hands on my shoulders.

"Tom?" she was saying.

I think I hung up on Dad.

.　　.　　.

The dream is always the same. Since Daniel actually died in a car accident, I don't know why the scene is never a road. The car was nowhere near water when it was broadsided. When I overheard the grownups saying that Daniel was thrown so far from the vehicle that they couldn't find him at first, I remember getting the most vivid picture in my mind of him floating in extreme slow motion through the air and never landing, as if the air were water, mercifully keeping him afloat.

In the dream, we're playing in the ocean and everyone else is on the beach. It's sunny, and we've waded in, fighting over some toy he's carrying. Every time I have that dream, I know that during the dream I'm aware of what toy it is, but when I wake up, I'll be damned if I can remember what we were bickering over.

The beach we used to go to when we were kids was pretty shallow for quite a way out until it dropped off suddenly from under our feet and became deep, dark ocean. At our age, we could walk out pretty far with the water only up to our chests. I loved walking out there because the gathering waves would swell and lift us off our feet, then place us down again like some invisible, gentle giant.

Daniel and I kept walking and being lifted, then set down, lifted, down again. And even though in reality we were usually surrounded by people, as soon as we started walking in the dream, there was suddenly no one around.

There were no beach sounds or screaming children or people splashing like there always were on vacation. There was only the sound of water and the sensation of our feet arriving at the edge of the deep.

At that point in the dream, Daniel always turns to me. I can tell by the look on his face and the way he holds his shoulders that he knows the giant has picked him up with no intention of ever putting him down again. He shoves the toy into my hand, and as my feet come back to the sand at the edge of the ridge, Daniel has floated beyond it, beyond any place where his feet will ever meet sand again. As he drifts backward and away from me, slowly, I grip the toy and dig in my toes while we watch each other from across the growing swell.

As many times as I've had that dream, we never call out to each other. He never looks frightened or cries or flails his arms. He doesn't even try to get back. He just floats backward and away. And when I wake up, I'm stunned all over again.

When Skype plinged, I tumbled out of bed and was sitting in front of the screen before I could even remember that just because a device plings, dings, sings, or even rings, it doesn't mean you have to drop what you're doing, like sleeping or dreaming, to answer it. I knew it was Deb—she's a rabid Skyper. Mel's strong roast was wafting up from downstairs. It was morning already.

"Hey, Tommy!" My sister's happy voice and face were there on-screen. I'll admit that I still like hearing my older sister call me "Tommy." It's comforting. "What's up?" she asked. "How's everyone up there?" Deb is a bigwig advertising executive "downstate" in New York

City. To her, we live "upstate," foraging in the wilderness for our nourishment.

"Yeah, well, we're doing OK," I said. "Actually, I'm glad you called."

"Hang on," she said, putting her index finger up to the screen before running out of the picture. There was music playing from somewhere and it became louder. It was ABBA. Deb poked her head sideways back on-screen. She was snapping her fingers and doing a mock-version of that old dance, The Jerk. "Got your favorite on, Tommy," she laughed. She knows I can't stand ABBA. Then she gave me the thumbs-up, laughed again devilishly, and went offscreen to turn it down. When she returned, she sat and said, "So how's my little brother?"

"Well, a lot's going on." My tone got her attention, something never easy to do with my sister.

"Yeah?" she leaned in to the screen and looked serious. "Whaddya mean 'a lot'?"

"Well," I started, "I wish I could explain some of this to you in person, but—"

"*Bonjour!*" said Mel cheerily as she walked in with two cups of coffee. She set one in front of me. I love it when my wife greets people in her native tongue, but she has a tendency to interrupt. So does Deb.

"*Bonjour*, Mel," said Deb. "*Ça va?*"

"Oh, *très bien—tant mieux, Et toi?*"

"*Va bueno, merci merci amiga!*" Deb doesn't really speak French or Spanish, and her accent is atrocious.

"So, uh," I burst in, "I'm glad we're talking, Deb, because I wanted to discuss Dad. And Lil. And Dad and Lil."

"So how's the family planning going?" Deb interjected. She leaned forward and winked as if I weren't

43

in the middle of another topic. She wasn't even looking at me anymore.

"We are still trying," said Mel.

"You can do it, *amigos*!" yelled Deb. "And what about *Grand mare*?" My sister's bad accent made Jo sound like a racehorse. "Will she still come live with you?"

"We are making zee plans. Tom is considering to *bump out* zee space over zee garage to make a room." It's cute, I admit, when Mel uses an idiom in English like "bump out." She slows down the sentence at those words so she can pronounce them properly.

"Well, we wanted to keep the guest room, and Mel has started decorating the other room for the baby, and Jo probably needs her own space and her own bathroom, so —" I wanted to talk it through, but Deb kept repeating the word "garage" over me, emphasizing the first syllable as Mel does. It was starting to bug me. In the meantime, Zoe appeared behind her mother.

"Aunt Mel, whaddya gonna name her?" asked Zoe. *Who said it's going to be a her?* was the question in my mind. My niece was in awe.

"We're not really sure yet," I said. Deb grabbed her daughter in a bear hug.

"Maybe they'll name her Little Zoe!" she teased. I turned to Mel—she was spellbound, watching their mother-daughter affections.

"You are a mama *très jolie*," said Mel in a soft voice to the screen. I don't think Deb heard her.

"*Gare*-azhe. Hang on—I'll be right back." Deb got up and left the picture. Zoe leaned into the screen.

"So when is the baby coming?" she asked.

44

"We're doing the best we can," I mumbled. Discussing my sex life with my niece was not the reason I'd gotten out of bed this morning. When Deb came back on-screen, she held a glass of wine and a Coke.

"A toast," said Deb, and handed the can to Zoe. "May your next test be positive!" she yelled. Zoe popped the can and we all drank.

"So Little Brother, what were you saying before?" It was suddenly quiet. I took advantage.

"Look, Deb, we need to talk seriously about Dad and Lil," I said.

"What about them?"

"Well, Dad especially is starting to get a little forgetful lately. I'm concerned because it's that time of the year again when they start to think about going to Vegas—"

"They always go to Vegas, Tommy."

"Yes, but when Dad ripped the phone off the wall, I never imagined that our neighbor would have to escape the assault, and I'd want someone to talk to if my wife were 84 years old, too, even though you can't just expect that the male nurse he attacked would understand that." By the end of my explanation, Mel, Zoe, and ABBA had all vanished.

"Nurses? Is he in the hospital?!" yelled Deb. I was confusing her—I should have started earlier in the story.

"No, I mean, he was, but not because of the arrest." I realized I was only scratching the surface. "It was because the car chase ended in a crash, so—"

"Tommy, what the hell is going on up there?!" I don't blame Deb for leaping out of her chair at this point —she's a busy professional who doesn't have time for action flicks starring Dad. I took a deep breath and continued.

"I haven't told you about any of this yet because I didn't want to worry you. Haven't you noticed when you call Dad that there's some, uh, slippage?" I liked throwing in that word "slippage."

"No," she said, putting down her wine glass crisply. I thought it was going to shatter. "Actually I haven't." That's fair. If you talk to Dad and Lil by phone, they sound like they always do, unslipped.

"Well, in person, he and Lil ... Deb, I'm just saying that their time is starting to come, I think. We'll need to take action at some point," I concluded.

"Action? I'm not even clear on the problem yet, Tommy. Why is our father acting like Scarface?" I felt I had to establish the main point, then bring the story to a close concisely.

"Because when hospital interns put on rubber gloves and approach him, he remembers he doesn't have anyone to talk to!" I insisted.

My comment was met with a silence. I admit that if you hadn't lived through the whole story, my version was probably muddled. But silence is something rare for my sister, so I put my coffee down to enjoy it. She picked her wine glass up.

"Tommy," she said calmly, "if he needs to talk, get him a cell phone."

I love my sister.

That's it. Game on. I put my foot down and insisted that my parents each get a cell phone. On Deb's advice, I got two matching basic phones and plans, then snuck over there and arranged them on the kitchen table, each next to its expensive leather casing, each turned on. I even left a nice card that said, "For Las Vegas and more" so that when Dad and Lil came home, they would know the devices are intended for travel in addition to everyday living.

Then I waited. All day. Nothing. I finally called—the cell phones, of course, not their landline. First I called Lil's. No answer, but I did get my own voice on the voicemail I had set up for her. I left a message, knowing that I'd be teaching them how to access voicemail. Having a real message to hear would be nice. Then I called Dad's. No answer *and* no voicemail, although I had set his up as well. I called the landline.

Lil answered immediately, bright as day. The sound of the TV filled the background.

"Hi, Mom," I said.

"Thomas, hello. How are you, darling? How's Mel?"

"We're fine, Mom. Hey, I left you two each a little gift today. Did you find them?"

"We did, and I'm so glad you called because we wanted to thank you, dear. What a wonderful surprise!"

I was encouraged—whenever Lil says something is "wonderful," at least she hasn't rejected it. You know you're way off track when she says, "Isn't that sweet." And I do mean without the question mark.

"I'd like to come over and show you and Dad how to use them. It's really easy." She consented, and I got in my car right away.

When I got there, I let myself in as I always do. Lil was upstairs at her desk checking off her to-do list, which always includes paying bills on time and other satisfying tasks. She loves doing that. Dad was in front of the TV.

"Hey, Dad."

"Hey, Tom, c'mon in."

"How're things?"

"Great," he said without taking his eyes off the screen. "Have a seat." I sat for a while and watched the *Frasier* rerun. I have to admit that, unlike Dad's latest episode, Frasier's was a very funny one, and much less dangerous. And Dad was having a good belly-grunt over it. I waited for a lull then hit the mute button.

"So Dad, I left you both some gifts on the table this morning. Whadja think?"

He looked up at me. "Think?"

I went to the kitchen. The leather casings were on the table, but the phones were not. Lil had come downstairs.

"Thomas, you're here—let me make you some coffee." I hugged my mom and watched over her shoulder as Dad unmuted the TV. In a coffee shop, Frasier and Niles were making an audience laugh heartily over something otherwise tragic, like erectile dysfunction. I used that time to chit chat with my mom, sliding naturally into the subject of the phones. She jumped right in, calling to Dad.

"Honey, where are the gifts Tom left for us?"

I didn't like her not using the word "phones." It said more than I wanted to hear. Dad lumbered over to us, sighing. He stopped at the kitchen table and looked around.

"Damned things kept ringing."

"They're supposed—" I started. I was glad Lil cut me off.

"But where are they, hon?" she asked him. In that next second, I realized he didn't know how to answer them and didn't want to say it. Fortunately, that also meant that he didn't know how to turn them off, so when I tried Lil's number from the landline, the muffled ring tone led us to two phones rolled up in a dishcloth and stuffed into the utensils drawer.

"No harm done!" Lil took both phones out of the drawer and explained to Dad that I was going to show them how to "make them stop ringing." Lil is clever, I have to admit—telling me how they felt about the phones and persuading Dad all in one short phrase.

Frasier was over, so we all sat down in the living room. I put the phones on the coffee table and began explaining how useful a cell phone can be. Dad listened from behind a poker face while Lil went and got the cups and coffee. I wanted to show them how to program all

49

our numbers into it, but a little voice was telling me to stick to the basics, so I focused only on how to answer and hang up. An hour later, Lil was getting it, but I couldn't tell if Dad didn't understand or was just being belligerent.

Mel called to see how it was going. I made a big deal out of taking out my phone, showing off to Dad and Lil that it was ringing, and saying, "Hello?" as if my caller ID weren't announcing that it was Mel. Teaching by example. I told Mel we were still working on our phone demo and asked her to call both Lil and Dad so they can have some "real world experience." Lil looked fairly interested, and Dad looked more irritated, but when Mel called them, they both answered their devices with relative ease.

I was proud. I had Mel call each of them once more to be sure they had got it. Lil was delighted and stayed on the phone with her. They chatted about baby wear while I asked Dad to stand so I could attach his phone to his belt. I'd purposely bought a casing that will attach my father to it.

When I was done, he stood stiffly, his arms held just away from his sides as if suffering from underarm boils. The look on his face was that of a 3rd grader who has to carry his lunch in an old Partridge Family lunchbox when everyone else has Buzz Lightyear, even though that analogy is backward if you really think about it.

When I got home exhausted, Mel recognized the situation for what it was: a quasi episode. We spent the whole car ride out to the cave dreaming up the title. We're calling this one "The Great Phone Caper."

.   .   .

We stopped at the local market cafe and picked up some groceries along with more lore on this place. First off, there are all kinds of sea motifs like strings of shells hanging in souvenir shop windows. There's a café-bar near the beach named "Pirate's Cove" and other silliness, even at this time of year, when none of the seasonal boaters or campers are around. We're not even near the sea. It's a lake, for God's sake. When you try to talk to these people about it, they act as if a local legend about pirates is just common knowledge, but they won't elaborate or say whether they believe it or not. When we asked Gregory about it, he gave us the old mumbo jumbo.

"They ain't talking, friend. Won't, neither. Not till a good soul brings the light. Then everthing'll be revealed." When he wants to emphasize something like the word "light," he tips his head forward and shakes it slowly from side to side as if proclaiming a profound truth.

After some head-shaking, he looked me up and down. "Whoever brings the light, friend, he'll be playful and wise." I felt my intelligence vaguely insulted. His comments remind me of those thousand suns again. I'm not buying it.

It's just that the people of this little lake community are acting like a bunch of backward, superstitious villagers from centuries past, all the while selling this flimsy myth to summer lake visitors. And here, in these most advanced United States of America. Some locals claim that in the summer, they find small pieces from the pirates' boat on the lake's more remote shores. One of the jewelry shops even has a piece of driftwood encased in glass and displayed prominently with some of the more expensive necklaces draped on it. While Mel was browsing in there the other day, the owner explained to me that she found it "in the area" and that it has been proven to be a piece of a hull from a very old boat. Then she pointed to a drawing on the wall. It was supposedly a re-creation of the pirates' ship based on research by the area's historical society. I've since seen that drawing around town in a number of places, like the background of the local diner's menu. It was floating behind the desserts like a watermark. I wonder how much the artist was paid to conjure that up. The jewelry shop owner compared the curve of the wood to the curve of a hull, as if that were a convincing argument. I said, "Curved? Like the Loch Ness monster?" but she kept right on talking over me.

The consensus in town seems to be that if you were to dive deep enough in the center of the lake, you would find the ship's remains. No one ever has, of course. I like this one: Various people in the town, like the mayor, claim to be the captain's descendants. Right.

I guess I shouldn't be such a pompous outsider. It does bring in cash. And so far, no one has even asked how we came to be staying there. The municipality hasn't sent a property tax bill, and Ol' Greg doesn't seem to be snitching on us. He doesn't ask if we bought the place or what we paid for it, and when we go into town, we're greeted like anyone else. Some people are starting to say, "So, you're up on the ridge. How do you like it?" with an air of curiosity but without using words like "buy" or "close" or any other phrases that would suggest a payment of property tax.

As we drove up there to haul more things in this evening, our quaint little squat-able seemed etched into the side of the landscape. Cute. This time we brought lots of tools and supplies, bedding, candles, a microwave, cleaning materials. I even brought the generator and got it going. It did feel quite therapeutic to dive in and work on the place. We hit on the idea of putting in a large bay window on the front wall facing the lake. That will change the whole look without ruining the rustic appeal.

Mel cleaned a bit and got the "bedroom" ready—a mattress in the middle of the floor—while I wrestled with the plumbing. Electrical current may not be running in this place, but cold water does. While I was busy replacing a faucet, Mel popped open the bottle of Pinot Grigio we had cleverly brought, then plopped herself down on the fresh sheets to entertain me with more "Jo stories."

Apparently, Jo worked the fields all her young life. Mel loved telling me that "she worked right zrough her pregnancy, right up to zee moment zee babies were born. All zee women did zis in zee old France," she said. "Zey helped each other and zey were good doctors," Mel continued. "Zey had to be—zere were no doctors." She took a sip of her wine. "She birthed *beaucoup d'enfants* in her life. When I was very young. I helped her ...."

I admit I wasn't really listening at first. I'm not sure I should put in writing here—in case anyone reads this— they won't, but if it they do—that men really do just pretend they're listening sometimes. Many times. But in my defense, I was wrestling with the new kitchen faucet at that moment. When it was finally in place, I went to turn the main back on. It's located in the bathroom. No cellar here.

"They sound like they were tough ladies," I said from the bathroom, referring to the women in her story, in the part I'd heard, anyway. I turned the rusty old crank. It was stuck, but I finally opened it. Water clanged and banged its way into the cave through what seemed like prehistoric pipes.

"*Oui,*" she said, "When zee baby moments came, zey stopped zeir work, got on zeir knees, and popped zee babies out," she said and snapped her fingers. "Just like *zat!*"

The kitchen faucet exploded off its base, shot up to the ceiling, and cracked off chunks of plaster. It all came raining down, the faucet bouncing off the counter and landing a few feet away from the small pile of chipped ceiling. Likewise did the bathroom faucet, shower fixtures, and toilet seat cover in the next room. After a stupefied moment, I noticed little rivers picking up the chipped plaster and running across the floor with it. I cranked the main shut, used language that admittedly ruined the wine-and-candles atmosphere—the one that was promising so much as soon as I was done playing plumber—and hopped into the car with Mel. We raced down to town to pick up a large squeegie mop, a bucket, washers, faucets, and other items, like a big fan to dry the floor. We luckily got there just before the town's only hardware store closed.

I know that Mel used the words "popped out" to be playful—and a bit facetious—but as I mopped up, I could also see the intense gleam in her eye. Even though I find "popped out" quease-inducing, the phrase kindles in Mel such a desire to grow life inside her that I decided that the punishment for child molesters should be to turn about 10 pregnant women loose on them in a small room. I feel sure that after such an experience, the offender would never do that again.

After much time spent mopping up, cleaning, and installing faucets and toilet parts, Mel and I fell on the mattress. There's nothing like candles, wine, the need to get away, a nice change of scene, and the successful wrapping up of a plumbing disaster to bring on romance. Even when you're exhausted.

I made love to my beautiful wife to the sound of an industrial fan blowing in the bathroom. It didn't bother us at all. It was mesmerizing, just a low tone humming soothingly in the background. It felt similar to falling asleep accompanied by the churning dishwasher back home. We drifted off very soon afterward with the generator and fan still going. Some time later, though, I woke to a new sound—Mel was weeping. I bolted upright to get a better look at her. Brushing a strand of her marvelous, soft, jet-black hair from her moist forehead, I asked, "What's the matter?"

"Tom, it is done." A tear rolled down her cheek. I felt like a soldier at the crucifixion.

"What's done?"

"I have zee feeling. I zink it is done."

All of a sudden, I knew what she meant. Now, I'm no woman, but my understanding is that no one can tell the exact moment of conception. Even pregnancy tests can't confirm until some weeks have passed.

"Zis place has made zee right mood, zee right ... magic ..." She was sobbing with joy. I drew her tight and hugged her, stroked her hair.

"That's amazing, honey. We might need to wait and see, though." That probably sounded like a downer, but I didn't want her to get her hopes up after so many failures. Recently, I had even been thinking about more drastic measures like adoption or fertility treatments, but I'm trying to give it a few more months. It's just that I don't buy into the idea that an outside influence, like location, can inspire internal biology. If it could, I'd be alerting my own seed to it, just in case. Her desire to conceive was pushing her intuition button a little too hard.

Later in the night, she became agitated. She kept waking, then waking me to insist that she heard the door creak. I didn't hear a thing. She swore by it and said it sounded as if someone was opening it. I went and checked it twice. It was closed and locked with the new deadbolt. Every time she thinks she's pregnant, she develops this overactive imagination that concerns me. I'm going to keep all these legends of pirates and hocus-pocus away from her, just to be safe.

But I couldn't sleep after all that. I'm sitting out here on a lawn chair using the tree stump like a footrest. Got the ol' laptop on my lap and a blanket under it. It's cold out, but the moon is full over the lake—spectacular —so I'm really enjoying writing. It's taken me so long to come back to the idea of keeping a journal. Most of my life, regrettably. This isn't really a journal, though. But even here, I can write words like "hocus-pocus" and when I go back and read them, it feels like all that living I'm doing is somehow recorded and reviewed. I don't need to wait until my funeral for some grieving relative at a podium to hash through my better moments like a movie preview someone forgot to put at the beginning.

In high school, I had my journal with me at all times. It was in the form of a beat-up composition notebook. I filled it with my thoughts and poetry and even my sketches and drawings. I was careful never to write anything too embarrassing in it—some pretty girl might find it and read it, and I had a persona to keep up. I was the junior editor of the school paper in my sophomore year, after all, known as something of a hip, up-and-coming writer, like maybe the Bob Dylan of the school's poetic underground. I commanded a kind of inverse fame, the kind the times back then bestowed upon rebels who claimed to be dodging notoriety while really enjoying the system and all its perks, perks like girls. It felt radical, and it got the attention of the girl whose attention I was trying to get, and of many of her friends as well.

Some of the guys in a band called The Lips were even putting some of my poetry to music. That's when I started calling my poetry "lyrics." I was at the top of the school's pop charts for a while until a bunch of other guys who thought they were cooler than all that money we were going to make tried to break my teeth. Poetry wasn't cool to everyone, even if The Lips were putting mine to music, good music, although they did go nowhere with that first album. By that time, disco had taken over everything anyway. I read once that ABBA has sold more records than The Beatles. That's just not right.

Then again, The Lips probably sucked. I don't know. I only remember not having a hard time trading my pen and notebook for a football that summer. If you can't beat 'em, join 'em is what I guessed. That was just a guess, though. You can be sure I'm not going to let this journal be read—I'm not going to turn it into a blog or post it on some dating site. God forbid I ever have to use online dating. I'm not going to post excerpts on facebook. I hardly ever get the chance to update my page, anyway. I'm not one to post my perfunctory deeds. "Finally got Dad poked today." I wouldn't post Dad's doctor appointments, even if my greatest accomplishment was to get him to one. That would be unbecoming.

I do remember missing my notebook after making the team. I wonder if I still have it somewhere. I'd like to read it again. I'd add some of those embarrassing stories I censored. They feel like they're still pacing back and forth inside me. Dealing with Dad recently is making me want to unlatch the door and let them bolt. Like that one time we Spartans were playing against the Coyotes in some serious October mud.

There I was, really moving, wide open, when something odd happened. My legs started feeling numb. Not numb, really, I just couldn't control them. They were locked into a pattern, one lashing forward while the other replaced the first and so on, until both legs felt like they were spinning like the legs of the Road Runner, the one on the Saturday morning cartoon of my youth. I guess I wouldn't know what a roadrunner was if it weren't for that cartoon. No one would, probably. But I did learn, just now, that those birds are also known as "chaparral cocks" or "geococcyx californianus." You've got to love Wikipedia. And smart phones.

So as I made my way down the field, I felt my whole body calm and smiling from the waist up while my legs spun beneath it, just like the cartoon character. Coyotes were coming at me from all sides, but the legs just kept spinning, and the calm just kept getting calmer, especially in my head, where it brought on a sudden feeling of futility.

It was a home game, so you would think that feeling futile in front of hundreds of screaming fans would slow the road running. But the more adoration I got, the more I ran. Futility poured like flood water into every crevice in my brain, but I pushed on, even though there seemed no point to it. The calmness even rendered uninteresting the regular glimpses I was getting of rosy-nippled cheerleaders bouncing in the extreme periphery of my view. I do realize that I was imagining the nipples —in reality, they were covered.

But I kept running. In fact, I couldn't *not* run. The ball had become a chicken in my hands, all feathery and ready to flap away toward a goal. It was then that I realized I was not needed to get it there. It had its own wings and intentions, so why were all those people cheering for me? I remember really clutching that bird to keep it from taking flight.

All of a sudden, something lumpy slammed into my chest. In the next second it got tangled in my spinning legs, but I just kept going, repeating to myself that I would never be caught dead telling anyone about the chicken. The guys would never let me forget it, like they never let that guy Eric forget.

No one could figure out how Eric had made the team, even though his size did make him more nimble. He was a pretty good, but not great, wide receiver. He used to talk like a girl, in this really femmy way that got on everyone's nerves. When a poem he wrote got into the school paper, I remember thinking, "Hey, that's a pretty good toaster poem." I secretly admired him for writing such a cool poem about a kitchen appliance. But I was glad that I didn't have my name attached to it there on the page because of what they did to him in the showers the next day. I never went near that particular stall again, and neither did Eric. The guys laughed when we got word about the lawsuit, which fired up a rush of confidential meetings and then fizzled out. If you're a fem-sayer in the middle of the wrong combination of lawyers-as-parents whose sons were being courted by some of the biggest names in college ball, then you'd better finish high school at Catholic Academy across town and forget it. Which he did, as far as I knew.

I let the chicken go at the end zone. It beat it immediately. I could barely make out through its squawking and flapping all those people pouring onto the field and yelling about clearing the way for the ambulance. Time momentarily halted while the ambulance folks scraped that star Coyote up off the ground, the one I had run over. All I remembered thinking is "Hey, that's great that they called in animal control" and "Coach is gonna be all over me for losing that chicke...ball."

I know the chicken-ball story sounds like maybe I cashed in my marbles for a minute or something, but after the confusion died down and the ambulance lights disappeared into the rain, some of us went and combed the end zone. The ball was never found.

So I watch my dad these days and tell myself that he's just not himself lately. Things can happen to a guy sometimes. He's probably just road-running toward his own personal end zone and enjoying a private moment with his bird. Everyone is entitled to that once in a while. But I also know that if he were on the other side, getting clobbered in a game, he would get right back up and maul his assailant, even if his assailant were his own son holding onto his own chicken. Lil has always insisted that "Martin is a kind and gentle husband and father who would never hurt a fly."

He wouldn't, but self-defense is a skill you need in hospital administration. Trust me.

. . .

I waited until we returned from the cave. Then I walked out onto the porch and took a deep breath. The cool air cleared my mind. I called the cell phones. Good thing I programmed them to ring something like 15 times before going to voicemail. Dad actually answered on the 14th ring. I'm hoarse, though, from screaming over and over, "Dad, turn it the other way!" and "You've got it upside down! That's why you can't hear me!"

Lil was shouting in the background, trying to get him to put it correctly to his ear. I put the phone on speaker to see if I could catch more of what was happening, but when the grumbling and shuffling noises finally stopped, all I heard was breathing. I debated whether to say "Hello" or not, but Lil's voice was suddenly there again, telling him to "Say '*Hello*.'" I heard more breathing, then an angry "I don't hear a thing here, Lil." Then the line went dead.

When I looked up, Phineas was standing there. I remembered seeing him approaching as I was yelling. He'd waited politely until the call was over before greeting me as he always does.

"Ay, sira, how goes the world?" he asked. I wanted to unload. I was fidgeting with the phone quite a lot.

"Ya know, Phin, my parents want to go on their annual trip to Las Vegas, but I'm really starting to worry about them, especially about Dad. I used to worry about Stephen like that when he was little, you know, that real sense of urgency. Like at any moment he could touch a hot burner or race out into the street in front of the nearest teen driver or—"

"Sir, pardon me in what I have to say," Phineas interrupted. "This speech of yours hath moved me. Didst thou speak with him? Know'st thou his mind?"

"I'm starting to know it more than I ever wanted to," I said. When you're the parent of little ones, you think their shaky grasp on reality is cute, but now I'm becoming the parent of my own parents. "I'm afraid Dad will wander onto the wrong plane and 13 hours later end up in Singapore. Or maybe he'll have an episode at the airport and somehow throw an entire anti-terrorism unit into action. I'll see him in handcuffs on the nightly news —"

"I see this hath a little dashed your spirits," he broke in again. I kept babbling.

"My sister isn't here to help, but she would, I mean, she lives in New York—"

"She's a good creature?" he asked. I stopped.

"A really good one," I said. "She's always the one who wants to jump in and help. She's the one who suggested cell phones."

"She is exceeding wise."

"And able. Ya know, it'd be great if she could go with them," I mused. I paused. So did Phineas.

"I think I saw your wisdom there," he finally said before I got it. Then I got it.

"Phin, we'll ask her to go—this is great!" I cried. "What a great idea—then she'd have the opportunity to spend some time with them and see what I'm talking about—"

"Fortune brings in some boats that are not steered," he said plainly.

"I'm gonna call her right now," I said and pulled out my phone again. The professor doesn't seem to have any family himself, but he does give spectacular advice on family dynamics. "Ya know, we really haven't had time to tackle this problem together yet."

Mel had stepped out onto the porch with us and was tuning in to our emerging plan.

"Zis sounds interesting," she said while I held up my phone and began scrolling to find Deb.

"Yeah, but I'm not sure Dad'll want a babysitter tagging along with them on their big trip. We might have to insist," I said.

"Why force you this?" asked Phineas. He stepped a pace away from me and looked up to the sky as if divinely inspired. Then he looked me in the eye. "If he were conveyed to bed, wrapped in sweet clothes, rings put upon his fingers, a most delicious banquet by his bed, and brave attendants near him when he wakes—would not the beggar then forget himself?" he offered. Mel looked to me and waited for my reaction.

"Butter him up—I like that," I said. "You know, maybe Deb could bring the kids up for a visit, and we could casually mention that she'll go with them," I mused. "They could join us for Thanksgiving or something."

"Zen it will be seem natooral to Dad," said Mel. She turned and smiled again at Phineas.

"Aye. Let our plot go forward," he said. "Everyone according to his cue." I nodded and touched Deb's number. We waited for many rings. Deb finally picked up.

"Hey," she said. My sister's face was on-screen clear as day, but she seemed to be at a loud party.

"Deb, hey. What's the noise?" I asked.

"I'm at an event for a new client. Look," she said. "I'll three-sixty you." She turned her phone all the way around the room. She was standing in some sort of posh meeting room in a hotel somewhere. There was a large spread of food at a central table, and an even larger bar.

"So do you have a minute?" I asked.

"Until the expensive new client wants to talk to me, I do," she quipped. "What's up?"

"Well, listen," I started, "Mel and I were doing a lot of thinking about the Vegas trip, and we were, you know, tossing around ideas about how, if one of us were to go with them, it might be—"

"I hate Vegas, Tommy," she declared. My sister is clever.

"But wait," I said, "All you'd have to do is keep an eye on them so he doesn't wander out into the desert and not come back."

"He'll never accept a babysitter on their trip—"

There was a sudden commotion nearby. The picture began swishing back and forth as if Deb were dangling her phone willy-nilly from a string. Someone seemed to be accosting her—I heard a lot of high-pitched cackling. After a moment, Deb pointed the phone again at herself.

"Hey, Tommy," she said. Another female voice was nearby. Deb began laughing with her. "Meet Rina," She whipped the phone around to the owner of the voice. "Rina, this is my little brother Tom and his wife, Mel."

"Hi brother and wife!" The woman waved with one hand and barely held onto a Martini with the other. Deb turned the phone back on herself.

"Mel is French," she said to Rina while texting to us: FAMILY OWNS 1/2 OF MIDTOWN.

"I speak French!" we heard Rina yell.

"Now, I didn't know that, Reen," smarmed my sister. I know she has to do that kind of thing with clients.

Another text came through: SKUNK DRUNK.

Then another: AS ALWAYS.

"Yeah!" More yelling from Rina—Deb turned the lens on her. "I love French!"

"That's great, Reen." Deb turned the phone on herself again and typed to us as she continued speaking to Rina. Her text read, CAN'T SPEAK A WORD.

The phone swung around to Rina once more. "You could talk here a bit with Mel," I heard my sister say. Rina was swaying side to side. Deb shot us another text.

UH OH.

What seemed to be Rina's voice, much lower and much quieter now, was welling up into song.

"*Non, rien ...*"

Text: LOVES EDITH PIAF.

"*... regret ...*"

Text: SINGS ENTIRE REPERTOIRE.

"*... good things ...*"

Text: MOSTLY IN ENGLISH.

"*... the past ...*"

Text: HAVE HEARD IT ALL   :   (

" *... memories ...*"

There was another assault. The picture went swishy again for a moment. Someone was crying. When it recovered, Deb was on-screen, pointing the phone at herself over Rina's shoulder. Rina was leaning on her and sobbing. Deb was rolling her eyes at us. A male voice sounded.

"Rina!" it said. "Sorry, Deb—you know how she gets." From what we could tell, the owner of the voice peeled Miss Rina off my sister. Now both the picture and the sound were muffled a bit. All we could hear was Deb saying, "No problem, Reen ... yes, yes. No problem ... You're right, Piaf was a god, surely ...."

It took a minute for the picture and sound to clear, but when it did, Deb was back.

"So," she said. She looked exhausted. "All in a day's work." Neither of us spoke for a moment.

"You're a natural caregiver, Sis," I finally said. A group of people burst out laughing in the background. Deb stared in silence.

"I'll let you go, Deb. But look, we're going to have a little warm-'em-up-and-feel-'em-out party here over Thanksgiving. You know, about the trip. Just come up and join in. We'll see how it goes," I concluded. Mel leaned into the picture.

"Deborah, we have already bought zee beverages for zee dinner—a beautiful Alsace Chardonnay." Mel interjected in an alluring, sing-songy voice. She's not beyond a good white lie for a good cause. And Deb is not beyond a good white wine.

"You and David and Zoe could stay this time at Dad and Lil's and not here with us. Stephen and Jamie will even join us—Lil will think it's great having all the grandkids together. And that way, you can help them out a bit around the house so they'll see that help can be a plus, not a 'babysitting.' In the meantime, we'll all slip into the conversation throughout the visit that you've always wanted to go to Vegas—"

"Yeah, except that I don't," interrupted Deb. "Why don't you just talk them out of going?"

I stared directly into the little camera on my phone and didn't speak. Mel leaned into the picture again. I'm sure all we needed was a quaint, decorative window behind us and a pitchfork in my hand for our Gothic look to say it all. On Deb's end, a waitress passed by with a tray full of drinks. Deb took one and downed it in a gulp. After hesitating, she spoke.

"When are they leaving?"

.   .   .

"I know that they usually stay with you and Mel, Tom, but please, give your old mother this time with them and let them stay with us. Now, when are they arriving?"

"The day before Thanksgiving," I said.

"We'll put Deb and Zoe in the spare room and David in the den."

"We can even move that contraption off the desk."

The way Dad and Lil were talking, you'd think their daughter and grandchildren had never been up for a visit. They wanted to be sure Deb and David and Zoe stayed in their home and not with me and Mel. Lil wanted to bake for the holiday, and the arrival of the "Deb contingent" a day early was met with great cheer. Lil's baking is reserved for only the most special of occasions, and this one was upon us before we knew it.

They all spent Wednesday together while Mel and I were at work. I purposely did not call until evening so that my sister and her kids could have that time with them. But on Thanksgiving day, Mel and I went over there early and helped Lil prepare the meal. She brimmed with happiness showing Mel how to baste a bird, American style. We made sure the wine was Alsace Chardonnay, of course, and we even broke out the old record albums from the cabinet in their console. Frank Sinatra was the unanimous choice. Did it really take a whole piece of furniture to play music back then? We couldn't believe the thing still worked. But it didn't matter where those tunes were coming from—everyone loved it. And as a wonderful addition to the evening, we invited Phineas. It seemed as if he would be alone again on a holiday, and Mel said she couldn't stand that.

I went over and picked him up right before dinner. He was wearing his bow tie and a suit that was straight out of the 1950s. I remember Dad's bow ties, and I've always liked them. To me, they scream "Real man!" and make a guy look as if he's from another, more confident age, like a real CEO type—the guy who has it together and is incapable of making a bad decision or becoming unglued.

As we ate, Deb chatted it up with Lil and Dad about their stay so far. It seems that yesterday they had a late lunch together, and afterward, Dad took David on a driving lesson. Driving lesson? I panicked—David is too young to drive and Dad is getting too old.

"We only went around the block, Uncle Tom," David assured me. He's only 14. I couldn't help picturing a lawsuit. Stephen jumped in.

"Don't you remember wanting to drive so bad it hurt, Dad?" my son asked me.

"Yeah, I do," I said, "but this guy here"—I pointed at Dad—"made me wait until I was a ripe old 16," I teased.

I haven't seen Dad that proud—or that happy—in quite a while. He and David, his grandson, had colluded to do something illegal together that afternoon and they did it and loved it. That kind of bonding can't be bought or planned. I felt like we were in an episode of The *Brady Bunch* for how well this was going.

After dinner, it was Benny Goodman all the way. The very first number—Dad kept calling them "numbers"—was *Sing, Sing, Sing*. That got everyone up and dancing. Even David and Zoe. I danced with Lil, Deb danced with Dad, Stephen danced with Zoe, David bopped around on his own; then Mel danced with David, Phineas danced with Deb, I danced with Jamie ... as I said, how well this was going.

Since Dad and Lil were so occupied, I cut in to dance with my sister. Phineas gave her up easily and waited off to the side like a perfect gentleman.

"So. Whattya think?" I said.

"We're skunks, Tommy," she answered. "Why don't we do this every Thanksgiving? Lil is the happiest I've ever seen her."

"We will," I said. We danced for a few minutes.

"Oh, before I forget—you might want to come back some time soon and put in another gazing ball," she said. The blank look on my face made her continue. "You know, that decorative purple ball on a little ceramic stand in the garden? It's trashed."

"Trashed?" I asked.

"Yeah. Dad smashed it," she said. "He backed right over it with the car. He seems a bit shaky behind the wheel, Tommy. You might want to keep an eye on him," she suggested.

"This must have been *after* he took David out for a spin," I said.

"You bet," she agreed. Deb would never let David get into a car with someone who shows even a hint of instability. "But you know, I gotta tell ya, Little B, I really don't see Dad or Lil as 'coming to their time,' or whatever you called it. They seem pretty good otherwise."

I didn't know what to say. I couldn't push her to go to Las Vegas if she didn't see a need. We danced quietly again before she continued. Benny's *Sing, Sing, Sing* had given way to *Moonglow*. Our step slowed.

"Ya know, Tommy, I always remember my friends in school thinking it was real cool that we called our mom by her first name. How did that ever get started?" she asked me.

"We just followed Dad's lead in calling her 'Lil' I guess. That's what I always thought," I said.

"I thought it was because of that time Dad was teasing her about being petite, so he shortened her name from 'Lillian' to 'Lil' and it stuck. Remember that?" she asked. "It was that day they took us to the zoo and it was really hot, and ...."

I didn't remember that at all. Sometimes Deb talks about our childhood as if she grew up in some other family. I nodded. When she was done reminiscing, I asked point blank.

"So should we nix the Vegas plan?"

Deb smiled. Her smile kept growing.

"What?" I said. "Did you already bring it up to them?"

"Guess what Lil said to me this afternoon?"

"What?"

"She and Dad want me and the kids to come to Vegas with them this year."

Just when it couldn't get any better. I didn't even wait to hear if she'd said yes or not. Smiling uncontrollably and in perfect step, I escorted my sister back to the professor. He was bobbing his head to the music and already lifting his hands to again accept his dancing partner.

"I like this place and willingly could waste my time in it," he said.

"Waste away!" I said as he and Deb whisked each other off.

I didn't mean that like it sounded. I meant that we owe all this good timing and success to Phineas for suggesting this plan in the first place.

Deb and the kids are safely back in New York, and our Vegas scheme is in the works. Since Dad and Lil went out shopping today for the trip, I thought it would be a good time to install the new cordless phone I've had in mind—a touch tone, of course. It was also a good opportunity to snoop around their house for problems and check that they're not investing in time travel, joining a cult, or taking a class on genital tattooing.

When I arrived, I saw—and smelled—that the toilet had overflowed in what Lil has always called the "powder room." Such a dainty name sporting such a mess. As I walked through the house and approached it, I saw a woman in there working away. She wore an apron and some overgrown, heavy-duty rubber work gloves. She was scooping up what had overflowed from the toilet and was dumping it back into the bowl with what looked like a garden shovel. It was not pleasant. I introduced myself—safely, from the hallway.

"Oh, hello," she said cheerily, "you must be Tom." She took off one glove and extended her hand. "You look just like your dad." I took a deep breath, extended my hand, and hoped that she'd been wearing gloves for the entire operation.

"Yes, and—" I said as we shook. I was going to ask her who she was and what happened, but I didn't have to.

"I'm Kelly. I just moved in. Here on the rock-garden side." As she emptied a last shovelful into the bowl, she motioned with her head toward that side of the house. I was not aware that the house next door had even been for sale.

"Your folks needed a hand here, and since they're so busy getting ready for a trip, I said, 'Marty,' I said, 'go on out—I've got some thick gloves and a good plunger.' So they're out running errands." She put the shovel down, picked up the large plunger that was standing there, and started plunging and grunting. After a moment, she flushed. The offending soup swirled away. "Pardon me while I go grab some cleaner to wrap this up." She smiled, set gloves, shovel, and plunger off to the side, stepped out of the powder room onto an old towel she had there to wipe her rubber boots, and went out the back door to her house.

No one can say that humanity is all bad when, suddenly, there's a new neighbor who cleans up your elderly parents' sewage just to be nice. I did not allow her to continue. When she came back, I had a hard time convincing her that I would finish the clean-up, but she finally accepted. I thanked her profusely. She insisted I keep the mop and gloves, then she left with a smile.

"Nice meeting you, Tom!" she called through my parents' open garage.

"Same," I said. "And thanks again."

When it was all finally mopped and wiped, I wished she'd left the apron as well. I went to the hardware store for a plumber's snake and some toilet parts to keep on hand. I brought them back to my parents' and tackled the installation of the cordless.

I hung the new phone in the same spot as the old one so they'd see it. Then I waited for my parents to come home. They didn't appear. I called Dad's cell. It rang faintly from its hiding place between the couch cushions. I pulled it out, set it on the coffee table, and tried Lil's. She answered. She was in the produce section of the supermarket. My mom doesn't usually tolerate being interrupted in produce, so that was an added plus. She asked if I would call her back in ten minutes when she's done. I almost asked her if she would call me, but I was afraid I'd never hear back from them. I waited nine minutes.

She picked up quickly again. I felt encouraged, but I heard a lot of noise in the background. I asked what was going on.

"Well, dear, your father and I are on our way home."

A constant whizzing could be heard in the background, as if they were in a moving vehicle with the windows open. I thought that was strange in this cold weather. Blaring car horns punctuated the whizzing intermittently. Then Lil's voice came through weakly, as if she were holding the phone away from her head.

"Careful. *Careful.*"

More horns. Then I heard Dad's voice, not near the phone, but clear as day.

"Fuck your own mother!"

"Ma, what's going on?!" I yelled.

Fortunately, the line didn't go dead, and for as long as the phone sat on Lil's lap, or on the car seat, or

74

wherever it was, I didn't hear any car-on-car impact. Just the whiz of moving vehicles mixed with Lil and Dad's occasional talking, other blaring horns, and Dad's shouting. I yelled a few more times into the phone but got no response.

I listened desperately, dreading each new sound. All of a sudden the whizzing noise stopped. I heard car doors open. I ran to their front door and flung it open. Dad and Lil were calmly getting out of their car. They began taking grocery bags out of the trunk.

I guess I lost myself for a moment. I ran out onto their porch and yelled, "God, I'm so glad you two are back!" I almost said *are back safely*.

Lil and Dad stood on their brick front walkway looking up at me. I looked down from the porch at the two people standing there. They looked so small. Each held a grocery bag. We stared at each other until Dad grunted, "Of course we're back. Where the hell else would we go after the supermarket? A brothel?" I held the door open for them.

As soon as they were inside, I went to the car and brought in the rest of the bags. Dad had already deposited his in the kitchen and was on his way to the couch. Lil was "aproning up" as she calls it to put things away and start dinner. I tried to help but she shooed me away.

I had only been sitting on the couch with Dad a minute when the landline rang. And rang. At first, I was thrilled—what great timing. I waited to see if he would get up to answer it, or if Lil would step away from her sink, dry her hands on the nearby dish towel, and walk over to answer it as I have seen her do a thousand times throughout my life, but neither of them moved.

I picked up the remote, turned down the TV, and lifted my chin to show that something was getting my attention. When neither Dad nor Lil responded, I started to worry that they had both suddenly lost their hearing. After yet another ring, I asked as calmly as I could, "Do you want me to get that?"

Both my parents looked at me as if I had blasphemed gravely. The call went to voicemail as we all stayed frozen in our places. We were pointed at one another like a circle of gun-wielding bandits surprising each other at a heist, then holding each other at gunpoint, unable to start shooting or stop pointing.

All my realizations came at once: (A) My parents will never be able to use cell phones because even landlines have become too high-tech; (B) My parents may have to be introduced soon to one of those "call for help" buttons some elderly people wear around their necks, but Dad would rather hang himself with it I'm sure; (C) I will never be able to substitute phones of any sort for the inevitable task of finding viable alternatives for keeping track of my increasingly self-menacing parents.

I turned to my father. He was absorbed in an infomercial as if it were a sudden death overtime. As I watched him, my mind suddenly hatched a plan. While Lil finished putting groceries away, I launched it.

"Hey, Dad," I said, "I was just thinking about how you and I used to have a drink every now and then, but we haven't done that for a while. Whattya say we go down to The Jockey for a warm up? I'm trying to be a father again, after all, so let's 'clink.'" An occasional "clink," as Dad used to call it, to "warm up" to things had been his MO all his working life. I turned to Lil and said, "Don't worry, Ma, I'll have him back by dinner."

When I turned back to Dad, he was lit up like their Christmas tree—the real one Mel insisted I set up for them this year to replace that fake one they've had forever. He was smiling uncontrollably. I turned to Lil for her approval, but she was a step ahead of me. She was happily washing vegetables, saying, "You boys have fun."

I didn't even have to say, "Dad, why don't you drive?" His good mood placed him squarely in the driver's seat in his own car, and his body and keys simply followed.

I'm always surprised that The Jockey is still around. The town is proud of it. It's been there for ages, and it looks and feels like a real English pub. Dad and his work buddies used to go there after important meetings and he loved it. I'd bet he hasn't been there since those days. For my purposes, it's not too close and not too far away. Just close enough so that I could get a good look at his driving.

I didn't mean to get that close. I should just concentrate on the great time we had. He was joking with the bartender and everyone else, exactly as if he hadn't almost run over a whole group of pedestrians, scared the hell out of a motorcyclist, and bounced off the stone curb a few times on the way into the parking lot. It was as if those things hadn't even happened. His high spirits—and the bourbon—made it easy for me to get his keys away from him after a few hours and offer to drive us home, which I did.

I'm not sure I would call Dad's bad driving display a full-fledged episode, but like the overflowing toilet, it could turn into one at any moment. Mel agreed with me on that, so we were up early today, throwing everything we might need for the cave into the car. We drove directly here from work. We thought that a little anti-episode breather out in the country might yield a plan for getting Dad off the road.

We got to work on time and pulled into our parking space right next to Jack. Jack is one of our best anesthesiologists and a real friend and supporter of my new life with Mel. We all got out of the cars to start our day. As happens often when our colleagues see Mel and me together, a few of them gave us tender looks that said, "How cute that you fell in love here at the hospital and now you're sharing your lives so completely." It's nice, but I'm not naive. There are also looks that say, "There's Tom Conklin, the a**hole who dropped poor Marla for that young French floozie." Mel ignores those looks really well. She tries to put my mind at ease by reminding me how readily Marla agreed to the split. Jack always jumps in and says something like, "She did? Well there ya go, Tom."

"That's great," I say. "Thanks."

Jack and I walked Mel to her office, then headed off to mine. I began telling him about Dad's mounting episodes. As we walked, I noticed that his resemblance to a star-nosed mole just won't subside. He's reminded me of one since I met him:

Maybe it's the way his face narrows to a strangely flat nose. Or maybe it's his narrow shoulders. Certainly those short arms don't help, the way they hang obliquely at his sides over a spreading midriff and taper to huge, out-of-proportion hands. One of them held a brown paper bakery bag. The other held a coffee. When we arrived at my office, I got settled behind my desk, and Jack sat across from me.

"Hey, lemme share this morning," he said. "You look as though you need it." He reached into the bag and took out two wrapped bagels. Jack tends to eat two of everything, so handing me half his breakfast was quite generous. I could feel the plump warmness through the wax paper, and it felt good. "Salt, with cream cheese," he said. He opened his and started eating. "You got me eating these—they're great with coffee." He popped open his coffee and washed down his mouthful.

"So," I said. I put the bagel down for a moment. "I'm not sure what to do about Dad," I guardedly continued our hallway chat. Conversations with Jack tend to stray into the philosophical or political realm, and when they go there, they may never end. If I looked like a star-nosed mole, I would probably wax philosophical each day. I reached for the comfort of my bagel. "He and Lil are planning their annual trip to Las Vegas. They're excited about it, but he seems to be developing some anger issues, you know, getting frustrated at things that didn't use to bother him." I started unwrapping.

"And he lashes out," said Jack.

"Yeah, and he doesn't seem to grasp new things or ideas like he used to."

"Like technology?"

"Yeah."

"And he probably can't drive either."

"He can't!" I yelled. Jack has a way of cutting right to the point, too. "Just yesterday, for example, I let him take me for a spin so I could see him at the wheel—"

"And you wished you hadn't," he deadpanned.

"That's right—I had no idea my dad's driving has gone so far south," I complained. I thought I remembered Jack mentioning once that his grandfather was having some similar difficulties.

"It's all a part of the human experience, Tom," he began, "it's unexplainable. And we're forced to accept it, to let go while at the same time taking responsibility for our own authenticity and remaining acutely aware of our unique choices in this hostile world."

"Hostile is right!" I dropped my bagel back onto its tissue paper without taking a bite. Then I jumped out from behind my desk. "That's what's wrong with Western medicine—we've built machines that can bombard a tumor or stone inside someone's body, obliterating the target without touching or even looking at what's around it!" I yelled. What did that have to do with my dad?

"We're used to putting things under microscopes," Jack added.

"Yes!" I exclaimed again. I forgot to sit down.

"We never zoom out and look at the whole person. We're always looking at what's sick and never at what's surrounding it that's probably well," he concluded.

"That's so right," I declared, "hospitals aren't set up to take care of *people*!"

Jack and I breathed heavily and stared at the wall for a while, neither of us saying one single word. Actually, Jack was chewing—I was the one breathing heavily. I became aware slowly of my upcoming meeting, of the people shuffling by in the corridors. A distant phone rang. My parents were being pulled from a perpetual wreckage in my mind, but I was removing myself for a moment, like an out-of-body experience. Or as Jack might say, an out-of-experience experience. My salt bagel was getting cold on the desk.

It was Jack who broke the silence. "Hey, give Motor Vehicles a call. You're not the only one who's ever had this problem," he said.

I called out to Andre. He poked his head in.

"Can you get me the number for Motor Vehicles?" I asked.

"It's 518-486-9786," he said, without hesitating.

I dialed in a frenzy before I forgot the number. New York State answered, then predictably put me on hold. I hit the speaker button. Muzak played for us and was punctuated intermittently by robo-announcements—their web address, reminders to keep our vehicle registrations up to date, and a countdown of our wait time, which was narrowed to less than half an hour. Jack and I actually enjoyed it as a restful pause. Then, a clerk was suddenly and prematurely on the line. I rambled to her about my elderly father needing a reality check for his driving habits. She was a patient listener.

"You may fill out our online form, sir. Then when we have it in writing, we'll send out a letter to the person in question. It will state that a review has shown that he's due for a vision check-up and a driving test," she informed me. I jumped all over that miracle.

"Will the person notified know who turned him in?"

"No, sir. Our letter only requests compliance."

Ingenious. When Dad doesn't pass, the ever-vigilant Department of Motor Vehicles—not his family—will revoke his license. And he'll never pass, of course. It's true that Dad's vision is extraordinary for his age so he might pass the eye test. But when he gets behind the wheel and takes three whole minutes to realize that his safe-deposit-box key will never turn on his vehicle, then has to shuffle through all his keys before he finds the right one, the examiner will surely conclude that the person sitting next to him should not be piloting nearly 4,000 pounds of steel down a crowded avenue.

Jack stood up, gathered his briefcase, his brown paper bag, and his coffee. He slapped his claw on the desk and said, "Hope that helped, Tom. Hey, one more thing—is his doc a gerontologist? 'Cause if he's not, you might wanna get him one who is."

My bagel sat cold and hard on its tissue. By the time Andre put together a list of the gerontologists associated with our facility, the idea of getting Dad to a doctor had canceled my appetite.

.　　.　　.

Deb email
Re: motor vehicles informant
tommy
 great plan. he'll fail. do it.
 ;)
 -Sis

It's 3 a.m. The moon is full here out on the ridge, and it's shining down on the cool lake. I have no doubt that if there really were pirates here who lost everything

—there weren't, but if there were—they would feel obliged to bow to nature's awesome power on a night like this. Or they'd get a little spooked, like I did last night.

I was sitting quietly outside, enjoying the crisp air when I suddenly felt a presence behind me. I knew it was Mel.

"Hey, didn't mean to wake you when I got up," I said. She didn't answer. I turned around.

There she was, holding a huge kitchen knife like a dagger, pointed at my head. The blade twinkled in the moonlight. I lunged away from it, even though I was pretty sure she was joking. "Ha," I said, "very funny." She just stared at me with a fuzzy look.

"Mel?" I said when she didn't speak. The blade wasn't going down. It seemed to hang in the air like Macbeth's. That's when I realized by her look that she was sleepwalking. Mel never sleepwalks.

Now, I don't know what to do with a sleepwalker, except that I've heard you shouldn't wake them, so I stopped talking. I got up slowly, took her gently by the back of her arm, and guided her back to our mattress on the floor. When we got there, I moved to take the knife. But I didn't manage it—she lowered it away from me, leaned down to the mattress, picked up the edge of it, and tapped the blade three times on the swirly pattern in the mosaic-tile-and-stone flooring underneath.

"Tile will tell," she said clearly.

She stood up. The knife was now limp in her hand, so I slid it out of her grip, set it aside, and tried to take her again by the arm. It wasn't necessary. She lay down by herself, curled up, and in no time was fast asleep.

In the morning, she denied ever having got up. She especially didn't like the part about the tile. "I think you meant '*time* will tell,' right, honey?" I asked, but she insisted she doesn't know that expression in English. Now she does. She also insisted that she's never had a sleepwalking problem in her life. I even showed her the knife.

"Tom, stop teasing me," was all she would say. I dropped the subject and suggested we go into town for brunch.

We arrived at the stretch of shops and cafes at the waterfront, and there was Ol' Gregory. Mel was happy to see him as always and asked him to join us. I was glad he had our company because I'm a bit worried about him. Every time we come out here, we stop in the village to get coffee or provisions and there he'll be, sitting at one of the cafes, dressed in spandex and flippers, or splattered with mud, or carrying some type of equipment like a shovel or a plumber's snake. This time, he was wearing goggles and had an icepick with him. We invited him into the nearest diner, managed to snag a nice table by the front window, and bought him a hot breakfast.

"So Greg," I said, "you're a busy man. You always seem to be involved in projects or extreme sports." Mel shot me a look. "Are you a sportsman?" He worked the goggles off his face as he spoke. Their imprint around his eyes made him look 100 years older than he already is.

"Nope," he said as his mountain of eggs and hash browns arrived. He began packing them away. He also waved through the window to every car, guy on foot, couple, family, and anyone else coming in or passing by. He seems to know every single person in the area, even the few tourists who wander in from the ski lodge and spa north of here. No one ever comments on his shoddy sports gear or his array of portable home-improvement tools. I guess eccentricity is what being retired can be about. Mel calls him "The Wise Man." He loves it.

"So, Mr. Gregory, my husband says zat I sleepwalk. I never sleepwalked in all my life."

"Sleepwalking. Goes to the gifted," he stated.

"What?" I said.

"Seers sleepwalk, my friend," he offered, and ordered more coffee.

"And who are these 'seers'?" I asked. My wife is a gifted person, but she has no crystal ball. The only true seer I know is our Channel 4 meteorologist. "Anyone I've heard of?" I asked.

"Course ye heard o' em," he said. "Jesus, Buddha, Muhammad Ali ...." He probably meant Muhammad.

"Well, Greg, I've heard a lot of things attributed to those people, even epilepsy, but not sleepwalking," I said gently, because Mel was kicking me under the table.

"Gregory has studied, Tom," she interjected. "I have seen you in zee library when I come to town, Gregory," she turned to him and said. The old man nodded knowingly and pointed to a small but quite modern brick building down the street.

"We got us a new town hall and library last year," he said proudly. His double stack of pancakes arrived. There must have been eight cakes in that pile. He slathered them all with butter and syrup as he spoke. "Got a great section on local history," he said. That was good information from the wise guy. I mean wise man. "Got a phone, too. They used to let me use it," he commented. I've never been to Ol' Greg's place, and I realized at that moment that I don't even know where he lives.

"Used to?" I asked. He nodded. Syrup was seeping into his beard.

"Don't got my own," he said.

After brunch, Mel and I went to take a look at the new municipal center. We stayed for hours in the library, and thanks to that great librarian they have, I was able to determine that our little cave-house falls within certain village limits—outer limits, but there it is—and is covered by an old by-law that states that any property abandoned for seven years or more may be taken up, free of charge, by anyone willing to move in and take care of the place. I had to dig to find anything about laws governing accompanying taxes. "Taxes begin accruing from the date of commencement of occupation," said one document on microfiche that I could barely read. So you can squat here in the good ol' capitalist US of A. I'll be damned.

The missing piece is that we don't know how long the place has been abandoned. It has *not* been here since the Age of Exploration, I'm sure. That's impossible. But no one seems to know of any recent long-term dwellers, not even Ol' Greg. And no one has asked for property taxes yet. No bill has been sent to the address—not that the place has an address—it's on a dirt path and has no number on it. So with a new cave-house that requires quite a bit of fixing and tax evasion, and a new addition on my old house for the new, old, great-grandma who might or might not arrive shortly, and a new baby hoped for, and new bills arriving monthly for my son's old college loans, and my new wife possibly taking an extended, mostly unpaid leave of absence from work to be with that hoped-for newborn, I'm not going to call anyone's attention to anything that might invoke a tax on both my houses.

"If anything happens, don't call me," I whispered chidingly into Deb's ear in the middle of JFK. She laughed. Then I laughed. I was glad she was taking this so much in stride. I even tossed a joke in there.

"I mean, if Dad gets abducted by an irate sex worker, for example," I added, "you might want someone to talk to." She laughed again, this time less freely.

"Don't worry, Tommy. I got this," she said. My sister's a confident sort.

We had driven Dad and Lil to the airport, and David, Zoe, and Deb met us there. The kids were beside themselves with excitement about the flight, and even Deb was looking forward to it. There was real satisfaction in seeing them all off. This week I'll go to work, come home, eat, make love to my wife, and undertake other baseline, real-life doings without feeling as if, at any moment, a small event in the life of my parents will explode into a full-blown episode in need of great attention.

We even watched the plane take off.

I've decided to call this "Tom's staycation and catch-up time." The first thing I did was pull out Andre's list of possible gerontologists. Slipping Dad's doctor out from under him like a rug while he's gone would make it easier, so I got right on it. Then I remembered that he has no doctor. Or if he does, no one knows who it is. He hasn't been to one in so long that I realized that getting him from one to the other won't be the issue—the issue will be getting him to one at all.

None of our associates are taking new patients. Especially at this time of year. And neither are any practices in about a 100-mile radius. Most of my conversations went like this:

"All-Health Group, how may I help you?"

"Hi, my name is Tom Conklin and I'm calling on behalf of my father, who is—"

"We're not taking new patients at this time, sir, but have a great holiday season, and thanks for calling AHG." Click.

After a total of zero receptionists took time to even hear my inquiry, I gave up. Then, in the afternoon, the office of a Dr. Galbraith finally called back, and we made an appointment for after the holidays. Maybe Dad will drop his life-long oppositional stance toward doctor visits by then. I doubt it, but right now, I don't mind waiting. It's my staycation.

After work today, Mel and I stopped to pick up a new garden ornament. No one is selling them at this time of year, but we did manage to find some discounted, left-over garden paraphernalia at a dollar store. There was one green gazing ball left. Green isn't purple, but we bought it anyway. Then we went over to my parents' house to put it in while we checked on the place. I wasn't prepared for the pile of rubble that was their former garden ball. Mel began cleaning up the destruction. Inside, I tried, and fairly succeeded, not to get upset when I noticed that on the dining room table sat both cell phones, neatly in their cases and not in Nevada. In addition, the cordless phone chassis was clinging receiverless to the wall. I pushed the find-the-receiver button quite a bit before giving up. I went out and helped Mel finish getting the new gazing ball into a nice spot, and when everything was in order, I re-set the alarm and locked the place up. We got in the car and pulled out of the driveway.

As we drove away, Mel turned anxiously and said, "Tom, who is zat woman taking your parents' mail from zeir mailbox?" She had seen someone in the side-view mirror, then took off her seat belt. She was turned all the way around, kneeling backward in her seat. I checked the rear-view mirror.

"Oh, that's Kelly," I said. "You know, the one who was cleaning the powder room?"

"Why is she stealing zeir letters?" she asked. Sometimes Mel can be very funny without meaning to be. I laughed.

"She's not stealing them—I forgot to stop their mail. And apparently, so did Dad." I should have thought to do that. Since we were still so close, I decided to turn around. Mel could meet Kelly, and I could collect from her whatever mail had come in the last few days. I was sure that letter from Motor Vehicles had come, the one summoning Dad to a driving test. It would be a stroke of luck for me to get my hands on it first. As we pulled in to Kelly's driveway, I noticed the last name on the mailbox: Pomeroy. "Kelly Pomeroy" sounds so familiar, but I can't place where I've heard that name before.

It began snowing lightly as we got out of the car and walked to the front door. Under our feet crunched the finely frozen layer of yesterday's snowfall. A lit Christmas tree shone in the daylight through the sheer curtains in her front window. We rang the bell. No one answered. We waited and rang again.

"But I saw her return to her house with zee letters," said Mel. We waited some more. Just as we were about to leave, Kelly came to the door.

"Hello!" she said cheerfully. "Nice to see you again. Tom, right?"

"Hi, Kelly. Yes, and this is my wife Mel."

"*Allô*," said Mel.

"Hello, Mel," said Kelly. "You know, I would invite you both in, but I was just on my way out—"

"No problem," I said. "We were just over here checking on the place and we noticed you picking up my parents' mail. That's nice of you. I'd actually forgot to put a stop on it."

"Not a problem," she said. I thought she'd offer to give it to me, but she just stood there.

"So I thought I'd come over and collect it for them," I said.

"Oh, yes, you know I don't have it right here. It's all the way upstairs. Marty did mention that I can bring it over all at once when they return, so—"

There was a sudden whining sound. She took her phone out of her pocket. A small ringtone was saying over and over, "I wanna go to the Ba*ha*mas."

"Oh—here's my daughter calling. I set it to 'whine' just for her calls, isn't that a hoot?" She tapped the screen and put it to her ear. "Hi Jule. Just a minute." She leaned forward, extended her free hand to each of us for a quick shake, then said, "So very nice to see you both." Then she backed into her house and shut the door. Mel and I stood there for a moment before returning to the car.

As I pulled out of Kelly's driveway, I got a view of the new green garden ball we'd just set up. It looked nice.

"The ball looks great," I said. Mel didn't say anything. "So that was Kelly," I added.

"*Oui*," she said. "Zee shit shoveler."

"*Shit shoveler*," I repeated and laughed aloud. And alone. "Actually," I continued, "I was the one who cleaned the toilet, mostly. She was there at first doing a lot of the dirty work, using her own shovel to scoop it all up. All the, you know. Shit. But I took over in the end."

"I don't know, Tom," she said.

"What don't you know?" I asked.

"Zat woman calls your father 'Marty' and not 'Martin,'" she said. I'll admit it does sound fakely familiar. Not even Lil calls him that.

"Some people get overly friendly with others, Mel," I said. "Here in America, we even give people pet names sometimes, like, you know, 'The Terminator'—"

"Tom, zis woman should not have your parents' letters," she interrupted.

"She was just on her way out, so I wasn't going to argue to get them," I said. I would have preferred to have that DMV letter, but then again, it may not have come yet. I shouldn't have got defensive with Mel.

"You should not have to argue to get zee zings zat belong to your family," she said. The conversation was getting to be too much work for a staycation, so I didn't respond. And anyway, at that moment, Mel's phone rang. It was Nick.

"*Allô? ... Oui*." said Mel. She listened for a minute or so. "*C'est magnifique!*" she squealed. I began my little charade to Mel to please speak in English—putting my hand up to my head and pretending as if it's talking to me while my mouth mimes "*En-gl-ish* please." I usually give her a big, dopy smile afterward so she'll laugh and not think I'm mocking her culture, although sometimes those French are a little snooty. Mel's half of the conversation switched to English.

"No, no, no Nikki, *mais, non*. We will be at zee JFK next Saturday to pick zem up ... *oui* ... I do not know, Tom's parents are flying on a crazy charter flight ... *oui*, a flying can of *sar*dines!" she said, with the accent on the first syllable. Like *gar*azhe. French can be gymnastics for the mouth. They laughed.

"Crazy, but *rea-son-a-ble*," I interjected, accenting all the syllables. My hand was talking to my head again. Mel ignored me.

"I will send you zee itinerary ... *oui*. Zat way, we will not drive into zee JFK two times ... *oui*, everyone together ... in one trip ... *oui*, Saturday ...."

I never expected Great *Grand-mère* Jo to arrive before the baby, so it's even more of a shock to find out that she will get here before the pregnancy. Now if I could just figure out where in the house to put a 90-something-year-old great grandmother, we'd be all set. I pulled into our driveway, wondering about that. And starving. I needed dinner. I hoped Great-Granny speaks English.

Mel's nice dinner went well with a glass of wine. Actually, it went well with two glasses. It made me forget about busted gazing decorations, cans of humanity at

35,000 feet, and mail-gathering neighbors named Kelly. I was lying in bed thinking blissfully about nothing when some hours later, my phone rang. I scrambled to hit the screen and answer it so the ring wouldn't disturb Mel. I saw that it was Deb.

Loud music and noise were coming from the phone. I got up quickly and went downstairs to talk at the kitchen table. I sat down and tried to wake up. As the fuzz in my brain cleared, I noticed a new box of pink pregnancy test sticks sitting on the table with other pharmacy items Mel had bought earlier. New toothbrushes for us, facial soap, ibuprofen. The test sticks box was open and missing one.

"Hello?"

No answer. "Hello? Deb?"

"Tommy?" My sister's voice was there.

"Deb? What's going on?" I looked at our kitchen clock. 4 AM. That means it was 1 AM in Vegas. I started to get a little nervous.

"Well ..." Loud music overtook her voice.

"Deb? Are you there?"

"Tommy, how did you reel in Dad last time he was arrested, because this time—" Here, the background noise was so loud I couldn't hear my sister at all. After a moment, her voice came back, cutting in and out. "He was so testy that ..."—garbled sound—"... cost a fortune —"

"*What* cost a fortune?" I said loudly. I stepped outside onto the back deck so I could yell freely and not wake Mel. "Deb, can you hear me? What's going on?!"

I switched to picture mode to see if I could get more information. The picture was dark and grainy for a moment. There was not a lot of light where Deb was.

When it settled, a very pretty woman's face with sparkles and lots of make-up was on-screen. She was staring at me. Her gaze was looking downward at me as if she were holding the phone low and peering into it. She didn't say a word.

"Where's Deb?" I demanded. The woman just smiled. The music was still loud in the background. "Who are you? Where's my sister?" I insisted. She blinked. Her huge fake eyelashes were like palm fronds. After a moment, she turned the phone away from herself and pointed it toward a stage. It was brightly lit, and when the picture adjusted, I could see clearly.

There was Dad, at the center of what looked like some kind of chorus line. He was shuffling his feet to the music. The colorful girls all around him were shuffling, too, but their shuffling was in sync with each other and with the beat of the music. I've never seen so many very tall, ultra-slim and sleek women. They were singing the words "It's raining men." Into the picture walked a woman who I think was Bette Midler. She walked up to the line, broke in, and put her arm around Dad.

"Martin Conklin, everyone!" she announced. The crowd was electrified. The applause was a din, smashing against the phone's small microphone. The singers seemed to be taking very good care of Dad there on the stage. A particularly glamorous one escorted him off to wild acclaim.

The picture went dark for a moment. When it settled, there was the pretty frond woman again. Again, she didn't speak. "Do you realize what time it is here in New York?" I said. I was exasperated. She smiled for a moment, then said, "Four A.M?" Her voice was a man's.

There was a jostling of the picture. Deb appeared.

"So as I was saying, Tommy, he's having a great time now, but I had to pay for it out of pocket, so—"

Beep beep. Gone.

.　.　.

"I've loved corn since middle school," I said.

Phineas had wandered over with his cup of coffee. It was steaming in the cold. He's seen me out here a lot with the contractors during this staycation week, making sure I know what they're doing to my house. Bumping out the space over the garage will yield a nice room for Jo. It'll yield a nice bill, too, because contractors are more expensive in the winter. I've also used my staycation to make more plans for the corn patch because I want to be ready when spring comes. I was taking a few final notes before Mel and I left for the airport to pick everyone up on this last day of my little break.

"I can even remember where I got the idea for a corn patch," I said to the professor. "Robinson Crusoe." When he didn't comment, I said, "He grew corn, too." Phineas didn't seem to know that book. I thought that was odd at first, but I don't know about every single thing under the sun in my profession, either. No one does.

"My middle-school friends and I loved that story," I said. "I think it captured the early merchant marine in me, longing to set out." Phineas sipped his coffee and listened as if he were captivated. He's a great guy.

"We were reading it in English class. About half-way through, our teacher gathered us into groups to identify events in the story that show how tough it was for Robinson to survive," I continued. "My friends and I started writing down anything we could find from the book that had to do with food because we thought food would be the big concern. But as soon as we wrote down that part where Robinson says, 'I resolved not to lose my corn,' we got off track quite a bit," I said. I stopped there. I couldn't tell if Phineas was picking up on the innuendo.

"You know, we couldn't write that anyone might lose his *corn.* I mean, we couldn't even write it down because we were laughing so hard," I said. Phineas was smiling broadly, but I had the strange sense that it was not at my story. "The teacher got so mad she put my buddy John in a different group on the other side of the room, Sammy in another, and then sent me to the headmaster's office," I concluded. Phineas did chortle at that.

"Then, when I was in college, we were learning about all the gods and goddesses in my mythology class, including the ancient corn goddesses. I didn't know there were any, until that class. In front of me sat a golden-haired corn goddess if ever there was one." I found myself stopped there for a second. "I dreamed about losing my corn to her throughout the entire course, but she went out with my best friend instead, and I had to take the class over again the next semester," I admitted.

Being a college professor, Phineas might have been able to relate to such student folly, I thought. "Aye," is all he said. The corn goddess seemed to have brought the conversation back to earth. My earth. I decided to return with it.

"So you don't ever use commercial fertilizer?" I asked, peeking over the fence at the sheer amount of gardens on his property.

"Nay," he said.

"I don't know. Maybe I used too much last year. Nothing grew out here," I said. I was looking down at my frozen soil. When I looked up, Phineas was shaking his head slowly from side to side as if someone had died.

"We must obey time," he said calmly.

"Yeah, well, timing's important. You've gotta wait until the soil's really ready in the spring," I said, "or maybe the problem was the viability of my seed."

I wished I hadn't said "the viability of my seed"— that phrase raged in my head all the way to the airport. It give me a headache, and depressed me. But only because I didn't know what was about to happen.

The plan was that I would drop Mel off at Delta to meet Jo, and I would continue on to the US Air terminal to get the gang. Then we would swing back over to Delta to pick them up. Thanks to Nick's planning, the flights were to land just half an hour apart from each other, so we had to be strategic. Mel made a thermos of French roast and some sandwiches for the ride in. We're probably the only people left on the planet who bring our own coffee in a thermos anymore.

Mel got out at Delta and went right in. I then drove around to US, found parking, finally got into the terminal, and arrived at the waiting area. It was full of hustle and bustle, of New York, of people, babies, baggage, noise. The flight was listed as "on time."

I paced. I will say that airports are good for pacing. I like the mindlessness of pacing. I texted Mel. She was pacing, too. I waited. She waited. She had the thermos. I wished we'd brought two, but I resisted the urge to buy a cup. My gang's landing time was fast approaching, and as planned, Jo had beat them.

Mel text
Landed

One down, five to go. I returned to pacing. I imagined Mel seeing her great-grandmother coming out to meet her, their tearful reunion. Last time she'd seen her was at Nick's, and before that, in France. I admit I was very curious to finally meet this elder matriarch of Mel's fine clan.

"Uncle Tom!"

The gang had landed slightly earlier than expected. David was running toward me. He waved, then turned and ran back to Dad and Lil to hurry them along. Dad was as cheery as could be, accompanied by an even cheerier Lil. They were ushering Zoe out in front of them. Both kids had some kind of cheap souvenir in hand and were sucking on ridiculously large designer lollipops— whatever happened to plain old candy? As we approached each other, I heard them bouncing around some joke about ice cubes and a bartender. We all began talking at once.

"How was the trip?" and "Hi Uncle Tom" and "It was great!" A few families near ours having similar reunions managed to be more discreet and quieter about it. They looked at us like a reflection in a cracked mirror.

"Where's Deb?" I asked.

I looked up. Coming out of the automatic doors toward us was my sister. She had the whole gang's jackets and sweaters draped over one arm. With her other arm, she was dragging more than one carry-on and not smiling. When she arrived at our little group, she offered me a look in lieu of speaking. The flight was not a red-eye, but looking at Deb's, you'd never know it. Hers were blazing, and glazed over.

Dad took out a designer pop of his own, unwrapped it, clinked it on Zoe's, then on David's. He plunged it into his mouth. It looked like a toast.

"Cheers!" they all yelled. It caught the attention of the couple nearby, the families, all passersby, the janitor coming out of the restrooms with her cart, and the strolling security guard.

Deb nodded at me. I nodded back in a show of empathy. Our little group yelled "Cheers" again. Deb rummaged through her purse for a moment before pulling out Dad and Lil's landline receiver—the one that was not in its chassis at their house—and held it out to me.

"Dad couldn't understand why 'this crazy mobile phone' you bought him wouldn't work out in Vegas," she said dryly. I took the receiver obligingly and shoved it into my jacket pocket. Our gang continued laughing and talking loudly.

"It was warmer there, Uncle Tom—"

"We went swimming—"

"The hotel had everything—"

"Grandma stayed up with us all night—"

I looked at Lil, surprised. She turned red.

"Only that one time," she said.

As they chattered, I noticed Deb peering at me with the most serious of facial expressions. I nodded again. She nodded knowingly.

"So," I announced, "Mel and *Grand-mère* await—let's go." Our group shuffled off gleefully toward the baggage pick-up. Deb was still lagging behind a bit. After retrieving luggage, we wheeled and pulled everything and everyone out to the car. I texted Mel that we were on our way.

We parked surprisingly easily and were finally into the terminal. No text from Mel yet, and no Mel at the baggage carousel or anywhere else. I texted her again and left the group to ask at a counter about Jo's flight, but before I could, my phone plinged.

Mel text
At end of sidewalk in smoking area.

Why my nonsmoking wife would be out there instead of at our designated waiting area was concerning, so I rounded up the troops quickly. We all piled out the doors, and I guided us away from the entrance, down to the far end of the sidewalk. During previous airport visits, I'd thought I'd seen the airways' employees enjoying their smokes out there. Zoe spied them first.

"Aunt Mel!" she cried.

There she was. She looked happier than everyone who has ever been happy combined. She seemed to have a glow about her, as if a spotlight were shining down on her, or as if a halo of pure joy were emanating from her and protecting us all. Near her were a couple of smoking employees on break. Zoe and David ran up to hug her. When we slowpokes caught up, I noticed that she was clutching something in her hands and holding it to her breast like a talisman.

Standing at the curb next to two beat-up, old suitcases was a tiny, frail, female figure. Her thin grey hair was pulled back tightly into a pony tail and her brown loafers, heavy stockings, and tightly buttoned-up wool coat—and what seemed like three scarves—were all wrapped around her like a motley swaddling. It was a bit of overkill on this cold but not frigid sunny day. When she turned, I saw that she held a lit pipe in her hand. By the time I realized that I was finally laying eyes on Great *Grand-mère*, Mel was already beaming at me and making the announcement:

"We will have a baby!" she cried.

Tears were streaming down her face. She took the talisman from her breast and held it high for all to see. It was a little pink stick, a plus sign boldly marking the sweet spot. Through the jubilation, I remember even the nearby employees stomping out their butts and clapping. *Grand-mère* Jo raised her pipe, put it between her teeth, and puffed.

Smoke trailed off in the breeze as she smiled, then nodded, confidently.

PART TWO

I honestly thought that having a 90-something-year-old granny named Jo in my home would be odd or would throw things off. Not so. Jo is entirely self-sufficient. She cooks, bakes once a week, cleans, fully expects to help when the baby arrives—feedings, cryings, fussings—you can never have enough help with that—and insists that she stay here alone to "relax" when we go to the cave. She dutifully steps outside to smoke because the smell of pipe tobacco triggers Mel's morning sickness. The only thing I've had to adjust to is her growing attachment to my corn patch.

Right now, for example, I'm sitting here at the window watching her. She and Phineas just finished shoveling the snow aside to examine the patch fully. Now she's on her knees with her ear to the ground as if she were listening for trains or buffalo. Phineas is holding her pipe for her. I was out there just a few minutes ago with her as she surveyed it.

"So you're saying you don't use fertilizer at all?" I asked.

"*Oui*, Toma," she said, "sometime, I put into zee soil zee natooral ingredients."

"Well ..." I trailed off. I admit that I like "Toma," but only from a nonagenarian. I wondered what "natural" ingredients she uses. Probably compost. "What's wrong with a blended formula of commercial fertilizer, balanced just exactly to make things grow?" I asked, but she was deep in thought and didn't answer. I'm still not sure how much English she understands. Mel was walking toward us from the house.

At that point, Jo reached down, swept some snow aside with her hand, and picked at the earth to loose some frozen dirt. She then drew her finger over the cold, open soil as if swabbing up a DNA cheek sample. Then she pulled her finger away and licked it as if she were tasting it. She *was* tasting it. I really don't want anyone tasting my dirt.

"Jo," I said urgently, but Mel reached up and put her hand on my chest lightly to stop me. Then she pulled me aside and lowered her voice.

"Tom, zis woman grew up on zee fields. She worked zem most of her life," she said. That phrase "popped out" was there again even though Mel didn't actually say it. "To make zee garden is zerapeutic for *Grand-mère*—I see her vibrant. You want to be zat vibrant when you are old, no?"

I don't want to be that old. But Mel's look made me not argue. We turned back toward Jo and the patch. I smiled at *Grand-mère* as if to say that tasting our back yard was OK.

"How was it, Jo? Good?" I asked. Again, she didn't react. She was outlining the garden's perimeter by walking around it in deliberate steps as if counting them.

Mel and I watched. When she finished, she was back around to our side again. She spoke to Mel in French and said something about the border. That much I caught. Mel was nodding enthusiastically while translating.

"*Grand-mère* suggests to take zee border out"—she walked over to the left side of the patch—"to here." She motioned with her hand along the edge of a new border that would be much further west. "Zee shed blocks zee early sun. To extend zis side is good." She nodded at Jo, who was smiling at me and nodding back. At least she didn't suggest that I move the shed.

We were all looking down at the patch as if tender buds would push up through the cold surface in fast motion, stream upward, and burst into flower like they do in nature documentaries. Phineas patiently watched the ground with us. When the buds didn't appear, he spoke.

"Let the sky rain potatoes."

Mel laughed and walked to him. She put her arm in his. "Professor Phineas, we do not need to wait for zat. Did you know zat Jo is a gardener *extraordinaire*?"

The professor and Jo hardly, but knowingly, nodded to each other as if they were members of the Weathermen. Or maybe they share membership in some other not-so-clandestine organization like The Over 90s Club, although Phineas's age is a mystery. He seems like a successful member of The Gardening Club. Maybe that was it.

"I am cooking a dinner, Professor," said Mel. Phineas stepped toward her and bowed slightly. "Will you stay?" she asked.

"I will your very faithful feeder be," he said.

Mel was pleased and returned to the house. Phineas and Jo began talking about soil, and I listened while Jo puffed away. Phineas kept talking, and I kept listening, and pretty soon he took a pipe out of his man-purse. I should stop calling it that. I don't like the idea of men carrying purses, and he does have it with him all the time. I've never seen him pull tobacco paraphernalia out of it, though. I've never seen him smoke at all, but there it was. Jo took out her pouch and offered her tobacco, and then both of them were puffing and talking, and I was still only listening. I noticed that the three of them—Phineas, Jo, and my soil—seemed as happy as could be without me. I left and went in to help Mel with dinner, but she was almost done and didn't need me. That's why I'm upstairs here typing and looking out the window.

While I'm at it, I've thought of a better word than journal: Memoir. I've started a memoir here without even realizing it. So, with so much literary freedom, with a new year well under way, with my house and my wife both expanding, it seemed right to jump in and call this PART II. Maybe I'll have the whole thing bound some day like a real book. I'll even keep sketching as I go— just like I did in my high school notebook.

Now Jo is holding Phineas's pipe and he's on his hands and knees, sniffing the ground. As far as I can tell, he's not tasting it, thank God.

When I called to remind Lil about Dad's appointment tomorrow with the new doctor, I didn't use the word "gerontologist." That word sounds as if I think she and Dad are old. They are, so I focused on the guy's name: Galbraith. It's a nice, solid-sounding name. Dad pays attention to that kind of thing. I thought Lil would say something like "Oh yes—the appointment. Such a good idea, Thomas," but instead she said, "Appointment? With a doctor? That's a bad idea, Thomas." Then she found an excuse to get off the phone.

I was stunned. She's the one who always wanted the men in her life to go to the doctor With my own kid on the way, with our own dealings with baby doctors, tests, morning sickness—I almost quit the whole endeavor. Too much doctor stuff. But then I thought, who's the boss here anyway? Now that Dad's getting on in years, I'm the head of this whole family if you think about it, and my dad needs to see a doctor, so I'm going to make sure he does. Lil dismissed it as though I'd never told her about it. I admit that I did slide it by her when they got back from Vegas, then dropped it on purpose. I decided to call her back and be firm. I tried her cell phone.

"Ma, hey, it's me." I heard the TV in the background. "You're both at home right now, right?"

"Yes, we are."

"Why didn't you answer the land line when I called just a minute ago?" I stopped. I remembered that Dad had brought the receiver to Vegas thinking it was his new cell phone, so pressing the issue during a conversation about a new doctor is probably not the way to go.

A shuffling noise was on the line, then Dad was.

"Tommy, is that you?"

"Hey, Dad."

"Look, son, I know you want to help, but I'm fine, your mother's fine—the doctor fixed me right up last time you and I went." I had to think for a moment. When was the last time? Then it hit me.

"That was a bar, Dad." I'm not even going to think about whether his reference to The Jockey was his long-gone humor kicking back in or something more alarming. Maybe he meant the hospital visit after his joy ride with the thugs. No matter—he continued speaking right over me.

"So if I have any issues I need to take care of, I'll do that ...."

The conversation became exhausting. We went back and forth about why he should see a doctor. I felt like a SWAT team negotiator on the phone with the kidnapper, trying all angles and running out of time. And my little extended family right here in this house wasn't helping any, bless them.

"Honey, tell him zat women go to doctors to get poked all zee time," Mel said in a loud whisper punctuated with lots of apologetic facial expression. She had no idea how bad that suggestion was. I didn't implement it, needless to say. Granted, she could only hear one side of the escalating conversation. Instead, I raised my voice to keep my courage inflated. That, however, attracted the attention of Jo. She put her pipe down on the deck table and stepped in through the sliding glass door.

"Toma, I'ave not seen a doctor in *trente-cinq ans*. Zirty-five years!" she yelled.

Shooing her and Mel away while trying to form an articulate counterargument to my dad was tough, but at least Lil stepped up. By the time I heard her comment in the background, I was exhausted.

"Now, Martin Conklin," she scolded, "don't make us roll you up in a carpet and toss you into the trunk to get you there, for Pete's sake!"

There was the most beautiful silence I'd ever heard after that. I stayed on the line just to listen to it. A minute or so later, more shuffling brought Lil back to the phone. I handed it to Mel to let her wrap up, then stepped out onto the back deck. She and my mother talked of other, more pleasant things, and for some reason I can't explain, I picked up Jo's pipe and lit it. I don't smoke, but I puffed on it until staring up at the crescent moon seemed like the only thing left to do. I slept uncommonly well.

When I picked them up this morning, no carpets or trunks were necessary, but almost. Dad was in a foul mood, I was trying to stay inflated, and Lil was trying to play along. Dad insisted on going into the examination room with the doctor by himself. I kept saying, "Well, Ma should come in with you, Dad, just in case you need something." Lil kept patting my arm, and patting his arm.

"Don't you trust me? Am I a child all of a sudden?" he kept saying. I couldn't really say yes in front of the receptionist, the nurses and aides, and the other waiting patients, but only God knew what the doctor would tell him that he'd never tell us. When a nurse's aide came out to get him, he got up with an air of authority that made both Lil and me stay put. I even forgot to give the nurse the list of episodes I had so carefully put together. I'll mail it in with a note to the doctor tomorrow. Then Dr. Galbraith can see patterns of behavior, things like that. I hope he'll read it, even though I only started writing things down to keep *my* sanity, not Dad's.

As soon as Dad was out of sight, I went to the receptionist. I explained to her that my father probably would do better if his wife or I could be in there with him. I said that we, the family, will need some direction regarding his care. I probably spoke with a careful—and a little desperate—tone that she'd heard a thousand times. I can't be the first person to bring in an ornery father.

"We get this all the time, sir, but it's patient privacy regs," she countered. "You've probably heard of HIPAA? Because you just helped him sign an informational sheet on it." Of course I know what HIPAA is, but we're talking about a man who does not seem to know the difference between a pub and an examination room. "You can't go in if the patient says no. The doctor does, however, encourage family participation, so the nurse might be out to call you in. We've noticed that when many new patients hear all the information they're given, they sometimes change their minds."

"Change." I muttered. "His *mind*." I laughed. The receptionist probably thought I was being sarcastic. She slid her plexiglass window closed. I went back to sit with Lil.

We waited. As we did, the door to the hall that leads to the examination rooms opened and closed occasionally, admitting and expelling various patients and their caring spouses, guardians, or adult children. Most were docile elderly people whose smiles seemed to say, "I'm so lucky to have my son/daughter here to help me." I tried to picture Dad looking like that. Some used walkers. One had a strap-on oxygen tank and was hooked up to it by the nostrils. I hoped Dad was noticing all these happy families. Every time that door opened, Lil and I tensed up.

Dad finally appeared. My fear that he had escaped and hid himself somewhere back there for 40 minutes— instead of actually seeing a doctor—was alleviated when I saw the balled-up piece of gauze taped to the crook of his arm. *They* had drawn *his* blood. I could see he wasn't pleased, but it was over. He walked right past us, staring straight ahead, even as he dropped some slips of paper into my lap. I picked them up, and he was already out the door. Lil jumped up and grabbed her purse and their coats and went after him.

The variously colored paperwork was a visit write-up in triplicate, white, pink, yellow, to be shown to the receptionist's nemesis, the check-out secretary. Two small sheets held prescriptions. While Lil and Dad made their way out to the car, I co-paid and asked a lot of questions. In return I got some half-answers as the secretary tore off the yellow copy and handed it to me. She said that the doctor needed to see Dad again in three weeks.

"Why?" I asked.

"He probably wants to follow up on whatever he found today," she said without looking up from her screen. "We have a Tuesday afternoon available at 2:15."

My mind raced to see how I could ask what it was he found and actually get an answer, but all I came up with was, "What's the date on that?" She wrote it down on a reminder card, placed it on the ledge, and slid her little window shut again.

I looked down at the prescription slips in my hand. One was something for high blood pressure and the other was something for high blood pressure. If I hadn't insisted on this doctor visit for Dad, he could've been dead by next week from a pressure spike. Something about that makes me want to put a pistol to my head and pull the trigger as soon as I turn 85. Instead, I'm writing this memoir.

.   .   .

It was great to wake up at the cave this morning and light a fire. Mel has already stocked the place with her French roast, a grinder, and a coffee maker. We even remembered to buy a small toaster oven and to bring our backlog of newspapers and magazines from home. I was up first, so I put on the generator. As I made coffee in our little kitchen area, I imagined the cabinets we wanted to put in. They looked great in my imagination. Stephen's neighbor is getting them for us wholesale so they can look great on our walls. I was enjoying that thought along with the paper when, flipping through to find the op-ed page, my eyes dropped right onto a full-page ad. It was Kelly Pomeroy's. That's where I'd heard her name before.

"Kelly is that successful attorney who specializes in elder-law," I said to Mel as she got up. I read from the ad. "We care for you" was their slogan. Mel was still fuzzy and shaking off sleep. She stopped and looked at me, then at the paper.

"Ah, *oui*. She works zee old people," she said.

"She works *for* them," I said. "You forgot your preposition."

Mel turned away, but I could see her devilish smile as she began her morning routine—pouring coffee, taking out a baguette and cutting it up into those small roundish pieces, then buttering them and putting marmalade on some and not on others "for variety" as she says. I cut my salt bagel, plugged in the new toaster oven, and slid in the halves. Mel used to like salt bagels—it was marmalade she never liked until she was pregnant. She used to pooh-pooh it as "British super glue," but now she eats it out of the jar with a spoon.

As I took out the cream cheese, she absentmindedly pushed her bread rounds into patterns on the counter. We have to sit at the counter on stools when we eat at the cave, or we sit on the lawn chairs we brought and eat from our laps out of Styrofoam containers from Mr. Wong's, whose fine takeout establishment is conveniently open in town most hours. That's where you eat when you live in a cave with a make-shift kitchen.

"So should we tackle the painting today or not?" I asked her. She answered without looking up from her breads.

"*Oui.*"

"I won't bother prepping the walls," I said. Then I waited, for effect. "I'll just lick them clean," I added. "I bet this place tastes good." I love teasing my wife. I've been teasing her about Jo's *au naturel* approach to all things, even garden soil. Even though she would not look up from her bread puzzle, I could see her smiling again.

"No. Zat would take too much time, Thomas." Sometimes Mel calls me "Thomas" to be playful or sarcastic. She hasn't done that in a while.

"OK, then. I'll do it the modern way, you know, the way us simple mortals make things happen—I'll go to the hardware store, get the necessary items, you know, paint and rollers and stuff, and then I'll actually prep and paint." Her puzzle seemed to be taking shape there on the counter. I took out my bagel halves and slathered them with cream cheese. They were so warm and fresh.

"Zat is a good plan, Thomas," she said. "I zink I will help you."

"No, you rest." I don't really want Mel doing physical labor during the pregnancy, but she insists on staying active, especially at the cave. "And we should leave soon—I think that hardware store in town opens at 9 AM," I said. I put down the cream-cheesy knife and went to take a bite.

Mel was suddenly sitting upright, cocking her head this way and that. She was staring at her bread-puzzle. She looked puzzled. I put my half bagel down. She walked over to the middle of our cave and pulled our mattress aside to inspect the floor. Then she came back to the counter. She took out her phone, took a picture of the breads, went back to the middle of the room, and began comparing the picture with the floor.

114

"Zis is strange, Tom," she said. She held up the phone. I walked away from my breakfast to look at it. I immediately saw that the pattern she'd made with the baguette pieces matched the tile-and-stone floor design perfectly.

"OK," I said. I admit I was buying time. I took her phone and checked the picture, but I wasn't sure what I was looking for. When people play checkers, they chat and push plastic red and black chips around a board, the mind humming along in the background. They decide how to jump and capture the other color, and a strategy and conversation happen. Someone wins. You then rearrange the board and start all over. In our case, Mel pushed little bread-and-marmalade players around our counter and ended up matching perfectly our Italianate-and-supposedly-crafted-by-15th-century-pirates-turned-monks mosaic-tile-and-stone floor. Right.

"Tom, I zink zis picture tells us something," Mel said, taking the phone back. She compared the picture to the floor again. I could clearly see what she was getting at. In both the bread design and the tile design, the pattern was pointing toward the front wall, right to the spot where we'll put the bay window. Neither Mel nor I had noticed that before. Mel became very animated.

"Stonehenge," she declared.

"What?" I asked.

"*Mais Stonehenge*, Tom. You know zat ancient place?" she asked. I know what Stonehenge is. "Zee big stones allow zee light to enter at zee summer solstice for zee sacred ceremonies."

"And?" I couldn't wait to hear what that had to do with our cave. I didn't wait, I just started talking. "No 15th-century version of ancient sacred building practices was resurrected here on a ridge in the middle of nowhere by some pirates made mad by the elements and instructed by some force to 'bring the light' as crazy Ol' Greg keeps saying," I insisted. It all burst out of me at once. Mel was laughing before I even finished talking and was on her way outside.

"But what if zey did? Come, let us look. We will measure for our own sacred opening." She grabbed her coat. I could still hear her laughing as she arrived outside. Then I got frustrated because I couldn't find my tape measure. And my bagel was cold.

We painted for what felt like the rest of the weekend.

We arrived home Sunday night as usual. Jo and Phineas were out on the deck having a smoke. It's nice of him to come over and keep her company, and it's nice of them to smoke outside, even though it's winter. Mel went inside first, but I walked out back to greet them. The professor watched me approach.

"Ah! Here comes the rogue. Sira, where have you been?"

He was quite cheerful, so I let the "rogue" thing slide. Maybe I should look up "sira." I guess I should know from my college Shakespeare course what it means, but I don't remember. It's probably something professors borrow from the plays and call each other, like some cabalistic greeting among the literati or something like that.

Mel came out to the porch. She began excitedly telling Jo all about our "Stonehenge experience," as she called it. She was so worked up that she slipped out of English and began yakking away in French. Phineas got up to go to the bathroom as I listened to Mel punctuate her telling with a few English words like "sacred rites." That way, I could follow along a bit. Jo nodded and puffed on her pipe.

At the end of the story, Jo put her pipe down. She started moving around it in circles, explaining something to Mel, gesturing and pointing. I expected Mel to laugh, or hug her, or wink at me while translating what was going on, or do something that looked like compassion for Jo in her confusion. Instead, my wife began following her around the circles, both of them alternately chanting and blabbing. In the next moment, they were on their way down the steps and out to my patch. When they arrived at its edge, they hovered over it, continuing to speak and gesture wildly. I brought them their coats, draped them on their shoulders, and went inside.

They barely noticed.

The letter from the Motor Vehicles Department arrived—
I had forgotten all about it. Dad kept saying that he
knows who the "informant" is, and just as he was getting
ready to name that person, just as I was bracing myself to
hear that he would never be speaking to me or Deb again,
he named instead "that guy at the mall."

"I saw him writing down my license plate number,"
he insisted, "and I knew he'd call the cops on me." When
I pressed Dad for more information, the guy at the mall
was suddenly not the informant, "the guy on the off-
ramp" was. When I asked if he'd had any problems
driving on the highway lately, the guy on the off-ramp
became "the woman at the entrance to the Cineplex."
When I pointed out to Dad that he's never liked going to
the movies and prefers TV, that woman turned into "the
crossing guard at the school," and so on.

That crossing guard reference really got me. Even
as I write here, I can see a crossing guard at an
intersection, smiling happily at the children and pleased
to have this part-time gig in his retirement years, bright
orange vest blazing on his torso and an overgrown stop

sign proudly in his grip. From across the street, a line of children come tumbling along, their youth and backpacks bobbing and bumping as they halt for the familiar red-and-white. As Dad approaches, he guns the gas pedal thinking it's the brakes, and as did not happen—thankfully—in reality, the crossing guard's body shoots through the air like a missile past the terrified kids, and Dad's front bumper crams the stop sign into the trunk of a nearby tree.

I almost looked happy as Dad lamented, but the image of those kids—I don't think Dad noticed it, but Lil did. She had been giving me quite the unusual look as Dad spoke. When we finally got Dad settled a bit, she took me upstairs to explain in the most agonized voice that *she* was the one who had contacted the DMV. I could hardly fight back my emotions at her pained confession.

"But Ma, no—I contacted them as well. Quite a while ago," I said. "They probably got my letter first," I added, but she wouldn't listen. I tried to make her feel better by making the analogy of a firing squad. "We don't know whose gun had the bullet," I said. Then I realized that wasn't the best analogy, so I tried another tack. "For all we know, the DMV got forms from me, you, the guy at the mall, the guy on the off-ramp, the woman at the Cineplex, *and* the crossing guard at the school," but the more I reasoned, the more she sobbed.

I praised her, hugged her, and reminded her that it's not only a matter of his safety but of others' as well, even her own. She's always in the car with him, after all. That helped a little, but she kept insisting, "Those poor children—what if something happened?"

She then walked over to her desk, pulled out the carbon copy of the letter she had sent, and handed it to

119

me. Despite the Mac I had bought them, she feels that she should type formal letters on their old typewriter, complete with a carbon copy as she's done for decades. I don't think she even knows that there is a form you can fill out online, but maybe the DMV takes letters, too. She wanted me to read it to see if she had been too hard on him. I couldn't convince her that it didn't matter—no one was ever going to see it except for one person at the DMV offices, and if it got Dad tested, then she did the right thing.

I put the letter in my pocket, and when she felt pulled together enough, we went back downstairs. I had a drink with them and waited until Dad was distracted before going home. I was absolutely exhausted, with a fatigue that seemed to seep right out of my bones into my bloodstream. I've never been that tired in my whole life.

Mel was in bed reading when I got there. Lately, she's been resting her tablet on her growing belly. It's cute, and if I weren't so tired, I would have taken that ebook off her and replaced it with my aching self. Instead, I started getting undressed, and when I did, I found Lil's letter in my pocket. I took it out and ran my hand over it to flatten it out. What I saw made all that exhaustion overtake me: Although the typed print made it legible, the words and sentences were gibberish.

I propped myself up on the dresser with both hands and stared at it. If I stared long enough, perhaps the letters would rearrange themselves on the page and make sense. They didn't. When I glanced at Mel, she was staring blankly at the ceiling. She looked tired, too. I quickly put the letter aside, finished undressing, walked over to the bed, and crawled in. She smelled so good. I thought she'd ask me what I'd just been reading there from my pocket, and I'd worry her by telling her, but she didn't ask, so I gave myself over to sleep's mercy.

Some time later, I sensed the light still on. I didn't know how long I'd been lying there, snuggled up to her side, but she was still staring at the ceiling.

"Zee doctor says I must make another ultrasound," she said flatly. I rearranged myself, trying to become coherent.

"Huh? Why?" I asked.

"She did not say why." Her body was stiffening as she spoke. She was wide-eyed. Her reader was wedged between us. I pulled it out, put it aside, and hugged her more tightly.

"She's just doing her job, Mel," I said, wishing our bedroom light could be dimmed. "Ultrasounds are common and they're used for so many things. She'd be negligent if she didn't check—"

"Zer is something to check. Zat is why doctors say zat word, 'ultrasound.'" She wiggled out of my grasp, stood up, went to the bathroom, and shut the door.

I decided to wait and see if this was one of those things that lighten up with the morning. There were so many reasons why I sure hoped so.

.   .   .

Lil's gibberish made me so nervous that I insisted on meeting her and Dad at the driving test. She had already taken Dad to his eye test. Apparently, he needs to wear his glasses, which he always does, so no problem there.

Maybe that clarity will just flow backward from his lenses into his eyeballs and then further backward into his brain, and one day soon, I'll have my father back.

Dad seemed in awfully good spirits. I tried to show good spirits, too. "Hey, Dad, I came to cheer you on. Go get 'em!" I said. Then something awful happened. Dad and the testing official got into the car, the official with his clipboard in hand and Dad with his keys at the ready. He immediately chose the correct key and put it into the ignition while dexterously hitting the button to roll up the windows. As the glass slid smoothly up, Lil and I watched our own reflections slowly filling the windows like cream filling a glass. Then we watched ourselves watch him pull his Lincoln out into traffic as confident as the sun. Lil and I were two stunned carjacking victims watching the perpetrators drive off, unable to do a thing about it.

We finally sat down on a bench. An occasional car went by. A squirrel darted up a tree. It all seemed too peaceful compared to the feeling that at any moment, a terrible smash might be heard from a distance.

When Dad's vehicle returned with an ease and fluency usually displayed in luxury car commercials, sliding up exactly parallel to and six inches away from the curb, I expected the tester to do what driving-test officials always do—open the door, get out, act professional but distant, not answer any questions, and assure us that the results will be sent to us. Laughing and handshaking and vowing to meet the examinee for a drink at The Jockey were not supposed to be part of it.

"So this is your son, Marty?" he said to Dad before turning to me. "Hey, how are ya?" he asked as he closed the passenger-side door. "Hey, your dad's a great guy. Sorry for the inconvenience."

My mouth was hanging wide open. It wasn't going to close any time soon because, when the tester shook my mother's hand and turned to go, she lit up, ran to the car, and peered into the passenger's side window to beam at her man as if he were just granted the Presidency. Then she opened the door, tossed her purse inside, and hopped in after it like a teenager on her first date. I watched the car pull smoothly away for the second smooth time. I barely remember Lil waving to me out the passenger's side as they left because that's when the bee flew into my gaping mouth and stung me.

I turned to run toward my car and that's the last thing I remember. According to eyewitness accounts, on the way to my car, I ran face-first into a tree. The eyewitnesses were two teens who apparently needed cash and thought that taking it off someone lying unconscious on the ground was the way to go with that. They took my cell phone, wallet, keys, and car, and went for a ride. But before they left, they called 911 to report a "screamin' crazy dude slappin' his face on a big-ass tree." That's exactly how the policeman repeated it to me. When he caught up with them, they reportedly said they called because they felt "bad for that muthafucka."

Mel brought me my laptop, and a nurse brought me a mirror. I really didn't need a mirror because I had Mel. One peek at her expression from under my swollen eyelid —the one I could open—and I knew I was a wreck. The way she caressed me spoke volumes. I did look into the mirror out of curiosity, though. The enormous, bloated, reddened, oozing blister on the front of my head barely resembled a face. It looked more like the cap of a giant toadstool.

Deb text
85-year-old man can't maneuver vehicle 2 min w/o bouncing off curb passed drive test + now keeps license??!!!!!!! I'll call u.

No sooner had I read the text than the phone rang. It was Deb.

"Tommy, Ma just called me. Is what she's saying true? An 85-year-old man who can't maneuver a vehicle for more than two minutes without bouncing off the curb numerous times actually passed a state driving test and now has a license to go back out on the road and mangle children?!" She was so loud I had to hold my phone away from my ear and turn it down. The bright pink of the new bee-sting allergy-alert bracelet they gave me contrasted nicely with the sleek black of my phone. But pink is so unmanly.

"Deb, watch it—your blood pressure—you've still got kids to raise," I suggested.

"Was Lil right there with him?" she demanded.

"Well," I didn't know how to describe Lil's reaction. "She really didn't have anything to do with it, Deb."

"Sure she does—she orchestrates everything for Dad right down to which socks he wears." She lowered her voice to a semi-conversational level. "Whaddya mean she—"

"Deb," I interrupted. I was getting too tired even to hold a phone, so I put her on speaker. An entire family was right outside my open door. They were waiting for the nurse, who was tending to their loved one across the hall, but I didn't think they could hear us. "She told Mel that she feels the DMV is justified in giving him his license back."

"Back? Did they ever take it to begin with?" Deb pointed out. It was a good point.

"No, but you should've seen her. And him. You'd think his success renewed his ability to drive and lowered his age by decades," I said.

"Get them a car service, Tommy—you can prepay. All they have to do is call for it."

"Yeah, but you're asking them to use a service they don't use well anymore—phones—to call for a service they can't use well anymore—cars," I said. "And anyway," I continued, "you know how Dad is about someone else taking the wheel." The middle-aged guy from the family out in the hall leaned in.

"They won't want a service, pal. My dad won't use one, either. Said it makes him feel unmanly," he informed me.

"Thanks," I said. Deb's voice was bleating compulsively out of the speaker as if her life depended on it.

"—sell their car. Did you mention that to Lil? That they should think about getting rid of it?"

"Yes," I replied.

"And?"

"She waves me away like a fly. She says in the most perplexed and hurt voice, 'Sell our car, Tom? Why?'"

"Well, then we need to buck up and play it straight: 'Because Dad can't drive safely' is what we should say to her," she said.

"I did." Now I was insisting.

"And?"

"And Lil answers, 'Tom, dear, your father loves his driving and that's a wonderful blessing. You know that he feels not manly when I insist on driving,'" I concluded for my sister. Quoting Lil made me realize how ungibberishy she can sound. There was a silence on the phone.

"Deb?" I asked. We'd got cut off. Or she'd hung up. The guy in the hall leaned into my room again.

"When my dad crashed into a lady's living room and wrecked the place *and* totaled his car, I didn't let him ever get near a dealership again. Eventually, he forgot about cars," he said. Then he peered with interest at my damaged face. "Hey, man, good luck."

In high school I read a sci-fi short story that I've always loved. A rich guy pays an exorbitant amount of money to a "safari" company that takes him millions of years into the past to hunt T-Rex. When they land in the Jurassic jungles, however, the guy chickens out. A real T-Rex turns out to be so awesome, so shocking, so terrible in its thunder and rush to slash human meat that the guy turns and bolts. To save their own skins, the safari scouts have to kill it for him.

It was the description of the T-Rex being taken down that I always remember. Rex starts to stagger, the idea of such mass and height pitching in any direction being enough to boggle the mind, but the author— Bradbury?—goes even further, describing the glistening skin, the slime, the putrid smell of the beast's bad breath as he blasts his intentions to not give up while fighting a slow-motion belly flop those skimpy arms will never cushion. He brings down everything with him as he goes, destined to lie motionless through the decay on the forest

126

floor, tiny gnats darting in the air just above twitching carrion while everyone else stands dumbstruck, covered with spewed blood and ooze.

My father will not give up even as he goes breathtakingly down, and as in the story, if I don't watch my step, the future will change unhappily, and indelibly, forever.

I think I'll order one of those silver-chained bee-alert bracelets. They're not pink, and they look military issued. That's more manly. I like that.

The hospital let me out as soon as they determined that busting the entire front of my head on a tree did not produce internal bleeding of any sort. That was good news. Mel helped me shuffle out to the car and drove us home. She dropped me off and went out to get groceries.

When I walked in to the kitchen, my great-grandmother-in-law was sitting at the table cleaning her pipe. Her tobacco, pouch, pipe cleaners, and other small implements and bags were spread out in front of her. Something was simmering on the stove. It smelled fabulous.

"Hey, Jo," I said.

She dropped what she was doing, got up, and came to greet me and inspect my face. I leaned down for her to better access it. She was stroking and prodding as if my mask were a mound of bread dough. My wincing didn't move her to stop, but she finally did pull away. I stood upright and waited for her assessment.

"I make zee ointment for zis face, Toma," she offered. "I put in zee vitamin E." I'll let her make it because I know she wants to. Mel can use it for small cuts—the doctor already called in a prescription for some cream that's probably much stronger, and I'd rather use that one.

Jo sat back down to fill her pipe. I walked over to the stove and lifted the lid on the pot of heaven cooking there. It was her stew—the best potato and sausage dish you'll ever taste. The aroma alone eased my pain. When I turned back toward Jo, she was flicking into her pipe a little gob of hashish.

She looked a bit like a teenager, sitting there with all her paraphernalia spread out in front of her, but unlike that time I came home early and caught Stephen doing the same with pot, she didn't flinch. She didn't suddenly throw all the evidence into her beret and shove it onto her head as my stoned son did with his baseball cap.

I passed my hand through my hair. I realized that Jo's little tin there on the table was a hash tin. She had it open for all to see. God only knows where she buys it. She walked over to the sliding glass doors, opened them, and stepped just outside to put the pipe to her mouth. She lit it, took a drag, and as she held it in, she spoke through her closed throat.

"Stew zis evening?" she asked. Then she turned her head to exhale outside.

A little voice in my mind said, "Talk to Mel first before asking Jo anything about her illegal drug habit," so I said, "That sounds perfect, Jo. Hey, whadja do all day?" My stomach was growling like a pit bull after my hospital stay, but I was able somehow to remain calm and pretend that Great *Grand-mère* was not engaging in an illicit experience in my home.

"I clean zee bathrooms, iron zee new curtain, cook zee foods, place zee teddy ..." she began. What? I asked her to back up.

"Teddy?"

"Zee *mauve* teddy," she semi-clarified. "I put zee teddy in zee *bébé* room." When I still didn't understand, she continued. "Zee *grand* teddy from Sister Deborah. *Très grand*." I have a little chuckle every time Jo calls Deb "Sister Deborah." I went upstairs to have a look. A massive purple teddy bear with red hearts on it was sitting on top of the dresser in the baby's room, its head mashed forward by the ceiling. It was bigger than Jo. Written on a ribbon around the animal's formidable neck was "FAO Schwartz." A card read, "We can't wait for the baby!   —Deb, Zoe, and David." I pictured our Great *Grand-mère* climbing onto the stool with a stuffed behemoth in tow and striving and grunting to shove it onto the dresser. Maybe she does deserve a little hash hit.

I returned downstairs to the kitchen. Jo was at the stove, tasting the stew.

"Smells great," I said.

"We will have a guest, Toma "

"Guest?" I asked.

"Zee doctor will come," she said. I was confused for a moment until she pointed to Phineas's house next door. He would come for dinner, but the word "doctor" had given me pause—it reminded me of our upcoming ultrasound. Mel's been on the Internet for days, obsessively trying to find reasons why OBGYNs order additional check-ups of any kind, and I've been obsessively trying to distract her. My smashed face put me in no mood for a formal dinner and guest, but it would keep Mel occupied.

The kitchen was soon a busy place. Jo's drug stash went quietly away just before Phineas arrived. When Mel returned from the store with a full grocery bag and two baguettes. I quickly forgot about Jo's wanton habits. We all pitched in to set out a gorgeous spread. Phineas was nice enough to comment positively on my facial disability. He shook my hand as he spoke.

"If the winds rage, doth not the sea wax mad, threatening the welkin with his big swollen face?" he asked. I've never been compared to such a mighty force as the sea. The guy's a character, really. First off, he showed up smiling. I've never seen Phineas smile. He wore his suit and bow tie and brought a huge bunch of assorted flowers and a bottle of wine, which he promptly presented to "the hostess Mel."

"Good sister, let us dine and never fret," he told her. He then turned to Jo and said something I found quite flirtatious.

"Let the world slip. We shall never be younger," he said and handed her the flowers. Then he turned to me, empty-handed.

"Aye, sir, the other squirrel was stolen from me by the hangman boys in the market place." I didn't expect him to hand me any gifts, but the large scratch he sported on his forehead made me picture some young thugs assailing him on his way out of the liquor store. Jerks.

We finally sat down. Mel poured the wine. We ate and chatted. Phineas is a remarkable storyteller, gardener, scholar, cook, and generally, a walking encyclopedia. Our conversation made me forget driving tests, twisted metal, and painful facial injuries whose painkillers don't allow me to drink. Watching Phineas make eyes at Jo throughout the entire meal, and watching Jo make them back, was distracting. I managed to ignore them by talking about the duplicate-me I've been wanting.

I explained that, if I could, I'd have a duplicate-me —someone who could take care of my career while I'm taking care of my parents and having a second family. I'd love for Mel to get herself a duplicate-her as well so we could take care of things together. For a few months or maybe a year, I could be a consultant to my double, directing him as to what needs to be done at work and he would do it, no one there the wiser. Then, when the time was right, I'd go back and fire my duplicate.

Phineas really chuckled at that. I'd never seen him smile, and now he's chuckling. He launched into a great story about a guy named Martin Guerre. I vaguely remember seeing a movie years ago that was similar. According to Phineas, there was a real-life Guerre, a French farmer in the 1500s who one day disappeared from his family. While he was missing, a talented imposter—one of uncannily similar physical resemblance to Martin—showed up and began sleeping with his wife and running his show.

The new guy managed his impostership for quite a few years until some suspicions began to appear—as did the real Martin. Apparently, claims and lies flew before the duplicate was finally fired. Hanged, actually, but that's the 1500s for you.

We got into all kinds of conversation regarding the imposter, the wife, the reason Guerre returned. Phineas threw in some interesting facts. He said that, for example, women were not allowed to remarry back then and that the fake Martin treated her well. We decided that she probably knew he wasn't her own Martin.

Can you blame her for playing along? And if you play along well enough for long enough, you might start to believe it after a while. In those first moments of dawn every morning, we wake up alone until our senses slowly come to us, and in the next few seconds, only semiconsciously, we put the world in order and remember who we love, and who loves us. Only then is the world even remotely right enough to face. That wife recognized the person she loved in someone she knew was not. The shell may have been there but the pearl was gone, and what would you do if someone you loved was now someone else?

Phineas politely left early. I think he could see I was exhausted. Mel and I went upstairs after seeing him off, and Jo insisted on cleaning up for us because "Toma," she said, reaching up and mashing my sore cheek flesh between her fingers, "you have zee face from zee blowfish." At least she didn't say, "Zee face from hell."

Despite my exhaustion, I awoke quite abruptly in the middle of the night. The urge to tell Mel all about Jo's hash habit was pressing, but my pregnant wife was sleeping so soundly that I gave it up. It hit me that once you reach the heights of 90 and beyond, enjoying a little hash hit in your day probably doesn't matter. What did matter was the unbelievable thirst I've had since leaving the hospital. I went downstairs to get water, staggered back up the stairs, and as I passed the window on the way back to the bed, a flash of movement in the moonlight caught my eye. I backed up. Jo was dancing around the corn patch. Since I've persuaded myself to get used to her rituals, I almost returned to bed without seeing the other woman dancing with her.

At first, I thought it might be Mel. Perhaps she snuck out while I was getting my water. Unlikely. And although I pride myself on accepting anything Mel does, I don't think she should be out there pregnant and dancing in the middle of the night. And she wasn't—she was in bed. I was so tired that I wrapped myself around her and fell asleep, glad she was in my arms and not outside howling at the moon.

Maybe there was no other woman. I could have dreamed it. She was taller than Mel, and blond. I probably was dreaming. Mel's not blond.

.　　.　　.

The tech was smiling uncontrollably. Then Mel was smiling uncontrollably. I was smiling a rather controlled smile, or maybe I wasn't smiling at all. I don't remember now. I only remember thinking the tech was referring to the baby's tiny, developing heart and Mel's heart when she said "two heartbeats." Then I thought "two heartbeats" was a metaphor for Mel's exceedingly good health. I looked up at the screen. I was seeing double. Then I became aware of the squeaky noises coming from Mel. She and the tech were sharing one of those knowing women-looks that make me so uncomfortable. Their smiles grew to gaping. Mel let out so many high-pitched *Oh, Toms* that I almost didn't notice the tech saying, "You didn't know?"

I didn't think my seed could do it. We could do it. I guess Mel did it, mainly. I felt my mouth hang open but nothing came out. I'm not sure I looked very happy—I wasn't sure I could do twins. Mel was, though. She became so high on the idea that riding with her to the cave afterward to meet Stephen and Jamie was like riding with a caged animal. I kept trying to call in our food order to Mr. Wong while she kept exclaiming, "Oh, Tom, zis is amazing!" between her own loud, French calls to Jo, and Nick, and France. I wanted to announce our news a bit more traditionally.

"Honey," I said, "when we get to the cave, let's wait 'till we all sit down to dinner to make the announcement." I liked the idea of announcing calmly and formally to my son that he'll have not one, but two new siblings. But asking the tide to clear out permanently would have been more successful. As we walked into Wong's small shop, Mel beamed at him until he could not ignore her.

"How you doing today?" he asked.

"We will have twins!" exclaimed Mel. The shop's harsh fluorescent lighting seemed to dim to a spotlight on her as she shared major portions of our recent life. I went to the cooler to get the drinks—a few beers for our guests and soft drinks and water for Mel and certainly for me and my face. Three other customers came in and were immediately absorbed into the audience. They were good sports, putting off their order to hear about a stranger's ultrasound and crowding around Mel to congratulate her. When I turned around after paying, they saw my damaged face and backed off.

With hot, delicious-smelling takeout in the back seat, we pulled up to the cave. Stephen and Jamie were already there. Brand-new kitchen cabinets were leaning against the outside wall, each wrapped in bubble wrap and dark plastic. I'd forgotten all about installing them this weekend. Stephen was inspecting them, and when Jamie saw our car, she waved and came toward us. She met Mel as we got out of the car, and they began speaking excitedly. I walked up the dirt path toward my son.

"Hey Dad," he began. His head was down as he checked a cabinet whose plastic had torn. "I had them leave these by the door." He glanced up. "God, what the hell happened to your face?" he asked. He stepped toward me, alarmed.

"Well," I started. I stopped and put my hand to my sore cheekbone. "I went with Grandma to Grandpa's 'check-up' driving test, you might call it, and—" There was a commotion over at the car. My daughter-in-law and my wife were alternately embracing and squealing. Then they were jumping up and down and laughing. Stephen and I watched them for a moment without saying anything. After another moment, we spoke over each other in nervous spurts:

"We're having twins."

"We're having a baby."

More women-laughing.

"A baby?"

"*Twins*?"

More squealing from the ladies.

"I'll be a *grandpa*?"

"I'll be a big brother!"

We stood for another moment, paralyzed. I don't know about Stephen, but I needed time for it to sink in. It's quite exciting but scary to become a father again at this late age, but at the same time, a grandfather? That feels like not going forward *or* backward—it's more like going sideways. Stephen and I looked to the women for guidance, or reassurance, or something. I don't know why —we weren't going to jump up and down and squeal, although that was the only thing I wanted to do. When they were done celebrating, Mel bounced over to us like a stray beach ball.

"Congratulations to zee *Grand-père*," she said as she hugged me.

"Uh ...." I said, sort of recovering. I walked over to Jamie and hugged her. She was appalled at the sight of my face. I tried to assure her that I would be fine, but Mel and Stephen were applauding loudly, and soon we were all yelling "Congratulations!" and hugging each other. For some reason, I realized at that moment that I am surrounded in my life by females who sport male names. I hugged my son and shook his hand. Then I turned away until the urge to cry passed. But I don't think anyone noticed—everyone was asking questions, alternately answering and beaming. Then we all got busy.

Mel and Jamie carried food and drinks in from the car while Stephen and I moved the cabinets just inside. He insisted that we drop our installation plans for this weekend because of my accident, and because I'm on strong painkillers. He said I didn't look that great and that I might nail my self—instead of a cabinet—to the wall. I had to agree. He said I probably shouldn't be driving, either. I didn't agree. We unwrapped the whole delivery and stored each piece in the corner while Mel and Jamie set the "table"—a checkered tablecloth on the counter— and finished calling the entire planet with the news.

For Dad and Lil's call, she cleverly dialed Deb in.

"*Allô* Deborah—it is Mel ... Yes, yes ... We are fine ... *oui* ... We have some news for you ... No, no ...

136

wait. I will first put your parents on zis call ... yes, I will 'add call' ...."

Ya gotta love technology. After a few moments, Mel continued.

"*Allô*? Dad? Yes. It is Mel and Tom and Ja— yes ... yes, we are at zee cave ... No, *mais* no, no bears here ... ha ha, yes, I know zat you are joking, Dad ... Dad, is Lil zer with you? Tom and I have some news ... Yes, please tell her to come ...."

While Dad went to get Lil, Mel beckoned me excitedly.

"Tom, Dad answered zis call on zee cell phone," she whispered loudly.

Stephen and I set the last cabinet down quickly but carefully and ran over to her—my father had engaged with an incoming cell call properly. That felt almost more wondrous and awe-inspiring than an egg splitting into two human beings in a womb. She put the call on speaker.

"Hey, Dad. Hey everyone," we heard Deb say. Jamie, Stephen and I leaned in. Before we could greet anyone, Lil's voice could be heard as if from afar.

"Who's there?" she asked. A long string of beeps began pouring over the connection. Lil—or Dad—was punching numbers as if trying to make a call. In between beeps, we heard Lil's voice, this time more clearly.

"Hello? ... *beep beep* ... no ... *beep* ... Martin, are you calling someone?" she was saying. We all began yelling at the phone.

"Lil! Ma! It's Tom and Mel and—"

"... *beep beep* ... Who's there? ... *beep* ..."

"Wait! We're calling you! You don't have to—"

"Who's ... *beep beep beep beepbeepbeepbeep* ..."

137

Mel managed to cut through the noise by yelling over and over the only thing that could be yelled.

"Tom and I will have twins! And Jamie and Stephen will have a baby! Zree babies—not one baby, but zree!"

The connection went silent. After a moment, Lil's voice was heard again from afar.

"Martin. *Martin*. Jamie's pregnant—and Mel's having twins." She began crying. Deb said not a word. We all stood back in our little circle around the phone and smiled. After a good minute of listening to my mom cry, Dad's voice came through clearly and somberly.

"Atta boy, Thomas."

Then the connection cut out. Only Deb remained on the line.

"Hello?" she asked after an awkward moment.

"We are still here, Deborah," said Mel.

"I'm so happy for you," she said. We now heard that she was sniffling. "I'm gonna be a great aunt—"

"You are a great aunt," said Stephen. My son is kind.

"Hi, Stevie—thank you, thank you," she said, recovering. "I was worried you were calling to tell me someone was dying, not being born." She blew her nose. "Now, how can I plan a shower for all these babies long-distance?" Mel was touched. So were the rest of us—Deb is not a crier.

"Deborah, zank you, but in my family, we have zee great party when zee babies are born. It is zee biggest celebration. You will like it," she persuaded. When she finally managed to keep her traditions in tact as well as convince her managerial sister-in-law that no shower was necessary, we all explained to Deb that we needed dinner. She understood. We promised to call her with updates, said our goodbyes, and turned to our makeshift dining table. We were soon adding a small vase with flowers and spreading out the food and drinks. It looked quite nice for a squatted, unfinished cave with no light. We drew up all the stools and lit candles. A toast was a must.

"To Conklins-on-the-way." We raised our glasses and drank, then we dug in. Mr. Wong did not disappoint.

"So you've told your mother of course, right?" I asked Stephen.

"It's so much fun telling everyone," commented Jamie with a mouthful. She and Mel nodded vigorously through their chewing.

"Yeah. Well," I said. "Lots of people involved." I admit I was still absorbing it all.

"Actually, Mom was the first person we told," said Stephen.

"Yeah, we Skyped her last night," Jamie added. Stephen gave her a fleeting but strange look. I was confused.

"Skype? Why didn't you just drive over there?" I asked. I know Marla—she'd want to know something like this in a formal, hug-you-in-person kind of setting. Jamie stopped her chopsticks in mid air to return Stephen's look. He finally addressed it.

"Uh," he said, "she's traveling."

"Oh?" I said. Marla always wanted to travel, but it never seemed like she'd do it. "Where?" I asked.

"In Tibet," said Stephen. Tibet. That's some travel. It's not like she went to Toronto for the weekend.

"What's she doing in Tibet?" I said. He and Jamie again exchanged a subtle look before Jamie swallowed to answer.

"She's studying a sort of meditation with Tibetan nuns," she said. My silence prompted her to explain, but it wasn't really an explanation in my opinion. "It stresses concentration toward mindfulness," she said.

"Zis is important, no?" asked Mel.

"Yeah," said Jamie. "She was telling us about it last night. She said that, in that kind of meditation, everything is the expression of your mind. Mindfulness slows time down so we can live in the moment," she added. I wasn't going to touch that.

"What did she say about becoming a grandma?" I asked.

"She cried," said Stephen. I wasn't even able to picture her in another country, much less crying at her screen in a Tibetan monastery.

"So how long has she been there?" I asked.

"She's only spending a month there, Dad," said Jamie. "The whole program actually lasts about three years if you want to become a real nun, but she said that some people go just for an introduction."

Only a month? I didn't know what to say.

"Yeah, so she'll be back for the birth, of course," said Stephen. I pictured Marla watching the birth on a screen at the monastery with all the other real and would-be nuns, all of them squealing and laughing and jumping up and down.

"Well," I said. "That's good news. We won't have to broadcast the birth live from the hospital," I said.

Both Jamie and Mel stopped chewing. Jamie looked disappointed. Mel looked confused. They glanced at each other, then at me.

"Tom," said Mel, "We will have zees babies at home, remember? *Grand-mère* will deliver zem."

I looked at Stephen. He shrugged. Jamie addressed us both.

"Don't you remember we talked about this when Jo first came here?" she asked.

I realized that I'd been absentmindedly going along with Mel's Jo-as-midwife idea because I assumed that Jo was a retired midwife, and that Mel's OBGYN would allow Jo to help *at the hospital*. I know we have midwives associated with our maternity clinic, but to me, the idea of midwives practicing at home and not in a state-of-the-art facility is from a bygone era. Jo's era. Mel and I are from this era.

My lovely wife then turned to Stephen and Jamie and uncharacteristically dominated the conversation by chronicling all the births in her family and in others' over which Jo has presided. She positively glowed while explaining that she herself had actually assisted in a few of them when she was very young.

"*Grand-mère* kept zee placenta after zee births to put into zee soil—it is zee best fertilizer."

Wong's Asian Delight began turning over in my stomach numerous times. I tried to stay calm. "Honey, Jo was born in a small, traditional village a long time ago on another continent. Modern hospitals provide sanitary disposal of things like that and that's why women to go hospitals to have babies," I said. I shouldn't have.

"Tom!" and "Dad!" cried Mel and Jamie simultaneously. "That's not why!" The nasty image of a corn plant lapping carnivorously at a puddle of placenta clinging to its roots kept me from picking up my chopsticks. Everyone around me was digging in just fine. Stephen finally noticed and tried a little humor to lighten my burden.

141

"Don't worry, Dad," he said. "We'll never be pregnant." He looked down at his belly, then added, "Pregnancy is something all the science and technology in the world can't do for us guys." Mel and Jamie laughed.

"That'd be great if it could," said Jamie, directing her comment at Stephen. "I could have this first one, you could carry the second one, you know, we'd do every other one." She and Mel toasted that idea with their iced teas.

"I guess it does seem more equitable that way," said Stephen. He began chewing again and glanced once more at his lap as if considering it. Mr. Wong's fried spring rolls are the best I've ever had, but I was still abstaining. I was watching the one on my plate.

"Yeah, but most guys wouldn't do it," I said.

"I bet some would," said Jamie. Stephen and I looked at one another.

"Yeah, I don't know," said my son. "It might be interesting for the first few weeks, but I don't wanna even think about how the little guy would get outta there," he said. He and I looked at each other and winced. Jamie took a big mouthful of chicken rice, then mumbled through it.

"Cesarean," she said.

Stephen and I both shot back a "No, thanks!" at the same time.

"Look," Stephen continued, "if it were more like one month instead of nine and I had all the right openings to get the little bugger out, I might consider it." Jamie turned to Mel and rolled her eyes.

"We don't really have the right openings, either, you know. Too small," she said. "Why do think they call it 'labor'?"

Mel suddenly decided to join the conversation.

"Tom, would you?" she asked.

"Would I what? Go into labor? I'm going into labor just thinking about it," I quipped. Stephen and I laughed. Mel and Jamie didn't. Fortunately, Jamie broke in. I felt grateful.

"Well, my sociology professor was saying that men are profoundly jealous of the birth experience—that's why they feel they have to make war all the time." She said it nonchalantly while she poured more iced tea. I started feeling ungrateful. My son swallowed his food hard before speaking.

"Yeah, well, sounds like he self-medicated before coming to class that day." He looked at me and laughed and nodded some more. Something told me not to nod back in agreement.

"You would have our babies?" Mel asked me again.

"Hang on," Jamie broke in, "he said it's because men know they'll never be able to approach the blood, or the pain, or the drama, or even the possibility of death—then there's the whole part about being able to give life instead of take it—"

"Was that Professor Huilly?" Stephen asked. "Everybody knows that guy took too much LSD back in the day and then beat it to Canada during the war. He probably can't admit his feelings of inadequacy."

Jamie looked at Stephen and put down her chopsticks. I could see Mel out of the corner of my eye. She looked unhappy.

"What does that have to do with it? Can you find one single other good reason for war?" asked Jamie.

"Profit," answered Stephen.

"I said good reason," insisted my daughter-in-law.

"Profit is a good reason to the people who make it," said Stephen. He shoved a loaded forkful of lo mein into his mouth.

"Not to the victims it's not!" asserted Jamie.

"How did we get from technology to victims of war?" I asked. My son laughed and rolled his eyes.

"It's easy, Dad," he said, "we do it all the time." He threw a look to Jamie. She smiled back in self-satisfaction. "We stopped for coffee on the way out here and the conversation with the barista ramped up from coffee to the economy in only the time it takes to say 'latte.'"

"These are important issues," insisted Jamie. She turned to Mel. "What do you think, Mel?"

Mel was looking down into her Styrofoam container and pushing fried rice around.

"Zee barista speaks about zee important issues—zat is nice," she said quietly.

"Yeah, and he thought gay marriage was just as important as job creation, can you believe that? What would ...." Stephen loves to pontificate, especially to his pro-same-sex-marriage wife. As he spoke, I was trying not to meet Mel's gaze. It was easy because she refused to look at me. I found it hard to listen to a word my son was saying.

Later, we went to see a movie in town, all four of us. It was relaxing. It took my mind off things. When we returned to the cave, it was actually fun to fire up the generator, light the fireplace, and spread out the blow-up mattress for them so we could all get some shut-eye.

Our little family pajama party was cozy, what with everyone tucked away until about an hour ago. That's when Mel got up. I thought she was going to the bathroom, but when she didn't come back, I crawled out from under the comforter and went searching. I found her outside sitting on the stump. She looked so beautiful sitting there in the moonlight, wrapped in our old, down blanket with the picture of Homer Simpson on it, but when I approached her and put my arms around her, she stiffened up like a board. That wasn't a good sign.

"What are you doing out here, honey?" I asked.

She didn't answer. That's always unnerving. Especially under a full moon. When men don't answer, it's usually because we're using it as a strategy. Or a cover-up, like that time when I was very young and Lil caught me stealing Daniel's allowance. I had shoved it into my mouth to cover up the evidence. I still remember her standing in front of me demanding that I spit it out. I finally did, but a dime slipped down my throat. To this day, she chides me about having to "wait for her change" to come out the other end.

I sucked in my plunged gut and resorted to my most tender voice.

"Mel?" I said. She stared straight ahead while speaking.

"You do not want zees babies," she said. She stood up.

"I don't?" I asked. I was thoroughly shocked.

"You do not look happy, and you make jokes," she said as she backed away from me.

"I'm not making jokes," I pleaded. I realize as I type here that pleading lost me the case right there. "What are you saying?"

"You were not upset when we did not get pregnant, and now you refuse to carry zees childs!" She started crying.

This was definitely one of those latte moments Stephen mentioned—I had gone from sleeping peacefully to my very own pregnancy in just a couple of minutes. I said the only thing that made sense.

"I'm a guy, Mel, and guys don't get pregnant." I heard myself getting loud.

"Zey do not, but zey could try," she said. Even though I was getting agitated, I will admit that her tears made me want to beat the odds and start trying. I wanted to say, "Mel, you're tired. Why don't you come back to bed and get some rest?" but last time I said that during an argument, I was accused of avoidance and shifting the blame to her fatigue. Arguing with women is sometimes like sparring with your therapist. Not only do you lose, but there's always a sound psychological reason why it's your fault, even though no one ever fully explains what that is.

"So, I don't know Mel," I said, "I'll try then." My intentions were good.

She stood up. The blanket fell to the ground. She tried to shake it out and wrap it around herself again, but she was having a hard time. For some reason I can't explain, I suddenly remembered that her birthday was coming up. Along with her pregnancy and all its related hormonal changes, getting older surely has something to do with her frustration. I can relate to that because my impending birthday is giving me all kinds of anxiety. I

146

tried to assist her with the blanket, but she snapped it away and threw it down.

"You are a man—you cannot have babies!" she cried, and stomped inside.

Now she's asleep. It's cold out here on the stump, even with Homer wrapped around me. But I want to get this evening down on the page because it might make me feel better.

So far, though, it doesn't.

"But Ma, is he OK?!" I was yelling as I drove.

"Well Thomas, he's been going to that Jockey's bar ever since you ..." I have to remember that my mom can never jump to the climax, especially when she's upset. I tried to remain calm as I tore into the hospital's ramp garage.

"But—"

"So he meets his group every Thursday—do you know that Buddy Wall meets him there? You remember Buddy, don't you? And James—"

"But what happened this Thursday, Ma?" I didn't want to hear a docket of the regulars at my dad's local hangout, especially while spiraling endlessly upward toward heaven just to park. The only spot available was on the top tier of the garage. I jumped out and ran to the elevator. "Closed for maintenance" said the sign.

"Well, you know it's good for your father to go out and socialize with the boys, Thomas. He's been in such a better mood. I don't go with him, of course," she said. I was thrilled about that—I learned later that the passenger's side of the car was completely caved in. "He

148

hadn't even had any alcohol yet. Then, well, he ... he never made it." She broke down. I took the stairs.

The other vehicle was a truck. A big one. Apparently, when Dad realized he had missed the turn at Anderson, he abruptly cut right from the left lane to go through the plaza parking lot. The truck driver was a contractor with one of those massive pickups with all his materials and tools in the back. It easily made a neat metal wrinkle of Dad's Lincoln by bashing in the right side like a stomped-on soda can. Miraculously, Dad was barely hurt. In fact, only his face was beat up from the air bag going off. No pedestrians were nearby, no children or crosswalk guards, and no other vehicles, even though it was early rush hour.

When I got to his room, my poor galled father was sitting up in the bed. He was staring straight ahead, his face a bloated black and blue and red puff of indignant wrath. I rushed to him as all kinds of thoughts collided in my head, thoughts like "He's alive—thank god" and "I don't remember Dad's upper body looking so frail—it must be that hospital gown" and "Gosh, Dad's face looks just like he smashed it into a tree." People have always remarked on how much Dad and I look alike. With both our faces ruddy and chubby with damage, we still do. Twin baboons in heat, bending over at each other.

At that moment, Lil came in carrying hot coffees, one for herself and one for Dad. She looked at me, then at Dad, then back to me. Her stoic, take-care-of-the-men-in-her-life attitude she's worn for a lifetime—the one that has recently intensified to combat-alert levels—stuck for a moment, then dissolved quickly into someone-take-care-of-me-for-once.

I managed to grab the chair from the corner of the room and place it behind her just in time. She deflated into it. I took the coffee out of her left hand, then the other one out of her right hand, then placed both onto the serving table next to Dad's untouched hospital food. I rolled it with much difficulty to the side. Who makes those damn unrollable trays?

Dad continued staring straight ahead. I sat in the other visitor's chair next to the bed, grabbed the small box of hospital tissues nearby, and handed a few to Lil. When enough tears had cleared the way, she whispered to me.

"We almost lost him, Tommy." I looked back at Dad. I didn't think he'd heard her. I turned back to her just as she finished blowing her nose.

"But we didn't, Ma," I said.

Lil got up and went to the ladies room. I moved my chair closer to my father, but he wouldn't turn his head. All around him, anger formed a tough, insulating bubble. I'm embarrassed to admit that I almost allowed it to repel me. I wanted Lil to come back and burst through it for me. But as that wall-mounted TV uselessly chattered to no one, I braced myself and slipped my hand through the invisible membrane and into my dad's. It went through more easily than I thought it would. The bubble didn't burst, and Dad didn't stop staring, but his fingers did squeeze mine, and he occasionally bounced my hand up and down on the stiff mattress. After a while, a nurse came in with pain meds, and he fell asleep.

I asked about his medications. She mentioned his high blood pressure as if that's news. "We've brought it down," she said, "but he'll need to continue those meds at home." I was irritated that they didn't know he was already taking something for his pressure. "It may have broken through due to the stress of the accident," she added as she turned and left abruptly. I was glad she was gone. I sat in silence until Lil returned. I spoke to her right away to keep her mind off the accident.

"Ma," I said, "remember when we first went to Dr. Galbraith and he gave Dad a couple of prescriptions for his pressure?"

"Yes," she said. That was all she said.

"We went out and got the prescription and he started taking it, right?" I asked.

For the first time in my life, and possibly for the first time in hers, Lil didn't have an answer. She just stood there. I got up and suggested she sit down in my chair. She sat, took Dad's limp hand in hers, and did not answer my question. I stepped out into the hall to call Deb. I didn't give the crash an episode name. That would seem like making fun of it. Deb answered right away.

"Hey, Tommy."

"Hi. Hey, listen, don't get alarmed, but Dad's in St. Cecilia's." Deb and I have lately mutually dispensed with how-are-you's.

"Oh, no! What happened?"

"Well, he was on this way to The Jockey and who knows why, but he tried to turn right from the left-hand lane there at the plaza, and a guy in a pickup was coming up on the right and couldn't stop—"

"Aah!"

"He's OK, he's OK," I said. "He'll recover. His face is kind of messed up from the air bags going off. And he's a bit stunned, really, and pissed off."

"Do you think I should come up?"

"Well, they're only holding him for observation, so it'll probably be just one overnight," I said. Then I thought again. "But if you did, you could help with the insurance stuff and keep Lil company. She could use it." I leaned into the room to check on Lil. She was passed out on the chair. "Sorry I'm always calling with bad news."

"Stop it, Tommy, it's not your fault. Look at it this way: Dad can't escape seeing doctors if he's stuck in the hospital, right?" she said. "And now he doesn't own a vehicle. He can't drive without one," she added.

She was right—a little quality senility had trumped the state driving test. I hadn't thought of that. The conversation paused while I took it in and peeked into the room again. I decided to put the phone on picture mode so that Deb could see both her parents in a peaceful state for once.

"Oh," she said, when she saw them. That's when I turned the phone back to my own face. "What's going on with your face, Tommy?!" It genuinely startled her. I had forgotten, in all the craziness, to tell my sister about my little accident.

"I ran into a tree," I admitted. "Long story." I could see Deb peering into her phone with a pained expression. "It's actually healed quite a bit," I added. We were both silent for a moment after that.

"Tommy?" she said.

"Yeah?"

"I'll take Friday off and come up for the weekend."

"Tomorrow's Friday," I reminded her.

"Yeah, it is." She paused. "So let me get going so I can figure it out. I'll text you with the flight time."

"That'd be swell, Sis" I never call her Sis.

"Tommy?"

152

"Yeah?"

"Go ahead and make plans to get outta there to the cave or something this weekend. Mental health is desirable."

"Yeah," I repeated.

The next morning, I went to check on Dad before going to work. Thankfully, Deb would arrive fairly early and I would hand things over to her. I got to the hospital quite early, parked, came up the elevator to Dad's room, and expected to see him still sleeping or eating breakfast on that annoying tray, or being toileted by a nurse. In that case, I'd wait in the hall until they finished. I try to honor my father's privacy.

When I arrived at Dad's floor, I walked quietly to his room and stopped. I peeked in. Dad was not uncomfortable at all. He was sitting upright in bed with a grande Starbucks coffee on that ugly tray. Sitting next to him on a chair was Kelly Pomeroy. She had her briefcase open on her lap and was chatting with him. She seemed to be shuffling some papers as she spoke.

"So that'll be fine Marty," I heard her say.

"Well, Lil's the keeper of our lives on paper," said Dad.

"She's wonderful. How is she holding up?" said Kelly.

Why did this woman need to know how my parents' lives are "on paper"? What would "be fine"? I waited and listened some more, but the conversation continued on pleasantries. A nurse was walking toward me suddenly.

"May I help you?" she said with a stern look. She had seen me spying. I immediately began putting one foot in front of the other to step into my father's room. That made it seem like I was just arriving as I answered her.

"I've found it now, thanks," I said to the nurse. "Hey," I greeted Dad and Kelly as I walked in, "all these luxury suites look the same in this hotel." Dad chuckled a little. I liked that. Kelly's smile disappeared even more quickly than her move to close her briefcase. She snapped it shut. I didn't like that.

"I'd rather be in my own suite at home," said Dad. He wasn't beaming, but he was fairly upbeat.

"Well, we'll get you there later today," I said. "They're releasing you. And hello, Ms. Pomeroy."

"Yes, I really—" Dad continued his lament about wanting to go home, but Kelly was up on her feet. I extended my hand.

"Hello, Tom, nice to see you again," she said, turning her back to me as she gathered her things. "I heard about Marty's accident so I ran over to see how he's doing." She finally looked up. At Dad. "He looks a slight bit tossed around, but no worse for the wear." She turned toward the door and continued, "So I'll be going now, Marty." I put my unshaken hand back down as she hurried by. "I don't want to interrupt a father-and-son visit. Bye bye!"

"You don't have to—" said Dad, but she was out the door.

"Bye," I called with a fake cheer in my voice. I turned to Dad. I was trying to decide if I wanted to ask about Kelly and their conversation or wait and concentrate on Deb's arrival.

"She's a great grocery girl," he said. I asked him to elaborate. "She goes to the supermarket for us, Tom," he said as if with admiration for a universal truth.

"And Lil lets her?"

Dad stared at me as if he'd just discovered his wife's illicit lover: homemaking. Lil is as married to her bill paying, cooking, chores, gardening and supermarketing as she is to Dad. She's arranged her life by those things for as long as I can remember—Monday is laundry day, Saturday is gardening in the spring, and so on. That she would hand any one of those tasks to someone else is blasphemy. Then again, this grocery report was coming from a man who can't wrangle taking pills or answering phones. Kelly probably went to pick up a few things once and Dad thinks she's a regular. I didn't push the issue.

"Listen, Dad, Deb is coming up to visit again. She'll be here later this morning to help Lil get you home. Won't that be nice?"

"Very nice, Tom," he said. That sounded pleasant. "You know, she can come with us to the dealership," he added.

"Dealership?" I asked.

"Of course," he said, "I can't rely on the same model again—that's what caused the accident." I looked at him in amazement, but he was not picking up on facial cues just then. "Those cars just don't handle well enough." He shook his head as if recently wrapping up a complete study of the industry.

"Dad, did your car malfunction? Is that what you're trying to say? 'Cause if it did—"

"I'm saying that I need a car that drives better," he said conclusively.

I decided to let Deb handle this.

.   .   .

Deb was right. Mental health is desirable. Jo packed us a huge basket of food and a couple of coolers of ice—no refrigerator yet out at the cave—and sent us on our merry way. It always feels good to leave town right after work. Before leaving, I noticed that Andre had left the tickets I had ordered to that *Stomp* show on my desk. I had them sent to my work address so I could surprise Mel with them for her birthday. It's not for a while yet, but buying now will help me not forget it, which I can't afford to do since she's so touchy lately. I also called a ritzy restaurant in the city that Andre had suggested and made a reservation. Mel will love that. I'm debating whether to tell her about her birthday dinner and show now or wait until the day of her birthday. It's probably better to not say anything unless she starts challenging me again to get pregnant. Then I'll have something to pull out as backup.

The ride out to the cave was therapeutic. As I drove, Mel kept taking snacks out of Jo's basket as if it were a magician's bottomless hat. She said Phineas was nice enough to help Jo prepare it. I mentioned to Mel how much I appreciate Jo and her care, but that I didn't think we should leave her in the house alone next door to Phineas anymore because of the flirting going on between them. I thought it was a reasonable concern.

"They'll be alone in the house with Ol' Smokin' Jo's pipe full of dreams," I said. That made Mel laugh very hard. I want to make her laugh very hard, especially lately. It almost made me divulge the birthday plans, but I managed to keep them under wraps. Mel is so cute when she laughs.

"Should zey not dream, either, Tom?" she said as we breezed down the thruway. Who said they shouldn't dream?

156

"No, but they make eyes at each other and he brings her flowers. They're always sitting together on our love seat on the back porch when I get home, and you know, no one's around all day because you and I work—who knows what they're up to there alone," I said. That part was not meant to be funny, but Mel was cracking up.

"Zen we can hire a babysitter when we go away. No, a 'seniorsitter'!" she said, so amused. Her laughing was starting to lose its charm.

"Look, I just don't want to come home and find my elderly great-grandmother-in-law and my elderly neighbor going at it like two teenagers on my living room floor," I said.

My words rang in my head like a rock guitarist's delay feature. I guess I did sound a bit paranoid, which made me sound silly—hysterical, in fact, judging by Mel's reaction. Sometimes we go at it on the living room floor, so I was wondering if she was thinking that. She was laughing so hard that she almost opened the door at 70 mph and rolled out to relieve her laughing fit.

"Just because you are not in a certain age and don't find zee older women attractive does not mean zey do not deserve love from zee gentlemen who do, Tom."

Still. I try not to picture elderly men having sex with even older, elderly women, OK? At that, Deb called. I put her on speaker immediately so she could change our subject.

"Tommy, it's me," she said.

"Hey, Sister Deborah," I said, "You're on speaker."

"What's so funny?" she said. I thought she was angry that I addressed her the way Jo does.

"*Allô*, Deborah," chuckled Mel.

"*Bonjour*." Deb greeted Mel dryly, rushing by an opportunity to practice bad French or gush over oncoming babies. "Tommy, Dad's driving me nuts."

"He wants a new car because his Lincoln made him crash," I said.

"That's all he can talk about!" she yelled. "As soon as I landed, I took a taxi straight to the hospital. When I walked in, he didn't even greet me. He just said, 'What do you think of the German models this year?'"

"And Lil is probably agreeing with him," I guessed. I was right.

"She keeps saying 'Lexus,' and he keeps saying 'BMW,'" she complained.

"And what do you say?" I asked.

"I say, 'Dad, is that catheter comfortable?'"

"Oh my," said Mel.

"Well, accidents produce results," I said. "Did that deter him? It'd be great if something easy would make him drop the whole idea of ever driving again," I said.

Deb's phone presence sailed in silence with us down the off-ramp, onto Country Route A, and to the stop light. We found ourselves behind one of those brightly colored Volkswagen Bugs with the big flowers decorating it.

"Now there's a car Dad would never be caught dead in," I said.

"Do not say zat, Tom," said Mel.

"What?" said Deb's voice.

"We're stopped behind one of those flower-power Volkswagen bugs," I explained. "Dad would never drive a fem-car like that," I said. Deb made a choking sound with her throat and started laughing.

"Lil would," she said.

Everyone paused. Bulbs were lighting up like a pinball win.

"*Oui*," said Mel first. "Yes. we must buy a woman-car for zem because only your mother will drive it."

There was only a short moment of silence before Deb began whooping and calling with happiness as if she were at a square dance. I was not sure how we were going to get away with it, but I admit there was promise in that premise.

"Mel, that's right," Deb yelled. "I'm going to hold Dad off as long as possible until we can figure out how to do this!" Deb was ecstatic. Mel was giggling. I wasn't doing anything except driving.

Sitting passively in the passenger's seat is not what real men do. Driving is a rite-of-passage for males. Especially in Dad's day, it meant picking up your girl and going out. It meant that ever-enticing mobility we all crave. I know it's only a few thousand pounds of steel, but it dominates the male sense of self. I couldn't bring myself to say that to my female co-conspirators. But at the same time, it's insane to believe that we can safely drive forever into the sunset while the evidence mounts so overwhelmingly to the contrary. If you notice people fleeing at the sight of your car, if other drivers swerve angrily around your vehicle and give you the finger on a regular basis, if the DMV is hauling you in for testing, then maybe that's telling you something. Maybe you oughta listen.

Maybe there's a reason why "humanity" rhymes with "insanity."

I was sitting out there on my lawn chair, feet up on my stump in the sunshine, enjoying the early thaw, mug in hand and laptop on lap when I heard a rustling in the bushes. I thought it was a small animal there at the ridge until I heard the grunting sounds. All of a sudden an arm flopped over onto the dirt. Its hand patted the ground like a big nervous spider until it found some small growth to clamp down on. I ran to the edge and began pulling up the person attached. Twigs snapped and branches broke and fell to their demise below. I almost let out a yell, but I managed to keep calm so as not to alarm Mel. In the next second, a bearded head and hairless frame inched over what looked like the edge of the Earth, and I realized only then that it was our pal Greg. I quickly bent down and hauled the rest of him up and over onto solid ground.

We both panted heavily. He stood and brushed off the dust and brambles. He was caked with dirt from the waist up with bits of Mother Earth embedded in his beard. His walking stick was fastened to his slim waist with a piece of rope, and he had a pickaxe strapped to his bony shoulder via a belt. That's why it was so hard to yank him up. He cursed to himself something about the numerous strains of creeping ivy that flourish in this area as he regained his composure. He was a compact Grizzly Adams, Johnny Appleseed, and Father Time all rolled into one. A twig was sticking straight up out of the back of his head.

"Coffee?" I asked.

"Love some," he panted.

He went inside to use our as yet unfinished bathroom to wash off some—but not all—of the dirt while I poured him some coffee. We came back out together and sat, I on the stump, and the old man on the folding lawn chair. Mel had just got up and was coming out to join us with her own coffee. She pulled out the other lawn chair and sat down.

"Good morning, Gregory," she said.

"A fine morning to ye," he offered.

"So what brought you here to us zis morning?" she asked. Ol' Greg answered that he hikes these parts all the time but that he's never had such a hard time on the cliff here.

"Musta been the thawing—washed out my path," he lamented. Things have thawed quite a bit, but it was his comment about hiking that piqued my curiosity. I got up and walked over to the edge of our little cliff to peer over it. It was not the vertical death drop I had somehow fixed in my mind, although I wouldn't be caught hiking it. There was a sort of second tier with a trail on it, if you want to call it that.

"Storm took alla them needles and such with it," he said. Mel and I looked at each other.

"Needles?" I asked him. He was busy picking out the last bit of earth from his beard. Then he started patting his head and found the twig. He pulled it out of his matted hair, stuck it in his mouth, and sucked on it a while before spitting it out to comment.

"Gonna storm, friends. Soon."

Now I really do like Ol' Gregory, and he certainly is fascinating, and I'm sure he knows his local nature and history, but it was promising to be the most beautiful day I'd seen in a very long time. Cool but not cold, only a few clouds in the sky. And I don't care how close to nature you live, you can't tell from sucking on some wood if the weather is going to turn. But arguing with our local nature nut didn't seem worth the time—I wanted to know about the needles. Greg continued.

"Like I think I told ye, there was teenagers living here. On and off, ye know, it was abandoned and all, so they been in here doing drugs and running away from nasty homes. Unhappy for them kids, real unhappy." Gregory paused there to loosen his walking stick from his waist. He held it across his lap. Now he looked like Jesus, if you ignored the pickaxe.

"They'd sit out here, just like we're doing now, and they'd toss the used drug stuff over the edge, just there." He pointed with his stick to the spot up and over which I had just dragged him. "I'd be hiking on a good lead, and then I hadda stop on accounna finding needles and such."

"What do you mean 'a good lead'?" I asked. I couldn't help myself.

"Well," he said, "folks 'round here suspect treasure. Gotta be here somewheres, 'cause where there's been pirates, there's been treasure. Gonna find it. Been looking for years and I'm getting close."

That explained the pickaxe and all his other extreme-sports paraphernalia. I smiled and nodded, then I

162

remembered the small burn marks on our supposedly pirate-laid floor. They do look suspicious, and they could have been made by runaways who felt the need to freebase crack in an abandoned house. That small mortar and pestle would have come in handy for drug abuse as well, so I'll admit his story made sense. I jumped back to it.

"If kids were doing illegal drugs in this place, why didn't you call the police?"

"Didn't havta," he said, smiling like someone enjoying a cold plate of savored revenge. "Pirate spirits, friend. Frighted 'em out."

Greg's ghost stories were something I decided to leave for another day because teenagers do crazy things like run away, break into abandoned houses, and experiment with drugs, and anyway, we had to dash inside because it started pouring.

As soon as we got settled inside, I typed the local zip code into my weather app. Rain all afternoon, it said. Cold rain. I chucked some logs into the fireplace and Mel took to the kitchen to make some breakfast. I'll admit it soon felt quite cozy with the smell of bacon and eggs cooking, the crackling of the fire burning. Some hardy chow inside and some rain outside would make a great day for work on the interior of the place. Mel asked Ol' Greg to stay for the meal, and I was going to enlist him for some help with the cabinets, but unusually, he turned us down.

"No little rain gonna stop my searching today, but I thank ye," he said. Before we could stop him, he hoisted his pickaxe onto his shoulder and casually walked out the door into the drops. No coat, no umbrella, an unhurried gait. From the door, I watched him stride easily to the lawn chair to pick up his walking stick as if he were not getting slowly soaked. Hair dripping, he turned and sauntered away down the muddy path, whistling.

A little physical labor makes an afternoon fly by. Mel concentrated on the bathroom, burnishing the floor, tile by tile. This crazy place has one of those old bathroom floors made of small, white, hexagonal tiles. I don't want her doing hard labor in her double-baby condition, so I propped her up on a huge pillow. She began calmly cleaning each ceramic piece with a stiff-bristle brush and plain soapy water from a bucket. It's tedious work, but effective. We put on some music to get into the "zone" as Stephen used to say. Mel chose Bob Dylan. She pronounces his first name "Bub."

Getting the cabinets up would allow us a real kitchen out here at the cave. I found myself measuring, poking, and tapping on the kitchen walls to the music. Jack has always said that Dylan's talky-singing vocals were a precursor to Rap. ... *foot*—TAP ... *soot*—TAP ... *put*—TAP ... CRUNCH! My hammer went right through the plaster. Plaster walls are supposed to be solid. I put down the hammer and cleared the broken pieces away with my fingers. *Look out, kid* .... I peered into the opening. It was dark, so I reached in. My hand met something cold and hard. I grabbed it and pulled it out: a black key. It was an odd shape, old, ornate, and heavy like iron, like something the Addams Family would use to open their dungeon.

I stopped for a moment to think. ... *weatherman* ... I didn't need a seer. That key likely belonged to the runaways. Who else? I peeked into the bathroom. Mel was humming along to Bub on her pillow, especially intent on a yellow stain. I was not in the mood for a conversation on what this thing might be, and I know Mel —she'd want to share such a strange find with Ol' Greg. Then they'd riff on it eternally. I shoved it under the sink and forgot about it.

By evening, the rain had stopped, but it was still cold and damp outside. Mel and I stoked the fire and cozied up on the mattress for the night. Some hours later, I woke up alone. It was especially dark because the fire had gone out. A gale storm had moved in—a whole lotta wind blew open the back shutters, and intermittent moonlight began shining in through the passing clouds. I rolled over, grabbed a candle, and managed to get it lit. There was Mel. She was kneeling over me holding that old key! She surprised me so much that I let out a whimper. She looked like a pregnant Morticia, hovering there with her long, diaphanous—quite sexy—black robe, holding the key in front of her face as if spellbound by it. I had to compose myself to speak.

"Uh ... Mel?" I said, "Honey, whattya doing?"

She was sleepwalking again. Sleepkneeling, actually. She slowly stood up, walked over to the foot of the mattress, lifted the edge, and tapped the floor three times, just as she'd done with that knife a while back. I decided to handle the situation the same way again. I slid the key softly out of her hand, took her arm gently, and helped her replace the mattress to lie down. She followed along easily.

"Just sleep now, honey," I whispered. She lay down. I let her get comfortable as I walked over to the chair where my coat was draped. I slipped the key into the interior pocket and zipped it shut. Mel grunted a little, squirmed around to pull the blanket over her, and mumbled.

"Tile will tell."

   .   .   .

It wasn't the phone call from Deb asking us to return early from my mental health break that concerned me, it was Deb's urgency and vagueness. Why I needed to come back early on Sunday to "meet with the lawyer" was not made clear. That made me nervous. Was the driver of the truck going to sue Dad and take everything he's worked so hard for all his life? That would kill him much more readily than not being able to drive.

Mel and I didn't even go home. We drove straight from the cave to their house. When we walked in, Larry was in the living room with Dad, Lil, and Deb. His secretary, Silvia, was also present. Having our family lawyer there accompanied by his professional sidekick did not put my mind at ease. Mel and I sat down. At the coffee table in front of us was all the necessary paperwork for Dad and Lil to give Deb and me their power of attorney. I was thoroughly confused because the last time I brought up signing a POA with Dad so I could help them with their finances, his reaction was "Get out of my house."

Not a mention of the accident, and the signing went smoothly. Almost with an air of devotion. When this communion was over, Larry got up, packed up, said he'd be in touch, and left. Sylvia followed him. Mel and I smiled as if nothing were strange or urgent. Not talking seemed to have blessed the proceedings. Deb's flight departure time was looming, and soon we were hauling her suitcase out to the car. "Goodbye" and "Come back soon" and "Kiss the kids for us" were all being said while Deb threw me knowing looks of ill boding. As soon as we were in the car, waving and smiling but with doors closed and windows rolled up so Dad and Lil couldn't hear us, she jumped right in as if having already started the conversation hours ago in anticipation of my arrival—and her departure.

"So anyway, after dealing with insurance claim information and paperwork and phone calls and even a call from the lawyer of the guy in the truck—" she said. I winced. Deb explained.

"Don't worry. He's doesn't want to sue or anything. His vehicle is fine, after all, except for his front grill. When his lawyer got back to me, he said that his client used to take care of his own father, so he understands what we're up against. The driver of the truck 'couldn't get his old man off the road either,' as his lawyer put it, until the father drove his car into a storefront."

All I could picture was Dad becoming disoriented by the sun's glare or some otherwise innocuous element of driving. Instead of casually lowering the visor, he simply continues along until a glass storefront is suddenly in his path and, in my imagination, he crashes right through it, drives over mannequins and displays, busts through the back wall, and keeps going. Bewildered and shocked employees watch the back of his car disappear around a bend through the pieces of glass and dust dangling in their hair. I groaned.

"Wait, Little Brother, it gets better," said Deb. "So as I searched in Lil's filing cabinet for things like their insurance policy, what did I see? Hanging folders, all neatly lined up. The most recent files were up top, the oldest in the bottom drawer."

"That seems reasonable," I said. "Lil's always been thorough."

"Yes, and it was very moving, Tommy, to see everything from tax returns and voided checks to copies of sick notes to our teachers and our finger paintings from kindergarten. All of it was arranged from our births to the present in exact chronological order. There was even that picture of a naked lady you drew in 7th grade."

"Lil's been a little too thorough," I mumbled. Mel grinned.

"Not too, Tommy—have you peeked into those files lately?" she asked.

"No. I've never had a reason to," I said.

"Well, if you do, you'll see that the top files start to fall into disarray. The most recent ones crumble into chaos, as if you're looking at a real-life timeline of Mom and Dad's decline. Like fossils caught in layers of sediment."

I do like my sister's analogies.

"And here's a kicker," she continued. "There were no tax returns in there starting about two years ago—"

Both my sister and I easily remember Lil sitting at the dining room table each year during tax season with all the right forms spread out in front of her. She had her coffee and her pencils and pens and Whiteout at the ready. It always got done. And happily, at that. People don't do that anymore. They go to the tax guy, but Lil loved creating that organized and well-oiled machine to live in. Dad left it to her. Who knew how important that piece would be so many years later?

"So they've not been doing their taxes for the last few years," I sighed.

"I guess not," said Deb. "And Tommy, there were things shoved in there that really don't belong in folders," she added. "Trust me." Deb is an astute, make-it-happen kind of advertising executive. I decided to trust her on that. She continued.

"Anyway, I grabbed the insurance policy and went downstairs. I waited for a moment when she and Dad were sitting together. Then I said casually, 'Ma, getting taxes done is really hard. I give you a lot of credit for doing it yourself all these years. But what with all the identity theft recently, I'd be really careful about filling out anything and sending it off.'" I can just see my cool and collected sister pausing here for effect. Then she continued. "How's it going, anyway? You don't seem to have all your usual stuff spread out in the dining room. Did you file for an extension this year?" she asked them.

Deb said she felt wicked as her own magic worked right in front of her. Her comments forced open the can of worms. While Lil didn't want to admit in front of Dad—or herself—that she hadn't been doing their taxes, the idea that someone could steal control of their finances became a steely thorn shot from a gun. It struck Dad's head at 90 miles per hour, imbedding itself in his brain. Deb said he became indignant. He muted the TV immediately, even though Niles was finally going to tell Daphne that he adores her.

"Theft?!" he thundered.

Deb remained calm and mentioned casually that she and I have put fraud alert protection on our own investments and credit records. "We could have Tom's tax guy easily pick up your tax stuff every year, then Lil could relax," she offered.

Although I can easily picture what happened next, my sister's description was golden: Lil offered a sad smile to her man that said "Please consent so I'm not shamed," and Dad leaned forward and put his hand on her arm as if having to defend her from his own children.

"Deborah," he proclaimed, "You call your brother this instant and tell him to get back from his crazy cave-dwelling or whatever he's doing and let's figure this out for Pete's sake—your mother should not be shouldering this all on her own. What's the matter with Thomas, anyway?!"

I don't mind playing the fall guy for a good cause. Deb and I are now the proud co-pilots of our parents' entire estate—checking account, investments, property, and eventually, destiny. I now realize that bumper stickers are the repository of some of the greatest wisdom of the Western world. The one that says, "Be nice to your kids —they will decide which nursing home you end up in" is the biggest truth this side of Heaven.

"It's Friday, whattya say?" cried Jack as he walked into my office. He'd been feeling guilty about not finding time to celebrate our "double jeopardy" as he calls it. "We're doing this—how often are you a double-father and a grandpa at the same time? Can Mel come?"

I said yes. Jack stood up and clapped me on the shoulder. It hurt.

"And a good drink'll clear up the last of your face dents in no time," he said. "Lemme go close up shop."

My dented face has healed almost completely, so it's not impossible that a much-needed drink after work might prove medicinal. As Jack walked out, Andre peeked in.

"The meeting tomorrow morning has been moved to 9 am," he said.

"Thanks."

"Your face has come along nicely."

"Thanks," I said again, "but it could use a drink." Jack heard me. I heard him laugh from down the hall. Andre stepped up to my desk and handed me some coupons for the new cafe downstairs. "I know this isn't the kind of drink you were referring to," he said, "but I want you to have them."

I like Andre a lot. I remember his first day on the job, and I'm still a bit embarrassed about it. I remember being sure that such an able and smart young man would only apply to be a secretary because he's putting himself through night school or something like that.

"Hey, Andre," I said, "nice to meet you. I'm sure you'll like it around here. You must be a student putting yourself through night school or something like that, right?"

"I just finished night school," was his reply.

"Oh. What did you study?" I asked. He was gracious when he answered.

"Secretarial sciences."

He's never held that against me. Anyone else would have been insulted by my question's innuendo—that intelligent, strapping young men shouldn't be secretaries. I'll have to admit that we've never had a better one. Ever. He's helpful, intuitive, discreet. I found myself asking for his help.

"Ya know, Andre," I said, "I wanna ask you something. D'ya know much about history?"

"I like it, but I'm no specialist," he said.

"Well, let's just say that, if you had a really interesting thing you needed, let's say, appraised, something that's been in the family for ages," I started. Talking things through was giving me good ideas. That key I found in our cave wasn't from my family, but it was from someone's, I just didn't have to say whose.

"What kind of thing?" he asked.

"Um," I stalled. Should I say it? I decided against it. "A trinket that could be, maybe, from the Age of

Exploration." I hoped he didn't notice my peering into his face to see if he was coming along for the ride.

"Oh," he said, then paused. "Are you one of those people who had relatives on the Mayflower or something?" His eyes widened. He was genuinely impressed. It made me want to say "Yes, I am," but I didn't.

"No, but we're looking into that as well," I said successfully. That sounded like I might come from such vaunted stock, and that I might have some belongings hanging around the attic that were on the Mayflower, and that I might not know for sure but am awfully keen to know. He stared at the floor and rubbed his chin as if to rub off information. He does that a lot.

"I think I recall from my classes at the university that their museum has a section on European history. You know, the link between their history and ours or something like that. You might try calling them," he said.

"Do you know the—"

"257-4260. Ask for Dr. Willows."

I quickly grabbed my phone and put the number in. When I looked up, Andre was staring at my face.

"I have a great organic vitamin E cream with aloe. May I bring it in for you for the last of those bumps and scrapes? It'll make the scars fade."

"That's nice of you, Andre, but don't go to any trouble," I said. "My doctor already gave me a prescription cream." I keep forgetting to pick it up. I'll have to do that.

"OK. Have a nice evening."

He stepped out. I waited until I heard him take his jacket and close up behind him. Then I wasted no time in calling the university. The doctor was in.

After some introductory niceties, Dr. Willows asked me to describe the "heirloom." I got up and closed the door. I sat back down and tried to say matter-of-factly that it was an old key made of iron.

"And you're sure it's iron?"

"I have no way of testing it. It could be an alloy, but yeah, it seems like iron."

"Well, what's it shaped like?" he asked.

"It's really odd. And decorated. It's shaped a bit like a sideways fork. Sort of," I said.

There was a solid silence over the line. I thought the call was dropped, and I was ready to call him back and apologize for my carrier.

"Can you bring it in first thing in the morning?" he asked finally. I said I would. Just then, my door burst open.

"Ready," Jack announced loudly. He rarely puts anything in the form of a question, even when it is. I motioned to him that I was on an important call. He mouthed back to me.

"I'll meet you at Bogan's."

Bogan's is one of the most popular restaurant-bar establishments in town. It's known for its French fries. They're home cut, homemade, double-fried, and superb. They are the main attraction, after the pretty waitresses, who are dressed in medieval wench costumes like so many St. Pauli girls. Over the years, the place began hiring guys as well in order to avoid a gender-discrimination lawsuit. Now the guys dress like a male version of St. Pauli girls, sort of, but they're not the reason Jack goes there.

Mel had been at a meeting and arrived just after we did. We sat outside in a nice breeze while a St. Pauli guy asked us what we wanted to drink. I would never appear in public with those forest-green shorts and suspenders.

"Are you our server?" asked Jack, dashed.

"No," he said. "Jenna is. She'll be coming over momentarily. Can I get you something to drink until she does?" Jack perked up. We ordered drinks.

When the drinks arrived, they were on Jenna's tray. Pretty, red-headed Jenna. She unloaded them, stood back, announced her name, then asked if we were ready to order. Jack was ready to order. And to talk to Jenna.

"Hi, Jenna. You look like a student," he said. She looked like the furthest thing from a student, but I had to give Jack credit for a solid opening shot.

"I am!" she answered, frothing like Jack's Guinness.

"What do you study?" asked Jack. His voice had the bounce of Jenna's all of a sudden.

"Policy," she replied.

"Like, government policy?" he asked.

"Uh huh. I want to work in foreign affairs."

I could see Jack starting to sparkle. Jenna was cute *and* intelligent, and I was sure it was going to be an interesting conversation, but my phone interrupted. The screen said it was Lil's number, but when I answered, Dad's voice was there.

"Tom?"

"Hey Dad," I said. Something in his voice was amiss.

"Tom, there are limits, dammit!" My father swore at me. He hasn't done that since I was a teenager. Limits to what? I turned partially away and lowered my voice. I didn't want to interrupt Jack—he was working it pretty well with pretty Jenna.

"Dad, what happened? What are you talking about?" I said. Jack asked Jenna if she'll be moving to Washington.

"I did not give you permission put my money under lock and key!" he roared. It really contrasted with Jenna's fine voice.

"I'd like to deal with foreign policy on the front lines, so to say," she said. Mel had been smiling at Jack's slick moves. Now she glanced at me with a what's-going-on look. I put up an index finger to her as if to say, "Hang on and I'll let you know what's happening," then I tuned back to Dad.

" ... at the Lexus dealership, and even Kelly was embarrassed ..." he was yelling.

"Whoa, whoa, wait a sec, Dad," I said, "Whattya mean 'dealership'?" I said. I heard Jenna elaborating.

" ... effecting change. I mean, take any of the recent conflicts—Afghanistan, Iraq ..."

"Kelly was nice enough to drive your mother and me down to the dealership ..." Dad asserted. I was so angry at Kelly I could barely hear what else Dad was saying. Jack's next move echoed behind Dad's ranting.

"... Eisenhower's military-industrial complex ..." he averred.

"Dad, look," I said as I got up from the table and stepped aside, "'fraud alert' is the kind of thing Deb and I were talking about, you know, to protect your ass—" I wanted to say "assets," but he kept yelling over me.

"I've never in my life not had access to my own funds, Tom!" he raved. Jenna commented.

"No congressional oversight at all ...."

"Dad, look, I'm coming over," I announced.

"You'd better explain yourself, Thomas, because this 'fraud alert' thing is a fraud if I ever ..." continued my father.

I turned to Mel and explained that Dad was in need of a private consultation with his son. She was worried, but she let me go. I wanted to say goodbye to Jack, but the twinkle in Jenna's eyes stopped me from interrupting. I heard him talking as I turned to go.

" ... profoundly jealous of the birth experience ..." he was saying.

As I walked toward the car, Dad's rant continued to stream out of the phone. He said he'll "never let people drive him around," and he'll never take public transportation "like Phineas does." He said he'll never forgive me. That image of Daniel floating through the air in slow motion was there again, and the grownups, who kept saying, "Tommy, it's not your fault."

I looked up to see my parents' home and Kelly's house sitting side-by-side in a foreboding twosome. Then I turned the car off. I was in Dad's driveway, but I didn't even remember driving there. I felt a rage at Kelly, and I decided that she's the one who needs a talking to. She may have thought she was helping, but she wasn't. I got out of the car and walked up her flower-lined stone path.

I rang the bell. She came to the door and opened it, then just stood there. She began peering at everything on the front of my head except my eyes.

"So what happened to you?" she asked. The upset with Dad made me forget that scars still decorate my face. Hers showed real concern, or maybe it was fascination. She invited me in for coffee and immediately led me to her kitchen table. We exchanged conversation about my accident, about how she works frequently at home—as she was doing when I arrived, she said—and hashed through other small talk while she made a large pot of coffee.

"I hope your face heals all the way," she continued. "I have a tube of vitamin E cream if you'd like it." I declined politely. I'd never got the one from my doctor, but she insisted that vitamin E will fade the last of the scars. I made a mental note to get to the pharmacy. "Cream and sugar?" she asked.

"Black," I said and got right to the point.

"You know, Kelly," I began, "I wanted to talk to you about your generous actions with Dad. It's really great that you want to help, but his mental state is slipping. I mean, he was in an accident. We feel he shouldn't be driving anymore, but thanks for taking him to the Lexus store." I chuckled at my own joke. It rhymed, and I liked the way it came out—Lexus "store." As if he's a kid going to a candy store, not a grownup going to a car dealership.

She peered at me as if what I'm doing with my dad is criminal. That's probably just her "lawyer" look. I did catch her during work hours, after all.

"So how will your parents get around and feed themselves without a car? You know I've been picking up groceries for them," she said a bit scoldingly. I'd forgotten about that.

"Oh yes, Dad called you 'the grocery girl,'" I said, again jovially, but her lawyer look held strong.

"Lil can still drive, so isn't it a bit confining to her that they have no vehicle?" she said. I remembered at that moment her firm's ad in the paper and that they cover elderly abuse cases. I pushed past the innuendo.

"Look, Kelly. The family has decided on something a bit unconventional, but we think it might work." This stranger had no reason to be in on our machinations, but I had nothing else. "We're going to buy Lil a nice feminine vehicle. Something she'll love, but one Dad wouldn't be caught dead in." I realized my unfortunate word choice and quickly moved on. "I mean, it's a gimmick, you know, to keep Dad out from behind the wheel. Lil will then be able to grocery shop and do anything they need, so you don't have to feel like the grocery girl anymore."

Kelly's face had lit up. It was quite a transformation. I didn't feel like a criminal, or even a mis-speaker, and she seemed to be back to her old, toilet-cleaning self. She was suddenly perky, very confident about Dad and Lil's continuing welfare. She insisted on making suggestions on which car would attract Lil and repel Dad. That grocery thing was probably a big imposition and now she'd be released from it. As we tossed around a few ideas, I reiterated often that we wanted something used. A solid vehicle in good condition, but reasonable so we'd buy it and be done—I reminded her that we're shooting for less bills and paperwork for my parents, not more.

When Kelly got up and poured a little brandy into our coffees, the ideas really started flowing—Grand Am, Grand Prix—I was beginning to see a pattern here, and it was all making sense. Even the brandy was Grand Marnier, so I took that as a good omen. We had a laugh over the idea of getting Lil one of those Volkswagen Bugs with the daisy on the dash and huge, 60s-style flowers stuck all over the outside. Maybe bright yellow.

Dad will never even want it parked in his driveway. That's when we realized Kelly's real insight: color. It doesn't matter what car we get Lil, she said, as long as it's pink.

In the end, Kelly settled on a pink Grand Prix. It was great to have some help on this one. And I admit that I greatly valued the female perspective on which car would be appreciated by their species, because honestly, sometimes I think women are another species.

. . .

"I don't know, Tom," said Mel at 1:53 a.m. I knew it was so late because I remember glancing at my phone as we drifted off to sleep. I had been explaining to her how gracious and intelligent Kelly was about the car thing. Maybe once we get Dad and Lil squared away with transportation again, things will calm down, and Mel will see that any help with aging parents is good help.

About an hour later, I got up to go to the bathroom. As I went by the window, I heard two voices outside in the back yard. The night was so clear I could actually see the two women out there. They were alternately chanting while circling my corn patch, then stopping to confer about it, or that's what it seemed. One was Jo, and one was not. The one who was not was Phineas. He was wearing a dress, for God's sake.

I can't believe I woke my pregnant wife, but I did. She came to the window, rubbed her eyes, and said, "Zee professor is a good sport, no?" and returned to bed. She fell back asleep so easily. I wasn't about to fall asleep, though. I felt my already tense muscles grab my body and run frantically down the stairs with it. I don't care how casually my wife takes it, or how used to her ancient relatives' ways she is, I don't want our neighbors thinking that we're carrying on with strange orgies or lewd parties every full moon. I love my wife, but I wish she would care about these things sometimes.

You would think that the screen door slamming behind me would interrupt Jo and her dancing daddy, but it didn't. They kept right on chanting and circling the patch. The full moon seemed to light up the night in the same way the sun lights up the day, if that makes any sense. I could see my patch perfectly and walked toward it. As I got closer, Phineas and Jo stopped their dance, bowed to the bare earth, turned toward the house, and walked right by me as if I weren't there. They sat down for a pipeful. Phineas's blond wig was shining in the moonlight.

When I got to the edge of the patch, I saw bare earth. Will Jo plant something, or is all this dancing delirium just to prepare the soil? Does she realize that I consider it my task to plant the actual seeds? Should I let her do it, since she's giving it so much time? I don't want another corn failure this year. Seeds should be busy for God's sake, like us humans. They should be doing something to get where they want to be.

I was alone with my patch for the first time in a long time. The cool, night breeze cleared my mind. I was reminded of Mel's placenta-as-fertilizer story. She did say that women back in Jo's era just hobbled over to the shade of the nearest tree to give birth and then returned to the fields to work. They would have the placenta right there. But where would Jo get it in this day and age? She hasn't delivered any babies recently. That I knew of.

I imagined her in dark sunglasses, knocking on an iron door in a back alley at night and looking around nervously for the cops. In my scenario, a female nurse opened up a small window and peeked out. They gave each other a secret sign, then the door opened slowly, and only far enough for a large Tupperware container of placenta to slip out. Jo took it and shoved it into a plain brown grocery bag as the door clacked shut quickly. It ended with the sound of a deadbolt slamming into place and echoing in the darkness.

Bizarre visions of tiny writhing humans on stalks appeared in my mind. They were growing in my garden. In reality, I was outside at midnight under a full moon in the same yard as a chanting old man dressed like a chanting old woman—none of that felt right. I felt small, "mortally aware in a temperamental environment," as Jack says. I felt the need to beat it.

It seemed to take forever to walk back to the house. I made it across the yard toward the dynamic duo. They were sitting on the swinging love seat, rocking and puffing. They didn't seem to notice me at first, even under that sun-like moon. But as I got closer, Phineas called out.

"What sneaking fellow comes yonder? Ay, sira! A word with you." I stepped up to the deck. I guess the look on my face made him explain. "My lady loves me. She did commend my yellow stockings of late, she did praise my leg, being cross-gartered, and in this she manifests herself to my love, and with a kind of injunction drives me to these habits of her liking. I thank my stars, I am happy," he stated. I vaguely remember that passage from somewhere. I looked it up just now, and sure enough, it was from Shakespeare's *Twelfth Night*. When I didn't respond, Phineas waited, then asked, "What grief hath set the jaundice on your cheeks? Ye've got a humour there does not become a man."

I really love the professor, but he was in no position to be commenting on what does and does not become a man. I thanked him for his concern and left them sitting contentedly out there. Now I'm sitting discontentedly in here at my computer. Since I've got my browser open, I'm going to click over to a dictionary site right now and look up "sira" since he keeps calling me that.

sir | rah (pronunciation: SEER uh)
noun — *Archaic*.
a title used to address people of inferior status; also used to convey contempt, misgiving, or the like.

I clicked off the dictionary site and stared at my twins. We've made one of Mel's ultrasound pictures our desktop image. Last time I started a family, I couldn't make my kid's ultrasound image my screen saver because there were no screen savers. There were no screens, unless you count TV or movie theaters. I guess there were no personal screens. This time around, there are personal screens galore. I don't generally go overboard with the social media thing, and I refuse to announce "just made coffee" and other patently banal tidbits on Facebook or Twitter, but my twin daughters are different. I've plastered them on every available screen. They're all cozied up in fuzzy black and white, and I can flick them on any time of the day or night to gaze at them. Each time, they take my breath away.

Jo just came in from her midnight gardening ritual. Phineas must have gone home. She saw me sitting here, made me a chamomile tea without even asking me, and brought it to me before going up to bed. It's good tea.

Deb email
Re: Girl car
tommy
if you just ignore dad long enough he might 4get cars
-Sis

Mel followed me in her car. I drove The *Prix*, as we're calling it. *Prix* means "prize" in French, so everyone wins —I win because I won't have to monitor Dad to keep him out from behind the wheel of a vehicle; Lil wins because she gets a car; Dad wins because he'll remain alive; Kelly wins because she won't have to be the grocery gofer anymore; and Deb likes it because it's pronounced easily "pree," so she feels as if she's speaking good French.

When we pulled up to the house, I felt sure that all our emotional and logistical preparations were going to pay off. I guess I'll have to be happy with what we got, because pink cars are not a dime a dozen, and what were the chances of finding that rogue, ex-Mary Kay lady who wanted to unload hers that cheaply? It was practically brand-new. Only 55K on it, and the paint job was exquisite. But I still had it cleaned and buffed and waxed and even sprayed with that new-car smelling stuff anyway just for good measure. It drives like a dream, too.

Dad and Lil came out of the house. As I pulled up and stopped in their driveway, Lil ran to the car. She seemed to instinctively know it was hers. I stepped out and handed her the keys. She got in and sat smiling behind the wheel, then began stroking the interior. At that moment, Kelly came out of her house, beaming. Her college-age daughter was with her.

"Why, hello, hello," she said with a smile and a wink as she walked toward me, checking to see if Dad was looking.

"Hello, Kelly," I said, nodding only very slightly to acknowledge her idea's triumph.

"This is my daughter, Julie," she said a bit loudly, trying to get Dad's attention. Mel and I greeted Julie, and she greeted us back. She seemed very nice. I couldn't help thinking how much "Julie" sounds like "jewelry" when I saw how much gold and silver she was wearing. Kelly nodded toward the car.

"I see you have a new addition to the family," she said again loudly.

Dad didn't respond. He stood apart from us there in the garage by about ten feet. He was focused solely on that car, watching it as if it made only partial sense. His weight was on one leg and his chin was in his hand, then he shifted to the other leg and the other hand. When Lil got it fired up and pulled away for a spin, Dad put his weight squarely on both legs and called me over. I pretended not to notice his consternation. He didn't say anything at first, so I did.

"So whattya think, Dad? Good looking *and* economical. Merry Christmas." I winked.

Even my father can see it's not the December holiday season. He picked his chin up, leaned toward me, smiled, and winked back. Then we both laughed at something that made him feel privy to a secret that doesn't exist and made me feel once again like a lying skunk. He loosened up and spoke.

"Heated leather seats?" he asked. I nodded confidently. That's something he can enjoy without even driving it. He looked impressed. "Infrared temperature sensor?" he prodded.

Now I was at a loss. I had to think fast. I just blurted the first thing that came to mind, and it was a doozie.

"Dad, all those extras are nice, but the faster you spend your money on too much luxury, the sooner you'll end up in one of those bare-bones nursing homes. Don't you think that something simple with less frills is more prudent?"

No one knows better about low-grade nursing homes than ex-hospital administrators. Especially those of Dad's generation. "Nursing home" in Dad's day meant low grade—there weren't many "high grade" facilities, so just hearing the words "nursing" and "home" in the same sentence was enough for him. He took several paces back from me, put his chin back in his hand, and stood squarely on both feet again, staring out toward the street and waiting for Lil to return.

In the meantime, Mel was chatting up Kelly and her daughter. When Lil finally pulled back into the driveway and stepped out of the car, Kelly introduced her daughter to Lil "so quickly zat your mother did not hear her name, zen she grabbed zee keys from Lil and tossed zem to zee girl, and after zat, zey jumped into zee car and—*zoom!*— zey were away." That's how Mel described it as we drove home afterward.

It's true that Lil offered them a test drive, and Kelly did look like she enjoyed riding along while Julie drove, but I don't recall any grabbing of keys or zooming.

"Kelly's probably getting a car for her daughter to have at college and wanted her to try something used but nice," I said.

Mel sighed. I thought she might say, "I don't know, Tom," but she didn't. Instead, she pointed out repeatedly that they were gone for 50 minutes, but I wasn't keeping track. I was busy skirting the issue of color every time Dad approached me with that look on his face. It's not like they didn't come back.

I have since gloated a bit to Mel that, without Kelly's genius for pink, Dad would not be staying away from that car like a sex-change operation. Lil is in charge and doing all the driving, so I have some time to get things done, things like gather up my parents' entire paper trail from the last 2+ years and shove it all into a box for our tax guy Arnett. He'll then happily sort it out for a fee. A rather large one. He'll probably sort it out unhappily initially, then take the fee happily when he's done.

When Mel first heard that I've had a tax guy all these years named Arnett Heatherington, she kept walking around the house saying "It is zee Arnett Heatherington Show!" in a low voice like the announcer of *Saturday Night Live*. Then, right before tax season, she adds, "Heeeeeeeere's Arnett!" and laughs like I've never seen her laugh before, not even with her sister. "He could be a member of zee House of Lords." Even though I try to defend him, Mel says "Lords" with the most parliamentary of British accents. It makes me want to roll on the kitchen floor laughing with her every time. I

188

always wonder if the guy would do our taxes—even for that fee—if he knew how battered his name gets in our house.

The other thing I've won time for is my garden. I went out to check on it this morning and finally saw it tilled but not sowed. Jo explained that late corn is better in our climate. I'll keep trying to believe her. I did notice, however, that there were no weeds. Not in the patch and not anywhere nearby. None in the yard at all this year. And I've never seen Jo or Phineas out there weeding, not with a hoe, or even on their hands and knees, and certainly not spraying any chemicals. Jo doesn't even know what modern weed killers are. Maybe a good chanting is all we need after all. Ha! Every year from now on, I'll get a couple of megaphones and have Jo and Phineas point them at the whole yard and chant. Poof! Weeds be gone! Or I'll get some really killer speakers and set them up outside on the roof and blast the neighborhood with "The Jo and Phineas Show" and watch everyone's weeds wilt. Yeah. I could charge for that service. The government will want a piece of that— they'll mount huge speaker systems on planes with Jo and Phineas inside at the microphones and fly over fertile lands before planting all that corn we need to fuel our cars.

I'm really tired.

.   .   .

When I arrived at the pharmacy this morning for the face cream, the young man behind the counter said there was no such prescription under my name. I pulled out my phone and read the name of it from my notes app where I'd jotted it down. My face only has a couple of light scars left on it, but I thought fading them as much as possible with a good cream was worth doing.

"Oh," said the young man, "That's an over-the-counter product. Here, let me show you." He came out through his little swinging door and walked me over to that aisle. It was a simple vitamin E cream. He pointed out the "organic" version, but I bought a tube of the regular one and left.

As I got to my office, I saw that I'd had a call from Dr. Willows.

"Conklin," I heard him say when the message began, "I'd like to talk to you in person about your family heirloom here. Please get back to me as soon as possible ...."

With all the brouhaha over finding a pink car and successfully slipping it into my parents' life, I'd forgotten I'd brought him that key. But before I could give it a thought, my phone rang. It showed Lil's cell number. I was thrilled at her continuing cell phone use.

"Hello?" I answered. It seemed no one was there. I was ready to hang up when I suddenly heard a female voice.

"Shit," it said. It was certainly not Lil's. Then another voice in the background sounded.

"Just hang up!"

The line went dead. I told Andre that I needed to go out and that I would be back for the review we had scheduled. I drove immediately over to my parents' house.

When I got there, there was no car in the driveway or in the garage, which was wide open. The front door was open as well with only the screen closed properly. I walked in as nonchalantly as possible.

"Hey," I said, "anyone home?"

"Come in, Thomas," Lil said. I followed her voice into the kitchen where they were eating an eggs-and-bacon breakfast out of Styrofoam containers, as if they'd gone out to get it. I was hoping they'd gone out in the new car, but where was it? Between the phone and the car, I'd rather they lost the former. After some small talk, I decided to start with that.

"I tried to call you just now, Ma," I lied with the most fake composure, "but no one answered. Where's your phone?"

"Phone?" she said.

"Yeah, your cell phone," I replied.

"Well, dear, I gave it to someone. How's Mel doing?" she asked. "Oh, and Thomas, when is the baby shower? Is Deb—?"

A car was pulling in. I leapt out of my chair and ran to the front door. I closed it and peered out the little round, decorative window on the side of the front hall, the one shaped like a portal in a ship's cabin that I'd always thought was a waste of time to install. It was now serving a stealthful purpose. Kelly's college-bound daughter sat behind the wheel of Lil's *Prix*. She was talking on a cell phone that, as far as I could tell, looked just like Lil's. What made it so brazen—besides the fact that the young woman was sucking down an array of fast food and drink and was depositing the wrappers anywhere they fell in the otherwise spotless interior—

was that the driveway she had pulled into was not my parents', but her own.

Luckily, she couldn't see me. I watched her gather up an assortment of overloaded key rings, jewelry, extra shoes, a grocery bag, two huge Macy's shopping bags, and her purse. When she got out of the car, I saw the small leather phone casing I had originally bought for Lil. It flopped around as Julie walked. The phone itself was in her hand and attached to her ear with an earbud. She talked as she walked casually into her own house, leaving the car easily in the driveway as if it were parked in the right one.

My mind raced through a number of options. Do I go over there and just get into the car and sit? You know, stage a little protest that way? No, too dramatic. I could just go over and slash the tires, but then I'd have to replace them. If I'd bought the car from a dealership, I'd simply stop paying for it and let the repo guys come after it. I liked that, but then my parents wouldn't have a car again. Before I could explore any other strategies, Kelly's daughter came out of the house. Still wired to my mother's phone, she got back into my mother's car and left.

As soon as Lil's car was out of sight, into view came Kelly. She was crossing her side lawn to come to my parents' house with the same grocery bag her daughter had just brought home. She had her head down so as to step cautiously with her high heels over the stone path through the azaleas. When she picked up her head at the end of the path, she was standing in front of my car.

She stopped dead. I was so glad I had come in the middle of a weekday morning, a time when she obviously did not expect me. Her panicked face darted from my car to the house, then swung back toward the azaleas, taking her with it. She sprinted back over the stones, ankles collapsing over the sides of her heels, and at the end of the path, she tripped on the border and fell face down on her lawn. Cans of soup and a milk carton went flying, and a huge head of lettuce was released. It rolled down her driveway and out onto the street. It must have been really fresh because crisp leaves came off in pieces, leaving a broken trail on its way down the blacktop.

But Kelly is a trooper, I now know. I watched her gather herself and the few groceries with speed and efficiency, not even caring that her expensive business suit and two faces were smeared with mud and grass. After she was inside for a while, and after I sat and had coffee with my parents and the remainder of their mysteriously begotten breakfast, I made a mental note to get them their groceries from now on. Then, without even addressing their missing phone or hijacked car, I climbed into mine and returned to work.

"Heeeeeeere's Kelly!" said Mel when I finished telling her the story. That was better—and funnier, I have to admit—than "I told you so." She was laughing so hard at Kelly's antics that I began laughing with her. It felt good to laugh like that. Mel had to hold onto her belly at one point and sit down. I became worried about the babies with her laughing that hard. I thought something might rupture, so I held onto her belly, too.

Pretty soon we were going at it on the living room floor. I can't hold onto Mel and her belly without being moved by the experience. Jo and Phineas were just outside on the back porch. At one point, the sliding door opened and Phineas came in for some water. On his way back out, he commented without even stopping.

"Proceed, sweet Cupid, thou hast thumped him with the birdbolt under the left pap!"

I couldn't look Phineas in the eye for the entire evening after that. I didn't know he was staying for dinner or that Stephen and Jamie were joining us, but Mel had invited them. We needed to discuss as a family the fact that we are now victims of a predator of the elderly. What we'd done—or as Mel kept reminding us, what I'd done—amounts to having ignored the warning signs while buying Kelly's daughter a college car. But I can't stop my mother from lending her new ride to her neighbors. Legally it's hers, and she can do with it what she wants.

"You know," I said after recalling the whole story to everyone, "the issue is that we don't know what else Kelly and her daughter have appropriated. Maybe I should go inspect the whole house to see if anything else is missing besides the car."

"And zee phone," interjected Mel.

"Do you think she'd be that brash to take things right out of their house?" asked Jamie.

"I don't know for sure," I said, "but when Dad was in the hospital, I found her sitting at his side with her briefcase open and commenting about his and Lil's 'paperwork,'" I remembered aloud.

"That doesn't sound good," said Stephen. "Who knows what they might've unintentionally signed over to her?"

"Scammers who rip off the elderly," said Jamie. "How low can you get?"

"And zis woman is a lawyer—she makes 'elder law' so perhaps she steals from all zee old people zat come to her," added Mel. I felt sick.

"Is she paying for their groceries herself? Because it doesn't sound like—" said Jamie

"Does grandma still do all their banking and stuff?" asked Stephen, breaking in. These were good questions.

"Well," I started. I began a quick mental list of an elderly person's day and what would be needed. "Since Aunt Deb came up and we did the POA, I'm paying their bills ...." I felt that skunky feeling again. Deb and I didn't think about their day-to-day expenses. "You know, I guess if I control their money like a parent, they need an allowance, like children." There needs to be some kind of class you can take to get through all this.

"So how can they be paying Kelly to be 'the grocery girl'?" asked Jamie. I didn't have an answer.

"You already sorta caught her in the act, Dad," said Stephen. "I'd be great if you could catch her actually taking money next time."

At that moment, I noticed Jo and Phineas packing food away as if they'd not eaten all day. They listened as if at a silent auction, nodding only very slightly and occasionally. I wanted to hear their perspective.

"Jo? Professor? Any advice?" They both finished swallowing, then looked at each other before Phineas answered.

"Be masked," he said. "A jest's prosperity lies in the ear." We all looked at each other. Mel put her hand on his arm and smiled. Everyone turned to me. Stephen spoke.

"Gathering some intel can't hurt, Dad," he said.

"ON" means I turned the camera on.

Me: "Testing ... test. OK. I'm hiding in the kitchen closet at 21 Walnut Hill Lane on Wednesday, June ..."

(OFF – this means I turned the camera off)

Although it was hard to maneuver in that small closet, I did have to turn Stephen's camera off at that point to laugh at myself. It sounded like I intended to put the tape into a time capsule, for God's sake. Or lend its plot line to *Spy vs. Spy*. And I don't really know how the professionals format video transcriptions on a page, so I went online and looked at a few. I think I'm close here.

Maybe that time capsule idea isn't so farfetched. Maybe someone from a civilization 2000 years in the future will dig it up and find our shenanigans utterly fascinating. Kelly Pomeroy and I will end up in some anthropologist's award-winning dissertation, and an assistant preservationist will spread out copies of our competing Powers of Attorney like a Faiyum on a protective surface, place them in a hermetically sealed casing, and display them carefully in a "special exhibits" booth. When museum goers step in for a viewing, a

196

scratchy version of my Kelly tape will be playing on multiple screens with the title, "Popular 21st century sport: Preying on the Elderly."

(ON)

Me (whispering to that little microphone): "Lil said that Kelly comes over every morning to bring groceries and 'help' them."

Here, there's a whirring sound over an almost black screen. I really don't know how to transcribe that. When you watch the video, you can see some light because Lil's pantry doors are panel shutters—those horizontal overlapping wooden strips. They let sound through, so it was perfect.

(whirr over black – 00:01:25 to 00:28:05)

Almost half an hour is a long time to stand in a closed kitchen pantry with the camera capturing the sound of my breathing and almost no light. I had to rummage through my pockets to find that backup tape. And battery. I only had one of each. I could have rewound, but that takes so long. And what if Kelly suddenly appeared? I had Mel drop me off so there would be no car in the driveway. Kelly would only know I was there if she heard me fussing with the camera. I had to time it right. When I heard her coming up the walk, I turned it on:

(ON – tape #2)

Me (whispering to self): "Is it on?"

(whirr – 00:01:15)

(background noise and voices)

Me: "Shit."

(OFF)

Not Kelly. The mailman chatting it up with Dad. I tried again.

(ON)

(whirr – 00:14:00)

(shuffling noise)

Me (whispering): "I just want to record here on tape for the purpose of identification that I'm standing behind a flimsy pantry door, waiting to capture a conversation between my parents' neighbor, Kelly Pomeroy, and my parents, Lillian and Martin Conklin. I'm hoping to hear their conversation and catch whatever picture I can."

(whirr – 00:15:10)

Me (whispering): "I hope Dad remembers to forget I'm here."

(background noise)

(whirr – 00:15:31 to 00:24:56)

Me (whispering): "Here she comes."

(sound of screen door opening; muffled voices becoming clearer)

Kelly: "... shrubs. You know I've got a whole hedge that needs trimming, too."

(laughing)

Lil: "One entire row of ours in the back yard seems to be infected, though. You'll have to look at it and tell me what you think."

Kelly: "I can do that. By the way, let me give you this."

(plastic bag crackling)

Lil: "Thank you so much, Kelly. What would we do without you? Martin, put these in the medicine cabinet. Here, let me put on some coffee."

Dad: "And whatta we owe you, young lady?"

(water running)

Kelly: "Marty, it's not a problem."

(more water running)

Lil: "We already paid her, Martin. Kelly, I'm sorry he doesn't ever remember. Martin, I gave her the check this month already."

Kelly: "We're all squared away, Marty."

(water running, laughing)

Kelly: (inaudible)

Lil: "But dear, you don't have to leave. The coffee'll be ready in a jiffy."

(kitchen chairs shuffling)

Dad: "Si'down, young lady!"

Kelly: "You're so kind, you two, but Julie's going to be home any minute and I'd promised her that we'd catch a matinee this afternoon."

Lil: "Wonderful. Then we'll keep an eye out for her. If she comes, she can join us for coffee before you both go."

Dad: "And Tom'll join us, too. Tom, come outta there, will ya?"

(whirr – 00:26:02 to 00:26:17)

(closet door opening / CLEAR PICTURE BEGINS HERE 00:26:19)

Lil: "Tom! Sit down. We're having coffee."

Dad: "You remember Kelly, don't you?"

(Kelly looking absolutely stunned)

Me: "Ms. Pomeroy, can you tell our audience what check my mother was referring to?"

(Kelly stands up)

Kelly: "Get that thing outta my face."

(Kelly tries to leave)

Dad (off camera): "Your daughter's not here yet, Kelly—where're you going?"

(zoom in to close-up on Kelly / Kelly speaks to camera)

Kelly: "Get the hell outta my way."

Me: "It seems like you're receiving checks regularly from my parents, can we say that's true, Ms. Pomeroy?"

Lil (off camera): "Thomas, how rude! Kelly asked politely for our Social Security check."

(camera swings to Lil's scolding look)

(sound of screen door opening)

Julie: "Hey, Mom, I'm ready to go—"

(camera swings to Julie leaning in door)

Lil (off camera): "She's been very helpful, so we give them to her—"

Julie: "Mom?"

(camera swings back to Kelly becoming enraged)

Dad (off camera): "There's your daughter now, Kelly. Hey, c'mon in, Julie!"

Kelly: "I said get that goddamned thing outta my face. Julie, go—start the car!"

(00:27:09 — camera follows Kelly as she tosses Lil's keys to daughter and walks quickly out the back screen door)

Me: "Whose car is she starting, Kelly? My mother's? Can you verify for our audience which car you're making a getaway in? And why are you even trying to get away?"

Lil (off camera): "Kelly, dear, I can make something else if you're not in the mood for coffee—"

Dad (off camera): "Where's everyone going?"

(camera on Kelly's back as she leaves through back screen door)

Kelly: (inaudible)

(screen door slams shut, hits camera)

(camera jostles, regains picture, follows Kelly across lawn)

200

Me: "Wait! We just want to talk to you, Ms. Lawyer. Hey!"

(Kelly's driveway: Kelly and Julie jump into Lil's car)

Me: "Hey!"

(car starts)

(close up on Kelly through window as doors lock)

Me: "I'll be calling the police, Ms. Lawyer!"

(car pulls away with a jerk)

(camera jostled—picture unclear)

Me: "Whoa!"

(horn blaring)

Me: "Sonofa—!!"

(crashing noise—lens damaged—picture blanks out)

(black)

Kelly and her daughter never came back. Fortunately, it was only the camera and not the tape itself that was damaged when I dove out of her way. A few days later, a huge van with no plates pulled up. A couple of guys got out and started loading things from her house into it. Dad said that when he walked over there to see what they were doing, one of them said, "Blow off, old man!" but by the tone in Dad's voice, the guy probably used some other, more offensive term Dad would never repeat.

Getting the video transcribed and down "solidly on paper" as Larry put it makes the evidence easier to review for legal purposes. And that's certainly true in this case— my spy video is mostly talking and only half picture. Larry is a good lawyer, even though he's dry as hell, and it's a plus that his last name is Clark—Mel can't mess with a simple name like "Clark." Once in a while, though, she'll call him "Clark zee Clerk" when he's being particularly fastidious, or boring, or both. Usually he's both. But his attention to detail is indispensable. He's making us re-do the will and POA because, he said, if Kelly did coerce Lil and Dad into signing similar documents, then whichever document is dated most recent is the "real" one. He also said that I should go right away to the Social Security office and apply to become the legal recipient of my dad's Social Security check, since we've "not secured that source of revenue yet." Mel suggested calling Dr. Galbraith to let him know about these recent events, which I did. He was not available, of course, but I did leave a long, rambling message with the nurse. I hope he calls me back. In addition, I filed a car-theft report with the police. Now it's in their hands.

For backup, Andre offered to make me a couple of DVD copies of the "Kelly Episode"—he's one of those multi-media-music-guru types. It's a serious hobby with him. I did feel a little embarrassed having to explain to him why I was taping my parents' neighbor from the inside of a closet, but he's the kind of guy who wants to give you a tube of vitamin E cream when you've smashed your face on a tree at your dad's driving test, and to me, there's something trustworthy about compassion.

. . .

I was growing from a little baby into an old man, but it was time-lapsed into fast motion like things are in dreams —weird. I could feel myself inflating while also being able to watch it happen from outside myself. At the same time, Dad was sitting opposite me. He was shrinking, going from old man to baby.

Then it happened: a confluence, a point in time when we were both the same age. The stream slowed briefly, just long enough to see the uncanny resemblance and the way the eyes search the other's face for understanding, for an opportunity to be not alone in the rush.

5953 52 51 50 **49** 98 97 96 95 94
44 45 96 97 98 **49** 50 51 52 53 54

Dr. Willows's call woke me. He's been calling a lot, and I have been letting it go to voicemail a lot. I let it go to voicemail this morning as well. This time he didn't ask me to call him back. Instead, he left a long message that informed me that the key I'd found in my wall was not a random find of no import. It was from the Viking age, and possibly from the Vikings themselves. I'm not buying it.

But he is, he said. Actually, one of the museum's backers is, or would like to, for the collection. He tried to impress me by launching into an explanation about how the Vikings braved so much to get to North America. Then he recounted all the theories about why they just abandoned their settlements and returned whence they came. It was a very involved voicemail. Then he went on about how the early explorers were a restless lot, and that even with the best navigational knowledge and tools of their time, they didn't always sail in the right direction.

"So much was chance," he concluded.

I lay in bed holding the phone in the air. I felt myself waking up more fully, then becoming aware that I was there alone. Mel had gone to work already. She had that early breakfast scheduled with a potential donor. That's when I came to the grave realization that it was her birthday. We had that stomping show and a swanky restaurant on the agenda for the evening. I was really not in the mood for a lot of rhythmic racket, but before I could brood over it, the phone rang again. It was Larry.

"Hello, Larry."

"Hey, Tom, my man," he said. He sounded so jovial I almost didn't recognize him. "I got your transcript of the incident"—I didn't like that word "incident"—"and it was great. Great. Those shot descriptions like 'off camera' and 'zoom in' and 'close up.' Yeah, that's real Hollywood stuff. Love it."

I sat up in bed. "I'm glad you enjoyed it, Larry."

"I did. Powerful."

Here he stopped talking. I could hear the copy of the DVD I sent playing in the background, the one of the "incident." I waited for him to say how we might move forward, but he didn't, so I got right down to business.

"So, then. How can we work this up into something that'll get Lil's car back?" I asked. "Because—"

"Ya know, Tom?" he interrupted.

"Yeah?" I said.

"'Green screen' is powerful, too," he said with a pressing sincerity. "Can you work that one in there?" This from a guy who never even smiles. I pointed out to him that he's our lawyer, not my agent, but he didn't seem to hear me. He just swung into a dissertation on the societal implications of his favorite film genre.

"You need to re-cast yourself in there as bit more hard-boiled, like those noir guys back in the day," I heard him say just before I hung up.

Now I need a new lawyer—one who can keep his mind on the issue at hand. Kelly was a lawyer, and even though she was moonlighting as a criminal, she was focused. And she knew how to keep food in my parents' refrigerator and their cordless receiver out of the trash. Now that she's gone, Dad and Lil will have to go back to a regular phone with an attached-by-a-cord receiver, since getting them on the cell is dicey. I called Andre to tell him I'd be working from home because it's Mel's birthday. I asked him to send her the largest arrangement of roses he could purchase and have it delivered right away to her office.

"No problem," he said. "What's the message?"

"Message?" I asked. I wasn't thinking.

"Yeah. You know, they put a little card in there if you want," he reminded me. "You'll probably want to if it's her birthday." Perfect. It was just the proper way to spring the show and dinner on her. I was so glad I hadn't mentioned it yet.

"Well, uh ...." It took me a minute to come up with something. "Have them say, 'Happy Birthday, Mel. Get ready this evening for a Stomp and a Gourmet Romp.'" Andre didn't react. "Should I add, 'Be there or be square'?" I asked.

"No," he said without hesitating. I didn't argue. I thanked him, said "Goodbye," got up, and marched to the shower with purpose to start my day. I would get a corded phone and install it for my parents. On the way, I just barely passed the babies' room before I had to stop and back up. There was now a second purple teddy bear on top of the dresser. Its size forced its head against the ceiling. A card dangled from its huge paw. I stepped in to read it. "Never thought it'd be a double header—you go

Little Brother! —Deb" I heard my own voice say, "Neither did I." I showered quickly and left for the hardware store.

At my parents' house, I started to feel better. I was busy getting things done. I had bought one of those phones with great big number pads for older folks and people who are visually impaired. And I made sure it had a really long cord. As I worked, a list of the many other things that I needed to do for my parents kept scrolling upward like movie credits in my imagination. I forgot to eat breakfast, there were so many. I'll write down some of the more pressing ones here: an allowance every week, transportation, groceries, a maid, a cook. Is Lil cooking lately?

I opened the refrigerator, thinking I might grab some toast and coffee. Or, if I was lucky, a salt bagel and some cream cheese. Instead, I found a flat Coke, a carton of milk, and the old-fashioned, squeeze-style horn from my first bicycle. The graceful little swoop of metal was sitting on the top shelf. I thought it would be cold when I touched it, but as it turns out, nothing in there was cold. I closed the door and stepped around the side. I tugged on the sticky, dust-clotted cord. It came up easily in my hands, unplugged. The overpowering smell of sour milk should have alerted me to that. In the vegetable drawer at the bottom, I found moldy carrots and the even moldier rubber horn squeezer.

I haven't seen that horn in about 40 years. When I asked Lil what it was doing in there—I didn't ask how she wrestled it off the rusty handlebars of my first bicycle, which is still in the garage—she said, "I needed a funnel." Never mind that right in the drawer next to the stove was an expensive stainless steel one we had bought her a few Christmases ago. Never mind that there was nothing cooked, so what she was funneling remains a mystery. And never mind that, when I was done cleaning out the moldy carrots and squeezer, the noise I had been hearing since I got there finally registered as a blow dryer.

It was coming from upstairs. Dad was up there. I know that for most people, a blow dryer is a wholly unremarkable piece of modern equipment, but you have to remember, my father has no hair. As I cleaned the mold off the rubber horn squeezer—it's amazing how much it looked like a moldy orange at first—that noise started to sound less like a blow dryer and more like an oncoming episode. I tensed up.

When I got upstairs, a long cord was hanging out from between the sheets of my parents' bed. It was plugged into the wall and powering the blow dryer, which was blasting hot air under the covers and dangerously warming them to fire-code violating temperatures. Dad was sleeping as soundly as a house cat, a quaint smile and intermittent butterfly twitchings on his peaceful face.

He's been saying that he's cold all the time. I calmly and quietly unplugged the blow dryer, slipped it out from under the top sheet, turned down the AC again —it's always up even though I've never seen Dad or Lil so much as touch it—and removed from the premises the blow dryer, a small toaster oven, an iron, and all the power tools I could find downstairs

I also took my squeeze horn and rubber squeezer. I stuffed it all in a bag before Lil could see me, left Dad asleep upstairs, and went to the kitchen to plug in the refrigerator. I vowed to come back with a bag of groceries, kissed my mom goodbye, and stepped outside to my car.

My phone was ringing there on the seat where I'd left it. I could see that it was Dr. Galbraith's office. I quickly opened the door and lunged toward it.

"Hello?" I said, out of breath and too urgently. It was the good doctor himself.

"Hello. May I speak with Tom Conklin?"

"Yes!" I said, then managed to calm myself. "Hello, Doctor Galbraith. Thanks for calling back. I just wanted to ask you about—" He interrupted with two words.

"Assisted living." He wasn't wasting any time. I liked that.

"How do we start?" I asked.

"Well, first you might want to take a look at a few facilities," he said. "ElderKeen is a great resource for 'all things elder.' Look them up. They have information on all the regional places." In Dad's day, there was no such a thing as "assisted" living facilities, as far as I know. Up until the moment I had to confiscate from their home all electrical devices except for the lights and the TV, I would never have considered putting my parents in one, either.

"Some of them are fine facilities, Tom. Bring your parents along, of course. Most of them have beautiful dining rooms, gardens, even workout rooms and events ...." His list went on and on. I pictured chandeliers, people smiling, a 24-hour staff, organized activities and outings. Dad will hate it.

I started my car and pulled out to get groceries as planned, but it occurred to me to pick up my "heirloom" first—I wanted to show up at Willows's office without calling, get the key without a lot of conversation, and store it until I decide what to do with it. Maybe even get a second opinion on it.

I didn't even stop to grab breakfast. I went straight to the university but found no available parking. You'd think the whole city was going to college at once. I managed to squeeze into a place between two cars that were offset in their spaces. I barely slipped out the door, then walked across campus to Willows's building.

When I arrived at his office, he was at his computer. There was coffee and a fresh, warm-looking bagel with cream cheese sitting quietly on an open piece of tissuey wax paper on his desk. It was salt. I tried to ignore it.

"Conklin! C'mon in," he said. "Have you been getting my messages?"

"Yes. I'm sorry I haven't been responding," I said. He sipped his coffee before speaking.

"So how may we proceed?" he swallowed and asked confidently, smiling so severely that his eyebrows seemed to be moving up and over his balding head like two caterpillars crawling sideways. He spoke as if my addition to their collection was a given.

"Well," I said, "you know, the piece I brought you has been in the family for generations, so I'll need more time to think about it." His eyebrows scurried back down to his forehead. He collected himself before speaking.

"That's understandable," he finally said. He took another sip of his coffee, then sat still for a long moment. He stared at his computer screen, punched something in, hit "enter," and began reading whatever had popped up. His hand went to pick up the bagel, but at the last moment, he stopped.

"You might want to consider leaving it here for safe keeping, Tom, not to mention further investigation into its origin," he finally said. "Would your family consider that? We'd keep it in our climate-controlled storage with other such items." I wondered what other "such items" they store and don't show. I pictured a room crammed with iron keys and other Viking paraphernalia like bows and arrows, axes, helmets, shields—even those heavy chains that have iron balls on the end with spikes sticking out in all directions. I think they're called "flails." I imagined him leading me to such a room, and when he opened the door, it would all attempt to tumble out. He would then press against the door with his whole weight to hold it open just enough to toss my key on top of the pile before forcing it closed.

"We actually store it ourselves," I said. I liked the way that came out. It sounded like we engage a professional service for all our valuable patrimony.

"Oh, no, but here you wouldn't have to pay for it— we would simply hold it until you're ready to ... to ...." He didn't have a word for it. Let it go? Negotiate? Accept a price? I just wanted my key back for now.

"I think the family just wants it back for now," I said. "But I'll get back to you."

My stomach growled at that moment. I was embarrassed, but he didn't seem to hear it. Without speaking, he stood and walked over to a safe near the window. I hadn't even noticed it. He entered a code, opened it, took out my key, and instead of handing it to me, sat down again at his desk. I stepped forward and held out my hand, but he pulled the key away and harbored it close to his chest. That was awkward. I didn't know what to do. I decided to put my hand down, not look aggressive in any way, then simply ask for it.

"So, I'll be going now Thank you for the information," I said. I put my hand out again. He put his out with the key in it, but when I moved to take it, he pulled it away.

"This is a valuable piece of history that should not be hoarded in some personal collection, Conklin. Because if you're thinking of selling it to a private collector, you're doing a grave disservice to historians. To history itself. You need to think of that before you let exorbitant prices sway—" I was stunned. Exorbitant prices?

"But it belongs to my family!" I cried. I had actually found it in the house I was squatting in. It probably did belong to someone's family. But squatting here in the U.S. is legal, said the town's library. I was becoming unbearably conflicted there, leaning further and further over his desk. I lunged my hand toward his and grabbed my key.

"Gimme that!" I heard myself snarl. Our hands were suddenly engaged in battle.

"Careful!" he said as we wrestled, leaning over his bagel and cream cheese.

As our fingers got tangled up in each other's, no one spoke. I grunted and squeezed—he grunted and lurched sideways to shake my grip. I held on tight and twisted to the left—he twisted to the right. A woman leaned in to the room and saw us—she let out a small yelp and fled. More grunting and growling over the desk, some of it from my stomach. That gave me an idea.

I let go. He staggered backward a step and looked at the key in his fist. Then he looked up at me. I waited a beat, then swiped the bagel off the wax paper. He shoved his right hand forward to retrieve his breakfast, but I cleverly held it just beyond reach while grabbing the key from his now limp and unattended left hand.

I turned and bolted out the door with both the bagel and my key. I remember running past the same woman who had peeked in previously. She had a man with her and they were hurrying toward Willows's office. As I sprinted by them, the man reached out to grab me, but he only caught my sleeve for a moment before I yanked my arm away and kept going. I headed down the stairwell and out the building. I made my way to my car, squeezed in, shut the door, and locked it.

Locking the door was a bit paranoid, I admit. Willows was in the wrong after all. I had every right to walk out of there with my key. That I found in someone else's wall. I pulled myself together. No one was going to follow me over a bagel, of course. When my heavy breathing subsided, I decided to simply go on with business as usual for the day. On the way to the bank, I drove through Dunkin' Donuts and got a coffee to go with Willows's bagel. It tasted great.

By the time I got to the bank, I was calmer and my stomach was happy. I could think more clearly. The young woman who signed me in to my safe deposit box may have caught a glimpse of the key, however. I didn't quite wait until she left me alone to pull it out of my pocket and inspect it. As she was leaving, she looked at me as if I had just looted the Museum of Natural History in New York.

Or maybe she didn't. I couldn't really tell. Perhaps I shouldn't have inspected it. I could have just put it directly into my safe deposit box and that would have been that. But I didn't. How many times in your life do you find yourself in possession of something that a

Viking touched? Not that I believe a Viking touched it. But it could still be a piece of history valuable to the area in some way. It'd be cool if it belonged to a Viking, though. I'm doing a community service by protecting it, even from the museum and Willows, until I find time to further investigate. I should get a second opinion because Vikings were like the merchant marines of the ancient world.

I almost forgot the groceries for my parents. I went to the supermarket, shopped for them, returned to their house to stock the fridge, made sure they were OK, then went home to collapse, thoroughly exhausted, on the couch.

The next thing I knew, a beautiful scented goddess was nudging me to get up. It was Mel. She was beaming. She was all dressed up for a dinner and show, and looking at her, I was dazzled. She pressed me to get dressed for our "date" and loved calling it that. I managed to pull myself together, shake off the dizziness, and we did make it into the city just in time for our swanky dinner. The show afterward was great fun, I have to admit. It really relieved the pressure I've been feeling lately. I lived vicariously well through all that mad stomping.

"Where are we?"

"Dad," I implored, then stopped. I didn't want to show him my exasperation in front of our host. "Remember I told you and Lil about considering a smaller place? It'd make things a lot easier because—"

"I'm not living in a nursing home."

"It's not a nursing home, Dad. Listen, we'll finish the tour, then we can go meet the director."

"Director? I don't have a 'director' in my home now, Tom, do I? Why do I need to move into someone else's who does?"

It's crazy how older folks can forget how to cool and warm their food, or their houses, or their sheets, but they can word a question in the most cleverly oppositional way possible. I asked the polite young woman who was showing us around if she would leave us alone for a moment. As she walked away, I turned to Lil.

"Ma, isn't it wonderful?"

"No."

"But you said when we drove up that it reminded you of Aunt Leena's."

"Yes. When she was in Brookhaven."

Brookhaven Meadows was the cemetery we buried my great Aunt Leena in until her daughter came back from Canada with a much later version of the will. It stated plainly that Aunt Leena wanted to be cremated due to her late conversion to Hinduism. We had to take her out of there and comply. That never really sat well with Lil or Dad. Especially the scattering of the ashes into the Ganges or, as the will stated, into a "similar body of pure water running eastward." The stream behind the pavilion at the park resembled the Ganges only with great imaginative effort, although it does run west to east. No one asked Lil herself to hike the Himalayas to the Bay of Bengal to scatter them, but she kept saying, "Sacred to Hindus? Isn't that sweet. Your family is the only proper resting place."

I turned to Dad. "Look Dad, since we're here, let's see one of the luxury apartments—they're spacious with big windows and lots of light, and they even have a unit available that overlooks the gardens."

"Leena's plot overlooked gardens, remember?" said my mother. Dad said nothing.

"Listen both of you, please. Here comes Bob now. He's the director and was nice enough to schedule a time to answer any questions you might have. Dad, you remember Bob Tritt, don't you? From Stanton, when I was first starting out? Dad? Dad!"

I don't have a name for this one.

Deb text
Can't u burn their house down while they're out? Then they'll HAVE 2 live somewhere else.

It'll never work because they don't go out. No car, remember?? Also, Bob said they need an evaluation by a social worker to get into any assisted place.

Lowering that gun-to-my-head age from 85 to 75—it'll put me out of Stephen's misery

Make it 70 I'll join u.

When I got back from showing my parents all the assisted living facilities they could ever possibly refuse to live in, Mel was at the counter chopping vegetables. She was tapping her feet and explaining the *Stomp* show to Jo. Even as Mel fills out with child and Jo seems to contract with age, I can see their resemblance. Jo's grey hair reveals a few remaining jet-black ones, like Mel's color. They both have the same uplifted cheekbones and surety in their step, not to mention in their personalities. Sometimes they act like sisters. The only difference is in the eyes—Mel's flash with life, but at 90+, Jo's are understandably toned down.

As we chatted, the cooking activity turned into a full dance session. Mel showed Jo some of that stomping stuff we'd seen at the theater. They laughed and stomped it up vigorously. It looked like so much fun that I started laughing and stomping, too.

Ba da ba da ba da BAM! Ta da ta da ta da WHAM! It felt great. Pom, pam, ta da SLAM! We were improvising our own rhythms. We had some pretty good syncopation going at one point. SLAM da da SLAM ba JAM!

"Tom!" yelled Mel at one point, "Stop!" Jo was leaning on the counter holding her hip. "Help her to zee couch."

I stopped immediately and picked her up, all 98 pounds. I walked her to the couch and let her down easy onto the softness. It was the first time I've ever seen Jo wane. Mel brought the footrest over and put her feet up for her.

Even now, hours later, I can't get the look on her face out of my mind. She sat on the couch without speaking and glanced around as if thoroughly bewildered. I've never seen Jo bewildered—she's been full of the power and purpose of an Argentinian soccer player since I've met her. I'm worried that this might be the beginning of an end. As if decline itself had lifted its head just above the waterline, blinked its large eyes once, then dipped back under to silently swim away. In a dream, I kept seeing Jo's face over a soundtrack, like a movie. The music was a song by either The Who or The Guess Who —I was confusing those two bands, and that feeling of menace woke me. That's why I'm sitting here alone at my computer at dawn.

Phineas showed up at the back sliding doors after I dozed off in the chair. His soft knocking woke me. I jerked awake and saw him standing there with a small, steaming pitcher. I let him in. He had seen our light on and come over, and when he saw me slumped in front of my screen, he went back home and made me some hot cocoa. Such a great guy. I invited him to sit at the kitchen table. I got two mugs and poured. We didn't talk at first, we just sipped. The cocoa was terrible. No sugar, just bitter baking chocolate in tepid milk. As I sat wishing for some whipped cream, I wondered if he's diabetic. I also wondered about his age and realized that I really don't know much about dear Ol' Phin. Our silence lasted for some time.

"Ya know, Phin," I finally said, "our time here is precarious. At best," I said. He nodded. I continued. "I had an orange squeeze-ball horn on my bike when I was little. I loved that horn. It made the most obnoxious noise —the other kids would dive out of the way when I was coming just to get away from it." I laughed. We sat in further silence.

"I'm turning 50 soon," I mustered. He sipped his cocoa and nodded.

"Melancholy is the nurse of frenzy," he offered.

I began telling him about stolen Mary Kay vehicles and North American Viking settlements, dangerous appliances and silver-chained bee-alert bracelets, Lexus sedans and Hindus' ashes overlooking gardens instead of flowing eastward toward the sacred. I couldn't help it— my brain just kept taking out the trash. "And I keep confusing some of the songs from these two rock bands, The Who and The Guess Who, and it's keeping me awake," I said. Then I took a breather. I don't like to blame my own mind lapses on those few LSD experiences I had in my youth, but sometimes I do wonder. I've been doing a good job of keeping this writing thing a secret, so I feel free to admit that here. It's my own memoir for God's sake. I didn't mention LSD to Phineas.

"When I was a teenager and first got my driver's license, I used to crank up the tunes and roll the windows down and sing at the top of my lungs," I said. I didn't tell him that I sometimes have the urge to do that now. "I'd have a song like 'Long Live Rock' blasting on the radio while I was flying down the highway. For some reason, motion takes all your cares away," I added. Phineas finished his cocoa, then took the perfectly folded handkerchief from his breast pocket, unfolded it, and patted his mouth. Then he blew his nose on it, loudly.

"By the time I was in college, though, disco was taking over. Everybody knows that stuff isn't real music. A good rock band usually sounds like it has some meaning. You know, a cool name, one that might beg punctuation. Like 'The Who,' which could be a question —*The Who?*—or 'The Guess Who,' which could be an exclamation—*Guess Who!*" I don't think the professor was following me at that point, but I kept going.

"I remember that album cover that showed the guys in the band walking away from what looked like a big cement wall—or was it a porta potty?—in the middle of nowhere, and when you're a horny teenage guy, for some reason, stuff like that takes on a cool that's mystical. Disco could never do that. But that never stopped Deb from blaring ABBA records on the stereo every time I was home from college just to rile me. She actually liked ABBA, and I know for a fact she's never gone tooling down the freeway with some cool music screaming out the windows so that she doesn't have to. That I know," I concluded.

I hoped I wasn't waking Mel and Jo with my yammering. Phineas listened intently, like a top psychologist. He finally commented.

"Perchance tomorrow you'll serve another master."

I thanked him for the drink. He nodded, and I stepped out onto the back porch with him. By that time,

219

there was the most beautiful sunrise in the making. The air was as sweet as I'd wished the cocoa could have been. Instead of going home, Phineas walked me out to my corn patch to show me what he and Jo had been up to. I couldn't believe my eyes.

Finally—the big daddy of vegetables—corn!

While I've been busy keeping up with my life, Jo and Phineas have been taking it upon themselves to plant. Now the little buggers are hard at work, muscling their way up. I dropped to my knees and touched them. Each was just barely poking out of its earthy lair. They were going to be mighty, I could feel it. Just as corn should be. I'll admit only here in my memoir and nowhere else that, since Jo and Phineas have been caring for my patch with their cross-dressing sideshow, the place seems more fertile. I'll even use that word I hate regarding plants— happier. The little squirts seem *happy*, but that's all I'm going to say about that. I likened them to my children, growing there in fertile ground, a nourishing and protective womb-like husk soon to form. I'm looking forward to all those kernels filling out eventually like cells. Our OBGYN calls growing babies "little corn huskers." I love that.

When I stood, I saw Phineas disappearing into his back door. I think he left me alone with my newborns out here on purpose. I stayed outside with them for quite a while. For some reason, it brought on an uncontrollable urge to run to my computer and organize the chaos that is my life recently, so I did. I made a spreadsheet. There's comfort in a good spreadsheet. I think I can get it done before Mel gets up.

Lil and Dad checklist	Done	Not done yet
Hire a cook		X
Teach Dad and Lil to use a microwave properly		X
Remove all hazardous items from the premises	X	
Hire a car service		X
Buy a pill organizer		X
Need an aide to check in regularly		X
Need an evaluation for Dad and Lil		X
Gun to head at 65		X

Now I understand Dante. He made hell in levels for a reason, and I've descended to the next lower. That never-ending class in college on the *Inferno* and all that lecturing never did the story justice—all the classes in the world can't teach you about hell. Only descent can.

Not that I consider myself religious or anything. I just think that going to hell when you don't have to is misguided. If you're going there, then you'd better turn around and come back because you're going in the wrong direction. Or as Winston Churchill said, "If you're going through hell, keep going."

I had gotten everything in order, found a cook, had her scheduled to make meals for the July 4th weekend—I had even stopped in before leaving town to reiterate the proper use of a microwave. I put a big sticky note on the only button they'd have to push to warm their food when the cook's not there—that was Mel's idea. I made sure the fridge was plugged in and cold, and I stocked toilet paper, milk, clean towels, dishes, clean everything. Stephen and Jamie would take them to see fireworks. I left my phone number written LARGE and taped to the wall over the corded phone. I removed the burner knobs on the stove, then left with Mel for the cave for a little temporary, desirable sanity via a simple Fourth of July weekend.

When we returned, we went right over there even before going home. As we walked in, the cook walked out. Out of the job of cooking for Lil and Dad, but mostly out of the job of cooking for Dad. He was yelling to me.

"The food that woman makes is always cold and has no taste!" he cried, pointing at her as she shoved past me out the door. "Lil is a much better cook!"

"Lil isn't even able to cook," the woman spat back as she opened her car door. Lil was sitting at the kitchen table looking utterly bewildered. That was frightening. "And I suggest you get a maid!" she called out before taking off.

I stepped further inside with Mel right behind me. The smell of old people and unflushed toilets overwhelmed us as we glanced around. Where did the microwave go? And Lil, who had stood up, was walking toward me with a slight limp. She couldn't tell me what had caused it. Mel kept her and Dad busy with calm conversation while I looked frantically around the house to see if there was any upended furniture or any other indication of accident.

All that did was open up a trap door through which I again descended with a crash to hell's next level. It was not called "The Wrathful" or "The Lustful" or "Heretics" as in Dante's underworld, but in the cosmology of caregivers, it carried an even more ominous and necessarily contemporary name: "Personal Hygiene Providers." Allowing your loved one to go unwashed is bad enough, but allowing that person to fall in the tub is a frightening and damning offense. Maybe Lil fell there. I whipped out my phone and put in a reminder to buy better, larger bath mats and one of those railings for the shower wall so that there is something to grab onto. Maybe I'll get one of those bath stools you can sit on when showering. Dad would prefer taking a shower standing on his head rather than use one, I'm sure.

When I was done making notes to myself, I was standing in front of their bathroom sink. Where did their toothbrushes go? Does Dad bathe or brush at all anymore? He does seem increasingly to be giving off that highly unpleasant odor peculiar to old people, but is it age or just dirt? Rotting or just a little crustiness? I can't tell. And even though he can watch TV, carry on a conversation about daily events, and ask about his grandchildren, I can't seem to make him understand a simple idea like cold food remaining cold until you actively warm it in an appliance designed to do so. It's as if some of my parents' faculties are disconnecting faster than others, and I don't know what I'll find unplugged next. The only salvation is that no one has said the word "car" in a blissfully long time. Then it happened—a slap-forehead-now moment.

Back in college, I had arrived at the last class for one of my courses without my final paper. I thought it was due on the last day of the semester, but our last class didn't fall on the last day of the semester. It fell earlier, on the day just before the professor would be on a plane to Europe. This was back in The Days of No E-Mail. It was also before the days of the Internet, the cloud, texting, and Internet-based ass-savers like easybib.com. My references were a mess of stray paper napkins and index cards shoved in a drawer.

As students handed in well-referenced work all around me, I slapped my forehead. I was honestly surprised at my mistake. The due date was right there on the syllabus, said the professor as he stepped down the stairs past my seat and headed toward the front of the lecture hall with an armful of completed papers.

So there, at my parents' bathroom sink, I slapped my forehead—there is a due date on a syllabus somewhere that has already passed. My parents need help with every part of their day and every aspect of their existence. I guess from now on, we'll have to put Stephen and Jamie on duty when we leave. I'd rather not do that when they have a little one coming. It's at times like these that I almost wish Kelly were back. She was a thief and a shit shoveler, but she was right next door for God's sake. And she brought food over regularly, even if she did take a 1000% commission and drive away with the bonus.

I cleared some dishes and generally restored order while Mel continued calming Dad down. That helped. Then I went out for groceries. Alone in the car, I called the after-hours number for Dr. Galbraith's office. When the doctor on duty called back, he was not pleased. He said to take Lil to the after-hours care facility if she is in pain, and that he didn't consider a cook's resignation to be an emergency. That's how removed doctors are from the experience of their elderly patients. He said to make sure that Dad takes his meds, and that I should get an evaluation done on my father as soon as possible, and that I should morph into a demigod and reverse world hunger.

I came back with goulash mix and hamburger. We cooked it up and ate with my parents. After the hot chow, Lil was walking better and said she had no pain. We cleared the table, put everything in the dishwasher and started it up. Then we went out to the living room to watch my dad and mom watch TV. They looked as content as babies. Lil glanced at me and smiled occasionally. Dad took out his favorite brandy. By the time a commercial came on, it was clear that facilities, no matter how many gardens are planted on the grounds, don't seem like home to me, so why should they seem that way to seniors?

When I got to work this morning, I made the decision to get that evaluation done. I didn't even consult Deb. If there is any way to keep Dad and Lil at home, then we're going to do it. I called ElderKeen. They were caring and helpful to a fault, except that they are swamped and under funded. They will not have an evaluation slot open for weeks. I asked about home services. While the young woman calmly explained all the services they offer, things like visiting nurses, aides, companions, and maids, Jack walked in. He sat in the big armchair Marla had bought for me, the one next to that freestanding lamp she also bought when I was first transferred to this building. She wanted it to look like a "little chunk of living room" right there in my office. A place where I can get my work-related reading done and feel at home. It still looks brand new because no one ever sits in it except, occasionally, Jack. Who's got time to read at work? And Jack doesn't even sit in it—he exists on it—fills the space between the arms like he means it.

He picked up my copy of last month's *Time* magazine and held it open in his huge claws in front of his face while I finished my call. They made the magazine look smaller than it is. By the time I hung up, my mind was racing. To get Dad to sit still for an evaluation, I'll have to lie again. Lie to the guy who, when we were little and Deb or Daniel or I were caught in some selfish tall tale to get what we wanted—has there ever been any other reason to lie?—made us sit together at the dining room table and talk as a family. The subject was always integrity—that it's something earned, worked for, not given, and that dishonesty and inconstancy are not integral. Not an essential ingredient in a life worth living.

"It's not just adhering to a code of ethics, Tom. 'Integrity' means being 'whole' or 'complete.' You want to be whole, don't you, Tommy?" Dad's words were ringing in my mind as if he'd said them just yesterday. Jack commented from behind the magazine pages.

"Ya gotta embrace it, Tom," he said. Somewhere inside me, I knew exactly what he meant, but my mouth wanted to pretend I didn't.

"Embrace what?"

"Being. In the moment. By both simultaneously embracing everything and admitting that it all has no meaning whatsoever. You'll feel better."

"What about death?" I didn't mean to jump so far ahead. He put my *Time* down.

"That's not what's going on in this moment," he said. I remembered an adage I'd heard once, something about how, as soon as you're born, you begin dying.

"How can I embrace something that has no meaning?" I diverted.

"Great individuals create their own values, Tom. Their own meaning."

I was thrust backward in time to my family's dining room table. Don't I want to be a great individual? Don't I

227

want to be whole? Don't I want to live forever and not smell like rotting garbage? Use a microwave to warm my food and not use a blow dryer to set my sheets on fire? When I'm my parents' age, will we even warm sheets or food? Will there even be food? I was jumping ahead again.

"So you're saying that in the broader world, there is no meaning."

Jack put the magazine back on my huge, mostly unread stack of periodicals. His response made me not want to live in this moment because it's so foreign.

"What broader world?"

.   .   .

Daniel was floating through the air again, and I was watching again. There was no sound, and time slowed to a suspended lull, like it does at the top of a roller coaster just before the big dive. As the dream both progressed and slowed, I remembered being on that huge coaster at that amusement park in New Jersey and how Daniel screamed, "I'm dead!" just before we went down—it was a terrifying drop—and how I teased him about that right up until the day we lost him. I've never stopped wanting to take that back. In my sleep, I made a deal with God.

Then I was sitting upright, drenched with sweat. There was some crazy storm outside and it confused me. I could hear the wind and rain beating on trees, and I finally recognized that I was at the cave. The flickering imagery on the walls and ceiling were due to the lightning. I realized that Mel was not in bed with me—

she was over at the front wall, drawing on it with my carpenter's pencil. I got up for a closer look.

She was sleepwalking, of course. Sleepdrawing, this time—outlining the spot where we'll put in the bay window. I was going to do that before we headed back, but she did a great job of it. Perfect, in fact. Her OBGYN has said that pregnancy can induce sleepwalking, but she didn't mention temporary onset of great carpentry skills. And come to think of it, Mel only sleepwalks at the cave. I'm going to let the doctor know that. I let her finish, then took her gently by the hand and led her back to our mattress.

In the morning, I called the contractors to firm up a time for the installation. I then started some other work on the place, namely, putting in the new toilet, but Mel cut our already short stay even shorter worrying about Jo.

"We should not leave her alone when she has pain, Tom," she kept saying. I reminded her that Jo herself had insisted that we get away. But in the end, images of Dad's and Lil's difficulties made me feel like the phone would ring at any moment, and Stephen or Jamie would be reporting from an episode well under way. On top of that, Mel got prickly about the bay window outlining job. She's still saying that I did it and that I'm playing a joke on her.

We found Jo on the couch when we arrived, asleep under the afghan. Apparently, she came downstairs for some water during the night and couldn't get back up. Mel and I were both pretty glad we'd come back. Since it was the weekend, I drove them to the off-hours care facility, dropped them off, then went over to my parents to check on them. I wanted to find a good moment to mention the social worker's evaluation. I wanted to prepare them so they'd not be taken off guard and barricade themselves in their home or hop the train to Canada.

I let myself in. I almost called Stephen to ask if anything went awry this weekend, but I didn't. He would have called me. Lil was watching TV. It was on. That was a good sign.

"Hey, Ma," I said.

"Hello, Tom, what a surprise! Here, sit down," she said. She sounded just like she always does. It was such a relief. "Is Mel with you?" she asked.

"Mel is with Jo today," I said.

"Oh." She glanced around the room. "Tom, when is the baby shower?"

"We're not having a shower, Ma, remember?"

"Oh," she said. She sounded disappointed.

"Where's Dad?" I asked.

"Upstairs," she answered.

"I'm gonna let him know I'm here," I said. I went up with all my senses on high alert. No suspicious smells, other than a constant but slight old-person smell that now permeates the house at all times. No funny sounds like a blow dryer. No wet floors, goopy handrails, or garbage strewn about. Dad was in fact, upstairs. He was in the bathroom cleaning his gun. I remained calm.

"Dad, how are ya?" I said.

"Hey, Tom," he said without looking up.

"Whattya doing?" I asked. He stopped. He looked at me in the mirror.

"What does it look like I'm doing?" he said. I laughed even though he didn't.

"It looks like you're cleaning your gun," I said. He put his hands on the counter and sighed.

"I'm loading it, Thomas," he said, exasperated. Dad has always kept a locked, loaded pistol in the house. I've always respected that. When I was young, I stumbled upon it one day under the bed. My friend Todd and I were so impressed we crawled under there to handle it for what I think was hours. If Lil ever knew that, she would have locked me in my room for weeks, then shot Dad in the legs for being so careless. I'd sneak into their room regularly after that to touch it. Dad finally put it somewhere else. There in the bathroom, there was nothing to load it with, thank God.

"What are you loading it with?" I asked. Dad looked around as if his bullets had all scattered suddenly like roaches.

"Yeah. Um ..." He looked around. "Would you go to the cellar, Tom, and—" I couldn't answer fast enough.

"Got it, Dad. I'll be right back."

What luck. I ran downstairs. I thought I'd confiscated the ammunition already, but it was a good opportunity to double check. I almost tore the small door off the cabinet down there as I opened it. I shoved any strays I'd missed last time into my pocket, then I took my time getting back upstairs so it looked like I'd searched.

"Dad," I said with a pretty good feigned disappointment, "you're out."

"Damn," he said. "I thought so." He placed the gun down on the counter as gently as if it were a newborn kitten. I was thinking on my feet.

"Let's go down and have a coffee with Lil. I haven't seen you two all weekend," I said. That seemed to get his mind off it.

When we got downstairs, Lil was making sandwiches. I was proud of her. They always eat lunch in the living room, so we took them out to the coffee table. As we sat, I noticed the sandwiches were baloney, which I'm not crazy about. The mayo was on the outside of the bread. The President was on a midday newscast, and Lil seemed to be studying him intently, so I made small talk as I turned the bread right-side-in. No one noticed.

"Are you following politics these days, Ma?" I asked as we dug in. She ignored my question.

"Who is that nice-looking man?" she said as she pointed to the TV. I didn't know which bothered me more —my elderly mother commenting on men's looks or her not recognizing the man in question.

"Ma, that's the President," I said. She nodded in what I took as recognition.

"Of what?" she asked.

The ElderKeen lady had said that as seniors decline, they finally embrace a move because of something as common as recurring falls and broken hips. But she also described situations in which elderly couples are forced out of their homes because the house burns down. Despite my pang of guilt, I wanted to suggest to her that those families were probably trying to smoke 'em out, but she seemed so soft-spoken and caring on the phone, I couldn't bear to say it.

"Is Mel with you?" asked my mother, again. "And Tom, when is the baby shower?" I resisted the urge to yell in a panicked voice, *Ma, you just asked me that.* I swallowed some baloney instead. I smiled at her.

"Ma," I said, "remember, we're not having a shower."

"Oh," she said again, disappointed again.

"But don't worry," I continued, "we're having a big party right after the babies come," I said, poker-face in tact. I changed the subject on purpose. "You know, Jo took a little tumble recently—"

"Oh—"

"—but she's OK, we think. Here, let's call," I offered.

"Please, Tom, let's talk to Mel. Is she here?" Lil looked around the room. "When is the baby shower?"

I told myself to be happy that my mother remembered we were having babies at all. I took out my phone and called Mel. Lil waited on edge. When Mel answered, I put her on speaker phone so Lil could hear her. Mel was animated as she talked of Jo's situation and quoted the doctor.

"Arthritis in zee hip," she said, but "in all other zings, healthy as zee horses." Lil was delighted.

"Tom," Mel added, "zee doctor says we must buy a 'chair lift,' you call it?"

"Of course, good idea," I said. Lil was nodding in agreement. Dad was staring at his sandwich. I decided to go for it. "So, honey, Ma wants to talk to you." I turned speaker off and handed the phone to Lil. As she and Mel chatted, I turned to Dad, and just as I took in a deep breath to begin the "evaluator talk," Dad spoke.

"I hate baloney," he said. It was a great moment. I'd found my in.

"Dad," I said, "you know, speaking of food, Deb and I thought we'd get you a real cook, you know, a much better one this time." I waited a beat, then decided that was dangerous. Don't give him time for negation. "I've made an appointment for you with a woman who will, you know, talk to you and Lil to see what your likes and dislikes are so she can match you up with the best darn cook possible," I declared. I threw in some other heroics as well. Dad listened for a while, then looked confused, then skeptical. Then he interrupted.

"And what does that cost?" he said.

"It'll be covered under your insurance," I said enthusiastically. I didn't say that coverage in this world depends on evaluations. In the void that followed, I noticed that Lil was done talking on the phone. She looked sad. She hasn't stopped looking sad since the previous cook quit. She's probably embarrassed. Lil cares about decorum. I turned to Dad again. He wasn't saying "no." The TV took their attention.

I was so elated that I excused myself for a moment, stepped outside, called ElderKeen, and left a message begging for an earlier appointment. I didn't want to wait weeks since Dad seems amenable now. They finally called back to explain that a cancellation allowed them to move us into that slot with an evaluator named Sharon. I thanked them from the bottom of my heart, many, multiple times, then made a plan to gear up during the next few days, psychologically, for her visit.

.   .   .

Sharon was just getting out of her car as I pulled up. We introduced ourselves, and she gave me her card and some preliminary information. She was very clear. She explained that it's a process, and it takes time, and that often the recommendation is simply for assisted living, sometimes for something more, sometimes not—seniors often stay in their homes with the right care. I said I understood.

As we strolled to my parents' door, I noted to myself that the fresh breeze blowing lightly all around us would only serve to accentuate the old-folks smell when we walked in, thereby alerting to Sharon right away to a potentially declining situation. The door was unlocked, so we let ourselves in. The curtains were drawn, and the darkness seemed fittingly foreboding. As if the people who lived there didn't know it was time to be up and around. My unwholesome self told me that was a good sign.

It took a minute for my eyes to adjust. I began to notice no old-person smell, as if my senses had converged to size up the situation. I felt the beginnings of a familiar panic. There were no dirty dishes or cups strewn around, no sound of running water pouring unattended out of a faucet anywhere. The phone was hung up, no loud mechanical voice reciting over and over from a receiver somewhere, "Please check your main telephone and extensions." There was no smell of an unflushed toilet. In fact, something good to eat was giving off a tempting aroma.

"Ma?" I probed.

"Tom, is that you?" Lil called from further inside.

Sharon and I turned the corner to the dining room. Spread before us was the table, clothed and alight with candles, arranged with Lil's best china, a bottle of wine, flowers. Everything sparkled, including my mother, who was suddenly there holding a dreamy-smelling casserole dish in her two hot-mitted hands. She was smiling and wearing evening black, heels, and her favorite pearls. Her hair was Jackie Kennedy's, her whole look was first lady, and as she carefully lowered the hot dish with ease onto a beautiful bamboo and ceramic hotplate I've never seen, she spoke.

"I knew you were bringing company, dear, so I cooked up a little something." She took off one hot-glove, extended her bare hand to Sharon, and said, "Hello, dear. Welcome to our humble home. I'm Lil. And this is my husband, Martin."

We looked up. Dad was there in the doorway. He was wearing a bow tie.

Deb email
Re: Why?
tommy
who knew? i'll be up on Friday
loved the frog analogy
-Sis

Suffice it to say that my email to Deb was largely incoherent and centered—fixated, you might say—on that Saturday morning cartoon of our youth. You know, the one in which a singing and dancing frog is brought in front of a showbiz agent by the guy who has discovered it and wants to make money off it. Needless to say, the frog does not perform. Both frog and man are tossed out of the agent's office.

I am not whole. I have no integrity. I do not embrace. The broader world holds too much meaning for me. I probably smell bad. I am not whole. I do not embrace ....

I did not realize that putting in a chair lift was so simple. I thought we'd have to tear up our staircase, but it's all about simple tracks laid down over it. It looks like Jo's own, personal railroad. I yelled "all aboard" when she tried it out for the first time, and that made her laugh, even though the chairlift company's installer scowled. He probably thought it was unmanly. Phineas liked "all aboard" and kept repeating it. It was the only time I've ever seen Jo laugh. She waved as she went up, smiling— she was thrilled. Phineas waved back and clapped, delighted. Mel got a little teary. I admit that it was moving to see technology step in and help someone in need so immediately.

Concentrating on the lift also took my mind off "The Last Supper," which is what I'm calling Sharon's evaluation session. It certainly was the most surprising— and perhaps revealing—of all Dad's episodes so far. I sat with Deb and Mel this evening to go over the report. The brandy we poured helped make our review clearer:

Sharon: Are you comfortable in your home?

Lil: We love our home.

Sharon: What do you like about it?

Lil: Well, we've been living here for so long.

Dad: What's not to like?

Sharon: Do you cook regularly or do you have someone do it for you?

Dad: My wife is a wonderful cook.

Sharon (smiling at Lil): She is.

Lil: I cook every day. How would we eat if I didn't?

Sharon: Well, I noticed that there's no car outside. Are you able to somehow get to the grocery store?

Lil: No, dear. You see—

Dad: Young lady, I decided after over half a century of driving that it's actually quite a boring and bothersome task. Gave it up.

The next questions went about the same. Then we got to one I didn't expect, and apparently, neither did Deb. But it sure seemed like Dad did.

Sharon: And what about incontinence? Do you ever have any problems with your bathroom habits?

Lil: Oh. Never.

Dad: Not a drop or a plop out of place!

Sharon is not going to recommend anyone for anything. Deb and I sipped more brandy, and Mel sipped her herbal tea. Then Deb pointed out the good side.

"Look at it this way, Tommy. Dad's crapping uncontrollably is a possibility, but not a reality." She laughed. Mel laughed. I didn't. Putting diapers on my own father was crossing a line I'm not even going to draw.

"What is zee next zing we must do, Tom? Did you ask Sharon or Doctor Galbraith?" asked Mel.

"The recommendation is for another evaluation in six months, unless something serious happens before that," I said. "Sharon said three to six months is the timeframe used to judge stability or decline." I saw Deb's crest fall before she even spoke.

"Six months?" she said. "Six? Aren't there any other options?"

"Well, she did say something interesting as she left," I remembered. "I guess she must have seen the dark circles under my eyes, because after she got into her car, she rolled down the window and said, 'Don't worry, Mr. Conklin, one of them may even break a hip before then.' Then she drove away."

We all stared at each other in a daze. After a few moments, Deb and I each pointed our fingers at our temples, as if we were holding pistols to our heads.

"I've lowered my age limit to 55," I said.

"Sixty," Deb shot back without hesitating.

That made Mel laugh because we both did it at the exact same moment, but Deb and I sat stone-faced. A sad silence crept over us. Stomachs growled. Mel and Deb got up and began pulling out pastas and cheeses and other things from the fridge and cabinets, but we were out of oil. Truffle oil, Deb insisted, so she and Mel could make parmesan truffle angel hair "for three," she said, and patted Mel's tummy. Then she admitted that she'd been craving Mel's pasta whether Mel needed to feed herself and two babies or not. I'm fine with butter on noodles, if you please, but I was the one sent on a mission.

At the supermarket, a nice young man who was stocking shelves passed by the specialties aisle and saw me wandering back and forth empty-handed. It was nice of him to help. I told him what I was looking for. He pointed out that truffle oil comes in very small bottles, so I was looking for the wrong kind of packaging. Since I was in a hurry, he walked me right to it. From there at the end of the aisle, I just happened to look up. Way across the store was Marla. She was disappearing into an aisle from the meats counter. That can't be *Marla*, I thought, *that woman has a baby with her*.

The baby was draped across her front in a brightly colored shawl. I remember the shawl because of pictures I've seen in *National Geographic* of those Andean mountain women with babies strapped to their backs, or fronts, just like that. The woman I saw even had jet-black hair, just like Marla's. I hurried quickly over to frozen foods to get a better glimpse—she wouldn't be able to see me there, but by the time I went all the way around, she was gone. I thought briefly that she might be toting our new grandchild, but it's way too early for that. And I would have known, of course. I darted around the corners of the aisles like a spy before going back to frozen foods where I picked up packages of freezing beans and peaches. I tried to look as if I were reading the ingredients as I stole glimpses this way and that, but each package has a picture on the front and no other ingredients, so I had to stop that nonsense.

I swear it was Marla. She was probably babysitting for someone's grandkid or something. She always did want more children. She's too old, though. There was just something about the way she was carrying such a tiny person across the front of her. It probably wasn't Marla.

As I was about to step away from the freezers, Mel called.

"Where are you?" she said.

"I'm in frozen foods," I said. I can see now, writing it here, that I probably sounded sarcastic.

"We are starving, Tom," she said.

"Honey?" I asked. She didn't say anything so I continued. "Since Deb is here, can we go back to the cave?" I asked.

"Sure, Tom. Zat is a good idea," said my wife. "Will you come back for dinner first and bring zee oil?"

. . .

"See? You're amazing," I said.

Mel leaned on the counter and held her belly with one hand while digging into the Goldfish® bag with the other.

"Stop it," she kept saying. She looks so beautiful when she eats Goldfish® by the fistful. And it's fun to type that little "®" in here.

"Yeah, this was a pretty good outlining job—centered, and a good height for the size window ya got here," said the contractor.

"Ye won't be calling the place a cave no more, neither," said Greg with a winsome tone in his voice. He was sitting cross-legged in the middle of our floor. With his grey, wild beard, torn jeans, and tunic pullover, he looked like a real Maharishi Mahesh Yogi. The window guys kept stepping around him, leaving as much space in between themselves and Swami Greg as they could. In fairness, they were trying to keep up their speedy installation because the sky was darkening at an alarming rate, and we were going to get hit with yet another storm.

At last, our huge bay window was in place. We all stood around it in awe. I was only disappointed that it was not sunny out, but even a brooding, ominous, evening sky over the lake and hills beyond was breathtaking. It changed the entire interior of the place. Even the carpenters were enthralled. Why no previous owner had done this is truly a mystery.

"We will call zis place 'Zee Villa' from now on," announced Mel. She looked so happy. I was, too. I ran over to the kitchen area and pulled out some beers for us guys, and a ginger ale for Mel.

"To The Villa!" we toasted. Greg looked thrilled, and the contractors seemed to enjoy the work break. When they finally left, I found myself wishing Ol' Greg would, too. The weather's moodiness was creating a cozy atmosphere. I lit the fireplace to enjoy it alone with my wife. Instead, Ol' Greg settled in with us.

"Found a shaggy grotto nearby, friends," he said as I brought in the lawn chairs. Mel brought over a tray with the Goldfish crackers, half a French bread, cheese, and more drinks. Greg plunged his dirty hand into the bowl and ate the crackers by the fistful.

"Yeah? And?" I said as we all sat down.

"Well," he started. He let out a little "sheesh" noise as if anyone could see what he was getting at. "Didn't know the thing existed. Gonna clear the ivies from it and climb in first thing in the morning to investigate."

"Why will you do zis, Gregory?" asked Mel.

"In case o' treasure o' course!" he declared. He was so invigorated that my subconscious socked me in the gut with a huge pang of guilt for not letting him in on my secret find—the key—the one I'd discovered with no effort whatsoever in a place I'm not even paying for on the outskirts of a village where I'm not even a native, as he is. Then my sub-sub-conscious relieved me by reminding me that there probably were no pirates or Vikings here, certainly none that left any iron-age items. It also reminded me that imagination, like hope, is a thing that flies. I raised my glass.

"To bountiful treasure!" I cried. We all drank. The fire crackled, and a huge clap of thunder and flash of lightning made me wonder if one of our trees hadn't been hit. I got up and went to the window. A pouring rain began drenching the entire area, which I could see clearly from our beautiful new opening. Only a lunatic would own a place in this location and not want to enjoy the view. We told Greg that he could stay the night, but he insisted on leaving as soon as the weather calmed a bit. He wanted to get ready for his expedition. When he stepped out to leave, I handed him an umbrella.

The next morning was glorious. The drenching night rains left sparkling drops on everything that could hold drops, including the umbrella. We found it unopened and leaning against a tree, but that didn't detract from the dewy private showing we were enjoying.

Our new bay window has smaller, openable side windows. I opened them. I opened the windows at the back of the place as well. The most mind-balming breeze came through. I propped open the door for even more circulation and made a note to myself to install a small bathroom window soon. There seemed no end to what could be done with this place. I hauled the new toilet in, measured for the bathroom window, got the grounds cleaned up—all before lunch. No therapy in the world can do for you what a good bout of villa-fixing can.

As noon came on, light was intensifying everywhere in the interior. At one point, Mel and I just stood there and took it in. Our patterned floor came alive in the sunlight. I'll have to admit, whoever laid it out was an artisan. I felt ever warmer rays approaching along with Ol' Greg—he was on his way back up our path. He had obviously accomplished his goal because he was covered in dirt and torn leaves. He was carrying his pickaxe, as always, and a huge knife. As the sun inched to its apex, he arrived. Mel immediately and graciously invited him in.

"Gregory, we are taking a break for grilled cheese. You will join us, of course?" she asked.

"Much obliged," he said and stepped inside. But as he and Mel made their way to the kitchen, they both stopped abruptly. They were staring at our floor as if into a chasm. Mel looked like she does when she sleepwalks.

"Tom, please come here."

I walked to where they were standing and looked down. It took my eyes a minute to adjust, to see that the colored tiles were not just mixed in with the plain beige stones to make a whorl of pretty patterns anymore. With the intense noon sun on it, it seemed to be a map of sorts with an "X" marking a certain spot in the design. We stood there so long that the sun began inching from its overhead position, and the "X" grew less and less prominent. As it faded, I looked up and saw the town's mail truck, way over on the far ridge, headed in our direction.

"And I been digging up nothing in wet crags, friends, while ye was holding the map right here," said Greg more to himself than to me. I was trying not to let that annoy me.

"What map, Greg?" I said, annoyed.

"Ye can't go telling me now that 'X' don't look like it's marking a spot here, friend," he countered.

"It does look zat way, Tom." said Mel. She was enjoying the conversation. Ol' Greg started circling the "map" and trying to "read" it. I will only admit here, and not publicly, that it did look like a map of the grounds with our squatted villa in the middle of the property. The "X" was marking a spot near the ridge outside, north-east of the house. Ol' Greg began jumping up and down.

"Friend—ye brought the light" and "The brotherhood's spoils is revealed" and "'X' marks the spot, just like us locals been knowing for years!" he shouted.

"You are Zee New Messiah," said Mel. She was winking and laughing.

Greg burst out of the house and ran to the place the "X" allegedly marked. He took his axe and began crashing it into the earth to no avail. It was very solid, despite the rains. I watched him through our new window barely making a dent in it. After a few minutes, I felt sick. I stepped outside to better think in the fresh air. When I did, the mailman came up the walkway. He stopped in front of me and handed me mail for the first time since we've been here. On the top of the pile was a property tax bill.

I did nothing. Mel went inside to finish the grilled cheese. Ol' Greg hacked away until he almost dropped. Birds chirped. A trickle of sweat came down my face and was absorbed onto my upper lip. The salt tasted good.

Greg was sweating too, profusely. It was all we could do to get him to stop pounding the earth and come in for a sandwich. By the end of lunch, he was offering to get his cousin to come over with a trencher he uses in his contracting business to break ground. I made him promise to go away and sleep on it, and for God's sake, don't hack our property while we're away. As we loaded the car to leave, he took a solemn oath, crossed himself, and bowed to us to seal his promise not to dig.

I couldn't get Ol' Greg out of my mind all the way home. He's way too invested, what with all his years of treasure-hunting, and Mel is way too entertained, since she loves Ol' Greg's antics, and I'm way too taxed. I can't bring myself to open that bill. So my mind just wasn't in the right place when we arrived home and found Jo on her brand new chair lift, stuck in a loop.

She was going up, then down, up, down, over and over, with no pause at the top or bottom to let her off. Phineas was pacing the entire length of the house with his screwdriver in his hand, yelling.

"O, ho, 'tis foul" and "How abhorred my imagination is!"

Jo looked quite content, however. Her pipe was lit, and she was taking a puff every other lap or so. While Mel calmed Phineas, I waited at the bottom and grabbed Jo off. It was as easy as picking up a doll. Mel helped her limp over to Phineas. They sat together on the couch, held hands, and looked into each other's eyes. He was so relieved that tears came.

"We that are true lovers run into strange capers," he said to her. I stood there staring until Mel gently shooed me away.

"Love does not dry up when you are old, Tom," my astute wife whispered to me in the next room. She's good at reading the looks on my face. "Dry up" really does illustrate what I was thinking. I don't know if it's the goddam media that worships youth culture and shoves it down our throats every day or what, but we really do expect to deposit our elderly folks in group homes of some sort and leave them there to dry up.

I just thought about how, if you lost your spouse at that age, you would have a very slim chance of ever meeting anyone you care about. I remember when I was a teenager, my plan was to be like Jimi Hendrix and somehow die before I got too old. And "old" to me back then was 30. Heck, it was 25. Now I'm almost 50 and starting a brand-new life and family. If you had asked me where I would be at 50 when I was 16, I would have said flippantly "in a nursing home." So if 50 seemed that way to me at 16, is 90 looking like it does because I'm a goddamn, flippant little 49-year-old? Will I want romance at 90? What if my kids had the right to put me in a home and they decided that 50 was the right time? What if they had the legal right to do that? That would be torture, and unfair! They would be acting from ignorance—they wouldn't know what it's like to be approaching 50 until they got here.

I spent the next half hour fixing the lift. As I finished, Deb pulled up on her way out of town. I stepped out to the driveway to meet her. I wanted to ask how everything went this weekend, but she addressed it first.

"So."

"Yeah."

"Interesting."

"I know," I said. "Anything happen?"

"Of course."

"Wanna tell?"

Deb looked at her watch. "No time."

"OK."

"Any word on the *Prix*?"

"None."

Then no one said anything.

"Tommy, I'd still love to throw a baby shower for you both. You know, happy people, lots of gifts. Get your mind off things. Celebrate the babies."

"Thanks, Deb, but that's for younger couples. And you know Mel with her traditions. We'll be OK. There's too much going on around here anyway."

Deb thought for a moment.

"Why don't I arrange to come up every other weekend from now on?" she offered. "You know, help out with Dad and Lil." Now that sounded like a party.

"Can you, Sister Deborah?" I asked. She smiled.

"Sure."

Again, a short silence.

"Lemme take you out to see my vegetables," I said. "It'll only take a minute." A weight seemed to lift temporarily as she shut off the car, got out, and stepped out to the back yard with me to my patch. We were not talking about Dad for the first time in a long time.

"My soon-to-be-mighty stalks." I introduced them. "See?" Deb leaned in and smiled. "They'll host some seedy meat," I declared.

"Tommy's got a garden," my sister teased. "Who woulda thunk?"

I guess I was showing my enthusiasm. I was also, unexpectedly, getting a little choked up. If Deb saw that, she'd never let me forget it. Fortunately, Phineas got her attention as he approached to greet her, waving. Deb waved back.

"Professor, I was worried that you might not be around, but here you are," she said.

"Good woman, how dost thou?" replied Phineas, stepping up to the edge of the corn patch.

"I dost good, Professor," said Deb as they clasped hands in greeting. Phineas looked down at the plants growing there by his feet. He seemed to grow with them.

"Nothing grew last year at all, and now, in the very same soil, we've got swelling little towers," I said. "Phineas and Jo sowed these." Phineas stood even taller. I clutched a plant. It was firm and straight. Reassuring. I could almost feel it bulging in my hand.

"And the green color's so vibrant!" exclaimed Deb. My sister was truly impressed.

"And when they're big enough, the leaves will rustle in the breeze—that's satisfaction only a huge vegetable can offer," I said. Phineas was nodding vigorously. He and Deb chatted while I bent over the patch to pull out a weed or two. There were none.

"Tommy, I gotta get going," said Deb.

"Ay, but why? Are my discourses dull?" Phineas asked. He was genuinely saddened to see her leave.

"Prof, I'm sorry. I can't *tarry*," Deb said to him, then winked at me. "I actually have to work tomorrow morning, and I have the whole drive ahead of me," she explained. Phineas understood that. She took his hand to lead him inside while she said her goodbyes to Mel and Jo. I got the hose out and watered, and when I heard Deb coming back out, I walked up the driveway to say goodbye. She got into the car, started it, and rolled down the window.

"So," I said.

"Yeah," she sighed, and backed out of the driveway.

I watched the car get smaller in the distance. Her leaving gave me that nervous urge to go ward off another episode if I could. Since Mel and Jo had dinner started, I gave in. I told Mel I'd be right back. I wanted to check on Dad before a new week was underway. I jumped into my car and called their landline as I drove.

Dad answered.

"Dad?"

"Yes, Tom," he said.

"I'm in the neighborhood and thought I'd swing by," I said.

"Fine. That's fine." He sounded a bit formal, but that's nothing to complain about. We continued chatting like old buddies about his weekend until I pulled into the driveway. Kelly's house next door looked as abandoned as ever. It gave the neighborhood a sad aspect. I was still on the phone with Dad.

"So you enjoyed Deb's visit?" I asked. As he answered favorably, I got out of the car, went to the door, and let myself in. Lil was sitting comfortably in the living room, but as I stepped up to her, I saw that she was crying alone in front of the TV, thoroughly distraught.

"Dad," I interrupted him, "hang on." I put the phone away from my ear. "Ma, what's wrong?" I asked.

"Martin called me 'Lil,'" she sobbed. I didn't know what to say.

"But Ma," I said, "that's your name. Dad's been calling you 'Lil' all your life. We all have." She burst into a fit like a child who needs a nap.

"You shouldn't have. I hate that name—it sounds like 'Li'l Abner'!"

Seeing my mother crumple over and sob into her own lap was heartbreaking. Dad's voice continued streaming out of my phone, and it brought me back. I put it to my ear. As I did, I looked up and saw the long phone cord stretched taut across the room from its base on the wall.

Since I already had him on the line, all I had to do was follow the cord into the pantry closet where I found him. We stood there, I on my cell phone and Dad on their landline, communicating face to face but using a technological device to do so. I like to think that in my youth I was something of a poet or amateur philosopher, but it was Mel who pointed out the symbolism in that.

I got him to hand me the phone by explaining that he could stay in the closet as long as he liked. The difficult part was persuading him to put the gun down. Even though I've taken all the ammo off the premises, the visual was unsettling.

Lamaze. Mel gets a little perturbed when I use that word. The method we're learning is some kind of updated Lamaze, so to me, they're all Lamaze. She wants to call the method we're using by its name, but all I care about is that it will deliver our twin daughters to us. That overpowers my imagination. Here they come—sprung from my seed. Two of them! So who cares about the name of the method? My twins' names are more important. One of them will be named after Jo, of course. Whenever the subject comes up, I gently insist that in using Jo's entire given name, it'd be nice to find a more pronounceable version. If there is one.

Mel pores over her list of family names nightly for a second name for the other twin. But as their arrival draws near, it's becoming important to me to choose a name from the Conklin side of the family. Personally, I like "Deborah"—it's a tried and true American name, but Mel was less than enthusiastic and Deb herself pooh-poohed it. My crazy but loving sister wants us to use "cool Frenchie names" for both twins. A name from the

Conklin side of the family would be great, though. I wish that list weren't so important to Mel.

Ever since Mel's doctor said we should take these classes, I've been thinking that someone should offer a Lamaze class for midlifers who are ushering their parents into old age. You could learn how to breathe, for God's sake. What I mean is, you could go to these Lamaze classes for middle-agers and they could teach you to "birth" your own parents—and yourself—maybe the word is "initiate"—into the rites and rules of aging. The course could be called "Lamaze for Lifers." It would offer a unit on creating a POA before back taxes start piling up. There could be a unit on "embarrassing moments" so you'd be prepared when you arrive at your parents' house to check on them and your dad is roaming around outside wearing nothing—and I do mean not a stitch except an old sweatshirt, inside out, with a tag sticking out that says "Void if detached." Another unit could be about "romance and love in later life"—the possibilities are endless. You would be taught what to do when your elderly neighbor cross-dresses and falls in love with your great grandma-in-law, or when your other elderly neighbor calls you daily, incessantly, to insist that you dig for buried treasure in your own yard. Or you would stay calm when driving down the street, explaining desperately by phone why you're late to meet the hospital's most recent major donors at that new, ridiculously expensive restaurant—because you were busy ministering care to a loved one—and out of the goodness of your heart, and your ever-evolving, newfound understanding of elderly people's needs, you decide to happily stop to pick up that old lady hitchhiker —the one with the thumb barely stuck in the air and holding a sign that says "Walmart"—and then realize that, when she climbs into the front passenger seat, it's your mom. A "Lamaze for Lifers" class could have also helped us with Jo's fall.

Yes, Jo fell. Jo fell. Jo fell. If I write it here enough, maybe I'll grasp it. Mel had come home at lunch to pick up something she needed and found this note on the kitchen table:

Lady Mel,

I scarce have leisure to salute you my matter is so rash. Post speedily to my lord your husband show him this letter. The army of France has landed!

"Dispose of her to some more fitter place, and that with speed," saith 911. By your leave, hostess, 'tis done already, and the messenger gone. But follow, my lord, and I'll soon bring her back.

I feel now the future in the instant. Prithee, hie thee hither, and farewell.

- Phineas

Apparently, Phineas found her lying in the back yard. She said she was on her way to check on the corn plants. He called for an ambulance, and they insisted on taking her to our facility. Mel and I met them at emergency. It took hours for them to test and check her thoroughly, and because of her age, they decided to keep her overnight. When the social worker pulled us aside to explain that they will only let her return home afterward if she has people to care for her, Mel didn't even let the woman finish. Of course she'll come home. Whenever staff saw her, they leaned in close to Mel or to me to speak in a lowered voice.

"In her 90s?" they'd say. "She's so with it."

If they only knew. And why they had to lower their voices, I don't know. As if *not* being senile at that age is a disease.

We took Phineas home when visiting hours ended. He was beside himself. When we pulled into the driveway it was very late, and no sooner did he get out of the car than he vanished. I checked his house and yard, but he was nowhere to be found. I got out my Markum Triple-E flashlight to scan the whole neighborhood, and as I shined it across our back yard, there he was. He was sitting among the corn plants. He squinted and put his hand up to shield his eyes from the beam. I quickly turned it aside and walked up to him. He sat stoically on that small stool from the garage, staring straight ahead. After I stayed with him for a while, he spoke.

"Lovers and madmen have such seething brains," he whispered.

.   .   .

It was the loud voices that caught my attention first. While Mel got dressed and prepared some things for Jo's return—an extra-soft pad on the chairlift and other amenities—I wanted to ask the professor if he'd come with us to pick her up.

There was an unfamiliar, beat-up car parked out front. The voices continued, so I felt the need to sneak over to the open window to hear what was going on before knocking on the side door. No one ever visits Phineas. As far as I know, he has no kids, no wife, no living relatives. No friends except us. As I leaned toward the window like a spy, I smelled cigarette smoke. Phineas doesn't smoke cigarettes. A dastardly male voice was speaking.

"But we been sendin' ya that goddam check every month—whattya do with it?"

Phineas's voice answered. "Mistake me not so much to think my poverty is treacherous."

"Stop with the mumbo jumbo already," replied the male voice, "I don't even know whatcher sayin'. Alls I know is, I ain't gonna be comin' here an' deliverin' you cash in person every time."

"We got our own problems, ya know," added an unfamiliar female voice.

I stood on my tiptoes and peeked in. Fortunately, the visitors had their backs to the window and were facing Phineas, who sat on the couch with his head down and his hands clasped in his lap. He began wringing them every time the man yelled.

"Ya got all that goddam Shakespeare crap in here, butcha don't got a goddam phone so's I can call ya an' not hav'ta drive all the way up here when there's a problem," complained the man. Phineas replied softly.

"Beat thy drum and get thee gone."

The man exploded. "Dad, ya ain't never been no college professor, so drop it, OK?! The college here don't even know who ya are, so ya can't go around sayin' ya worked there when ya worked in a factory, for Chrissakes. I'm sorry the plant closed, an' I ain't any happier than you that Ma left us back then, but—" My ears burned as he went on to list all kinds of things that apparently went wrong in their lives. "The line's the only thing ya ever been qualified for—ya ain't never taught college," he said, "an' like the doctor said, ya ain't never gonna." Then he talked about bringing Phineas here with some woman who, as far as I could tell, was Phineas's daughter, but from what he was saying, she apparently beat it after a while, just like their mom. "So ya can't go back an' work the line no more even if there was one—you're too damn old!"

The man turned suddenly. I ducked. Then he yelled again.

"Here, this is so ya can get a goddam phone." I heard some fumbling and walking around. I ran over to my own yard and started inspecting the spray attachment on my garden hose as if it were old and faulty and not brand new. The son and the woman marched out of Phineas's house and slammed the screen door. The woman stopped to light a cigarette as the son got in the car and gunned the motor. She jumped in, and they sped off.

I went back to the window. Phineas was still sitting with his head down. He had stopped wringing his hands. I've never seen someone look so alone.

I immediately ran home to tell Mel. She pushed aside the mound of sheets and bedding she was putting on the couch for Jo. We sat, and I told her what I'd just heard. I think it was the first time I've ever cried in front of her. I was embarrassed. First, she put my head between her breasts and large belly. We stayed on the couch like that for quite a while. I know people who pay big bucks for therapy sessions to clear up their deepest traumas, but Mel cleared up mine with one sweet nestle. When I'd recovered enough, we made a plan. We'd go pick up Jo, and when we came back, we'd bring Phineas some dinner.

"He may not want to see people at zis moment," said Mel. I went with that.

Picking up Jo was a smooth affair, thank God. I was in no mood for rough ones. When we got to the hospital, the gerontologist on duty gave us directions for her care and praised our getting a chair lift.

"Do you have a basement? You may want to put in a second lift for that flight of stairs as well," she suggested. Mel loved the idea.

"In addition, we could have a makeshift emergency room set up in our garage, you know, like a M*A*S*H unit," I said. That woman didn't know humor when she saw it. Mel shoved her elbow into my side and smiled at the doctor. I smiled and ignored my phone, which kept vibrating in my pocket. Each time, I let it go to voicemail.

"We take care of all zee old people in our family," stated Mel, "and some who are not in our family, too." This perked the doctor right up. She looked at Mel's belly and smiled. Mel beamed.

"Twins," I said.

"Now there's a challenge," she said to us before motioning to a passing aide. "Janet, would you get these folks an ElderKeen packet?" Janet went to grab one. I didn't have time to tell her I already had one because my phone's vibration took my attention once again. I thought I should answer it, even though I didn't recognize the number.

"Hello?" I said, exasperated. Someone was talking, but it was muffled. I couldn't make out what he was saying. "Hel—?"

"Friend," I heard more clearly. It was Ol' Greg. "Dirk can come next weekend. Friday night. Ye in?"

"Who's Dirk?" I asked angrily. He was the cousin with the trencher. "Alright already, Greg, fine, fine—next Friday," I said. "I'll have to be there because it's my property." Or it must be by now. That tax bill told me so. "Look, Greg, if we get a machine to dig the X-spot, the guy might mistakenly crash right through the middle of whatever's buried there," I said, turning away from Mel, and from Janet, who was on her way toward us with a packet in her hands. "And don't forget he'll be privy to our find, and who knows how much of a cut he'll want to keep his mouth shut?"

"I'm swearing him to secrecy, friend," whispered Greg. I could hardly hear him. "I figgur we can do it after dark." Another voice was suddenly there, loud and clear.

"Sir, this is a library—what are you doing behind the desk? That's the librarian's phone!" We were cut off.

I love it when you're going along in life, trying to take care of all the generations around you, and you're expecting a third generation any time soon, and you're steeped in problems of all sorts, and right in the middle of handling one of them, a doctor or nurse or social worker says, "You don't know about such-and-such?"

That's what Janet asked. She opened the packet and showed us the literature for the support group. I guess I had missed that when I looked through my copy.

"When do they meet?" I asked. In my mind, I was saying, *Why the hell didn't anybody tell me about this before?* and Is it like a *"Lamaze for Lifers"? Where do I sign up?*

Janet took the packet back, grabbed the pen that was dangling noisily from her neck with her keys and ID, took the brochure I was looking at, flipped it over, and circled the date and time of the support group printed on the back.

"The information is on their website, too. You don't have to pay or sign up or anything, just come. A woman named Crystal runs it. You'll like her," she said as she was paged. She was on her way before we could ask any questions. "It's specifically for people who are dealing with the care of their elderly loved ones but who are also trying to juggle their own kids and family obligations," she called as she left.

I love that. "People who take care of their elderly relatives." There should be a word for us, just like there's a word for "people who fix your pipes and toilets" (plumber). Or, "people who stand in front of musicians and wave a wand at them" (conductor). Or even, "people who oversee a vast network of mind-boggling bureaucracy in the medical profession" (hospital administrator). It would just be easier to refer to us if we had a name. We'd feel naturally more of a group. We'd have an identity, I thought. Then my phone plinged. Deb was texting me.

Deb: How's it going
Me: We're at the hospital getting Jo
Deb: Why?!!
Me: She fell, but it's not serious. I'll call you later.
Deb: Oh no—hope she's OK.
Me: Got some info about a support group for caregivers who are parents giving care to their own parents.
Deb: Sandwich!
Me: ??

260

Deb: There's a name for it Tommy the sandwich generation

Deb: Where u been?

Me: Sandwich! That's perfect!

Deb: How are dad & Lil?

Me: Ha! We must be a double-decker then.

Deb: Forgot to tell you he was constantly looking for bullets when I was there.

Me: With horseradish all over it! It stinks!

Deb: And Lil got weepy watching TV.

Me: Actually, I'm a triple-decker if you count Stephen having his first kid.

Deb: She wouldn't tell me what's wrong.

Me: And then there's Phineas and Ol' Gregory, who aren't even related to us.

Deb: U OK, Little B?

Me: They're all in my dreams lately!

Deb: ??

Me: So my sandwich is a triple-decker turkey deluxe—and I'm the turkey!

Getting Jo home and settled helped take my mind off things. I went immediately over to Phineas's to invite him to dinner. We realized it would be easier than taking Jo and dinner to him. He was still glum, but I talked up the meal and the great lemon cakes Mel had made in honor of Jo's return.

As soon as he heard that Jo was back, he was cheered. He came right over. Of course, no one mentioned his rude son or his big life lie that he was—wasn't—a professor in the literature department over at the university. We didn't tell Jo, of course. And it was so easy to check up on. All I did was call the main number for the campus this morning.

"I'm doing research about higher education for a graduate class and was wondering if I may get some information on the literature department and its distinguished faculty over the last 40 years," I said. Forty years is a lot, but I was trying to sound like I was really doing a research project. The woman proudly referred me to the alumni office, who proudly referred me to the Dean's office, who annoyedly referred me to the department of literature. When the secretary answered, I repeated my inquiry and then tried to elaborate. "I'm interested in the professors and their areas of expertise, specifically those researching Shakesp—"

Before I finished, she rattled off easily the individual names of the entire literature faculty of the last half century with an air of intimate knowledge as if she were naming exes. She did not mention Phineas's name, or any name that sounded even remotely like his. I thanked her and complimented her thorough knowledge of the department.

"Nah," she said, "I'm new this year. They're all lined up on plaques on the wall right here in front of me. They've got their pictures and everything."

I was shot through the heart with a longing to see Phineas in his bow tie, smiling in gradations of bronze on a nice wooden plaque, mounted on the wall of a distinguished institution as if he were the proudest guy in the world.

Her name is Allison. It even sounds like a home-health aide's name should sound. I found her through the support group. It was quite a group. They told me we can get an aide without the recommendation. That's what support groups are for. To tell you things you didn't know. There was one woman there who kept repeating her own personal mantra.

"One day at a time. Lordy. One day," she kept saying as people told their stories. I was first up because I was the new guy. I began talking about Dad's decline much more easily than expected—like slop spilling out of a bucket. Even so, those nice support groupies really did support me. I couldn't stop rambling, and those total strangers couldn't stop listening, as if I were giving them the password to Eden. They were sucking up nourishment from my crazy anecdotes, and when they shared theirs, I could see why. Whew. Some of their nutty tales about their declining loved ones made Dad look like a fully functioning CEO.

At the end, the "Lordy" lady came up to me and gave me Allison's card. Other people approached me, too, and they generously offered all kinds of help and tidbits that are only available in the elder-care community from people who've actually been there. Support groups are probably the closest thing we're going to get to Lamaze for Lifers. Or to Eden.

Allison seems to have lots of experience. She stepped into my parents' home graciously and was not put off by the smell or that Dad's bathrobe kept opening as he moved around, revealing his full-frontalness. The best thing was that Dad liked her, and so did Lil. I tried to sit her down and explain things, but she kept getting away to sit with them and chat. I liked that, too. Compatibility. What I didn't like is that she kept asking where the absorbent products were. At one point, she lowered her voice.

"You know, adult diapers?" she said. That's when I told her that I know what those are, thank you, but my father doesn't need them. She chatted some more, then got to work. I had made sure the fridge was stocked and dinner was ready to go. As Allison took over, I suddenly realized I wasn't needed. That felt good. I was leaving my parents in good hands, and they seemed to like it. I wanted to let Allison do her thing, and at the end of her shift, I would go back to thank her and see if she needed anything else. I ran some errands, went home, and ate dinner with Mel.

By 7 p.m., I was back. Allison was sitting in the kitchen having tea and doing her paperwork. The place was clean, the food was in the fridge all wrapped, and Lil and Dad were in the living room watching TV. Allison seemed to know how to get out of her clients' way and let them live with dignity in their own home while still making sure they got the care they needed—Dad was watching the news just exactly as if there was no woman sitting in his kitchen writing a report about how many pills she got him to take. Maybe he's just too fed up to react anymore. I can relate to that.

I sat with them in front of the TV for a while. At one point, Allison poked her head in and said goodbye. Dad and Lil politely waved.

"Do come back!" said Lil. I was in heaven. Allison slipped out the back door.

When I went into the kitchen to make Dad coffee, I saw the note she left. She had sketched a little diapered doodle on it. I took a picture of it before throwing it away:

It was cute and showed her professional style and friendly personality, even when asking me to get a box of adult diapers. I'd told her repeatedly we didn't need them. She's probably just trying to cover her bases.

.   .   .

Mel didn't want to come to The Villa. She wanted to stay with Jo and Phineas in case they needed anything. She packed a little dinner for two—enough for both Greg and me—complete with beers, bottled water, and a tablecloth. She also gave me other things to ferry out there, like towels, some trinkets for the fireplace mantel, and a bathmat. We got it all into the car, and I climbed in after it. I put the window down and she leaned in.

"I want a string of pearls and one of zose big diamonds, Tom," she said. Then she burst out laughing.

"It won't necessarily be a treasure chest like the ones in Hollywood movies," I said. She stopped laughing. Then she kissed me.

"Good luck," she said.

I pulled up to The Villa as the sun was setting. Ol' Greg and his cousin were already there. The twilight gave us just enough light to orient ourselves, but it was disappearing fast. I noticed that Greg had already outlined the X-spot with sticks stuck in the ground in formation around it. It looked like a mini Stonehenge.

"I come early friend, noon-like, and I used your big window to see the map," he said. I could picture him pressing his nose against our new bay window to read our floor. "That way, I could mark it, accurate." It did look accurate, if my memory served me. We went into the house to look at the map once more. There was no noon sunlight, but we could see that we were digging in the right vicinity.

Cousin Dirk was a large guy with a long beard. As it cascaded downward, it seemed to blend into the rest of the hair on his ample form. He was sitting and smoking in his small trencher, a one-seater. Ol' Greg put his back to him and lowered his voice to speak to me. He nodded backward over his shoulder toward the machine.

"Cousin thinks we're digging a well for ye," he said. "I'll have him loose the spot, then me and ye'll go for it."

"Water it is," I said. I looked up toward the machine and waved at the man—he didn't reciprocate. What he thought we were digging for didn't really matter—conversation didn't look to be his strong point. I'd follow Greg's lead.

"Got the flashlight?" he asked.

I went to the car and took out my Markum Triple-E camping light. "A floodlight you hold in your hand," I said. I really like that advertisement, because it's true. They aren't always true. We walked over to the smoking cousin, who perked up.

"Won't be needin' that," he said. He turned the trencher's headlight on. With darkness upon us now, it illuminated the whole area in front of his machine and beyond. "Like a thousand suns, this here," he said. He then flashed it on and off for show. I turned off my wimpy little hand-held light. Greg turned around to me again, leaned in, and lowered his voice.

"Gonna need that for our own digging so ye done good bringing it," he said, pointing to my Markum. He whirled back around toward his cousin. "Let's go!"

The machine rolled easily toward Greg's twig monument. Its sound crashed through the evening calm we always enjoy up here.

"Glad we're up on the ridge, friend—no one can hear us up here!" Greg shouted. His cousin maneuvered the machine a few feet this way and that to center the cutter. Then he plunged it toward the ground. He yanked backward to slit open the Earth like a birthday cake. Chunks of soil climbed out of their own way and gave up the ghost. He only needed to plunge and yank a few times for a considerable opening to be loosed.

267

When it was, Greg ran toward him, arms waving and mouth shouting. "Whoa, Dirky, whoa!" he yelled. Cousin Dirk stopped digging with a puzzled look on his face. He pulled the trencher back slowly and turned the motor off. Peace and quiet clapped into place all around us like thunder. He removed his large body from his machine with some difficulty and walked over to Greg with his head cocked.

"That ain't near deep enough for no well," he said.

"Water's close up top near these parts," Greg said immediately, thinking on his feet. I was impressed. He pulled a wad of cash out of his pocket and handed over a number of bills from it. Cousin Dirk immediately saw it our way, and I wondered for the first time what crazy Ol' Greg did all his life for work and where he gets his money. I made a mental note to give him some toward the expense.

Dirk wedged himself back into his machine, put it in reverse, backed up and twirled around, then pulled away. Greg and I waited for the noise to fade down the dirt road. Then we grabbed my floodlight, ran to the wound, and peered. Dirt. Lots of loose dirt. I hung the light from the nearest branch and aimed it while Greg grabbed the shovels. We started digging furiously. Much to my back's dismay, we dug until the hole was wide enough to maneuver in. It was a lot of earth to move— almost as deep as Greg is tall—only 5'2" or so. I wanted to give up, but Greg wouldn't allow that.

"Friend, I can feel a commandment upon us. We gotta finish!"

His fortitude carried me. Besides, I hadn't done all that reading up on those private collectors for nothing. I wanted to see how much they might be willing to pay on the hush-hush as compared to the established museums for something like a Viking find. That would keep Willows honest, if I ever went back to him. Selling Viking spoils would help pay for my new twins' education, and I could save a few of the nicer pearls and such for Mel and Lil. And Deb and Jo. And Jamie. I'd almost forgotten to get the key, but thanks to extended bank hours on Fridays, I got there in time. I kept feeling my pocket to be sure it was still there.

Under a bright moon, our digging became a rhythm that my body seemed to be matching. The sound of shovels slipping under dirt—*harrrumph*—then being lifted to hurl the dirt away—*shooom*—became so soothing that when the metal of my shovel collided with the hard metal of something found—*clang!*—it shook me. It electrified Greg. He dropped his shovel, leapt out of the hole in one bound, grabbed his pickaxe, jumped back in, and started pulverizing the earth in a circle around whatever it was I'd hit. He was huffing and puffing, and repeating thanks over and over in a high-pitched whisper that was in sync with his pounding.

"Such luck, friend!"—*phmph*—Much obliged!—*dmph*. Glad to be here with ye ...."

After quite a bit of pounding-shoveling, shoveling-pounding, we managed to yank an iron box about the size of a small air conditioning unit out of the ground.

We stood stunned. I barely remember hauling it out of the hole. We drew it across the ground and hoisted it onto the stump for examination. I grabbed the Triple-E off the tree branch and shined it on the box before you could say "Leif Ericson."

It was a small iron trunk with, unbelievably, a lock on the front. A clasp like one that any modern-day trunk might have on it, but older. Much older. Greg lunged at it and pulled, but it didn't open. I reached my shaking hand into my pocket and slipped out the key.

"Ye got a key, friend?" Greg's voice half whispered.

There was awe in it, and humility. I couldn't even begin to explain to him at that moment where I'd gotten it. He began shuffling around behind me, mumbling and pacing, but I have no idea what he was saying—I was having a hard enough time holding the light with one hand and fixing the key into that lock with the other. I finally cracked enough dirt off the clasp to find just the right angle. I slipped the key in. It turned ... *clack*. The damned thing popped right open.

I was afraid to peer inside. The musty smell was expected, but when I shined the flashlight inside, the contents weren't: A simple stone.

It was a weird stone. I took it out and held the floodlight to it. It was white but clearish, and rectangular, like Mel's facial soap, and about the same size. I didn't know what to make of it, but I did notice that holding its smoothness calmed me. My hands weren't shaking anymore. My mind cleared a bit. I remember thinking that if there were a lot of them, I might get excited. Instead, I was disappointed.

"So whattya think?" I said to Greg. He didn't answer. I thought he'd been peering over my shoulder, but when I turned and scanned the darkness, he wasn't there. I shined the flashlight all over the surrounding area. After only a short search, I found him—he'd fallen into the hole and fainted.

It took me some time to get him out. I had to revive him first, but I had no smelling salts. I was wishing someone could revive me as well because there was a

Viking treasure chest sitting on my stump, goading me like a wink. It was making me dizzy, so I stopped looking at it and rushed to grab the only thing available. Eucalyptus.

I tore off a small branch and ran inside to find something to tear it up into besides my hand. As I burst through the door, there was the mortar and pestle on the mantel. I tore the leaves off, quickly tossed them in, and starting mashing. As I did, their aroma filled the air. The smell was beautiful. When I was done, I stuck my nose in and inhaled. I felt an immediate clearing in the brain, and the residual, dizzy lull lifted. Then I ran back out and climbed into the hole.

Ol' Greg was lying on his back. Fortunately, we'd been sloppy and hadn't chucked as much extra dirt out as I'd thought, so he'd landed on a pile of soft earth. I slipped my hand under the back of his head, tilted it upward a bit, and shoved the mortar under his nose. He came around and sat up rather easily, as if only from a very light sleep. He shook his head out like a wrinkled sheet.

"Was I dreaming, friend? I saw a key, and ye were there, surrounded by all the mates from the ship ... ye was taking a diamond out o' a chest .. there is a chest, ain't there?" he said as he rubbed his face roughly with both hands.

"Yeah. There is," I admitted quietly.

I climbed out, then helped Greg out. As I walked over to the stump, Greg staggered. He put both hands on the rim of the box to steady himself. I shined the light in. He reached in and took out the stone, held it for a long time, and stroked it like a pet. He held it up to the light.

"Ain't no diamond," he said finally.

"No," I agreed.

We stood in silence. The breeze moved the clouds along, and a bright moon came out. It was peaceful.

"Whattye gonna do with it?" he asked.

"I don't know, Greg. I think it'd be a good idea to put it away somewhere until I decide, maybe in my safe deposit box," I said. That seemed to please him. We locked eyes. With not one word spoken, we swore each other to secrecy and shook hands.

He helped me load it into the trunk. He was still not steady on his feet, so I told him to go ahead and stay. I led him into The Villa. He lay down immediately on the mattress and was out. I put one of our blankets over him, patted his head, and left for home.

.　　.　　.

Mel and I got up together this morning. She got ready for work, and I got ready for work. We both ate with Jo, then we both grabbed our lunches. I drove us. We chatted a bit about the coming day. She didn't ask about last night, or about Ol' Greg or our dig, but I could detect a snicker in her voice, even when she reminded me that the contractor would be coming to work on the deck. I nodded and didn't say a word. I didn't bring up the treasure chest at all.

We were running a bit late, so I dropped her off at the staff entrance and kissed her goodbye. I'm sure she thought I was going to park. I didn't. I drove toward the parking garage as if I were going to park there, but when I saw in my mirrors that she had gone inside, I drove home. I didn't even call Andre to tell him I wouldn't be in. I wasn't feeling myself. I should have gone to work, and I should have called him. Instead, I went home, took my Viking treasure chest out of the trunk of the car, checked to be sure the stone was in it, wrapped it up in large black plastic garbage bags, strapped it carefully to our old set of luggage wheels, and loaded it back into the car. Then I drove to our bank.

I went in without it at first and stepped up to the counter. The woman there was very nice. She was new. She did all the paperwork right there to get me access to a very large safe deposit box in addition to the small one I already have. I asked for one of those huge ones that are like half a storage locker. She waited patiently while I went out to get the treasure chest and wheel it in. It just barely fit into the new box, minus the luggage wheels. She was discreet enough to leave me alone while I taped the iron key to it. Then I shoved it in. I called her back in, she locked up, and then she handed me two copies of the deposit-box key before we both came out.

After that, I came home. I sat at the kitchen table to think. Jo and Phineas were outside as they had been all morning, harvesting my corn. I let them. Phineas was wearing a dress, and Jo was in the recliner on the deck. Phineas must have dragged it out there for her so she could rest her hip while still being a part of the harvest. She was giving him directions, happily, and Phineas was taking them, happily. I was sitting at my kitchen table watching them through the glass doors and deciding I wouldn't go to work at all. Happily.

I hoped my colleagues wouldn't miss me. I know Mel would worry if she knew that I stayed home to research semitransparent stones from the age of the

Viking explorers. I was dressed as if I'd gone to work so that, at the end of the day, I could just go pick her up. I liked the idea. Even though I'm a skunk, I admit it. Time seemed to be slowing down. I love it when time slows down.

The Internet is such great tool. It showed me pictures of stones exactly like the one I found in the treasure chest. I made a sketch of it:

The Vikings called it a *sólarsteinn*, which translates as "sunstone" in English. It's made of calcite, and it allowed sailors to navigate like some insects do—by seeing polarization patterns in the sky. The Internet told me that the early navigators used the stones to sail within accuracies of one degree. That's how they reached America first. Who needs Willows when you have the Internet? Who needs modern equipment when you've got the sun and a perfectly good stone?

Each time Jo called out directions to Phineas, the contractor, who I also watched easily through the sliding glass doors, glanced up. He was trying to repair our deck's railing, but he kept staring at Phineas, especially when Phin began circling the harvested corn with a burning stick of incense. If I were the contractor and didn't know Jo's and Phineas's personal stories, what they've lived through, what accomplishments and disappointments they've suffered, I'd also think that I was witnessing some raw mental decline. Especially because Phineas forgot his wig, so it was really obvious that he was an old guy dressed like an old woman. The contractor touched the cross around his neck and inched himself further away from Jo every time she yelled.

"Smoke zee base!" she'd yell to Phineas. The contractor would back off a little. "Tweest and *snap* zee cob off zee stalk." Phineas looked so happy blessing and harvesting corn, so it was a shame when the contractor ran away. I'll pay him anyway, poor fellow. Then he can be happy, too. And I think I would have been as happy as Phineas and Jo if my phone weren't ringing nonstop all morning. It was Allison.

I ignored her at first. Then I couldn't. I thought maybe she'd found Dad's pistol in the house and wanted it removed. I wouldn't blame her, but I just don't consider that an emergency. Then I started thinking that maybe Dad or Lil fell. If I didn't respond, I'd stink even more, so I decided to do the only thing a good son ought to do— just get up and go over there. So I did.

When I pulled up, Lil was outside watering her flowers. She looked happy. I waved, and she waved back as I stepped inside. Dad and Allison seemed to be upstairs. I heard water running up there in the tub. They sounded happy as well. I went up to greet them. At the top of the stairs, I called out to them.

"Hi—anyone home?"

"We're in here," said Allison.

I stepped up to the bathroom door. There was Dad, standing in the middle of the floor, Allison helping him into his clothes. He was wearing diapers.

"Tom, thanks for coming," said Allison as calmly as if Dad were wearing briefs. "I had to run out this morning for a box of absorbent products, so I tried your number a few times to let you know—"

"How dare you put diapers on my father!" I screamed.

Now, I'm not exactly sure what happened next. I remember raising other, similar concerns. I remember Allison shuffling me out of the bathroom rather gruffly. I remember phrases like "Who do you think you are?" coming out of my mouth—I think I really screamed that one. There were many others that are just now coming back to me.

So I thought it would help me to recap here because I got a little lost after that. I admit it. That I was lost. I remember tearing out of the house and jumping into my car. Before I knew it, I was driving around in circles outside of town and couldn't get out of the circles to come home. I kept coming back around to the same intersection whichever way I went, like a guy lost in the woods who keeps coming back to his own campsite debris and realizing he's gotten nowhere and gets that sinking feeling of utter vulnerability and self-loathing because he knows there is NO WAY OUT.

I guess if I were the cop who stopped me, I'd be concerned—I'm turning 50 soon, but I had the radio blaring and the windows down like a teenager. I was singing at the top of my lungs, and swerving the steering wheel to that tune *Starbaby*. You know, that oldie but goodie:

> *Well I've never been much for admitting things,*
> *That's why it's all so hard to say—*

But when you swerve the steering wheel, the car swerves as well, so the cop thought I'd been drinking.

That I'm head over heels in love with your kind of
insanity—

At first, I didn't see his lights flashing or hear that punchy POP! sound they make with their sirens when they want you to pull over. So naturally I didn't pull over. Then I did.

And if it please your highness on a sunny day
sometime
Can you take me ridin' babe I'll tell you what I'm
thinkin' 'bout you—

"May I see your license, sir?" he said as he leaned toward the window. He spoke loudly over the music, but I was in another sphere, like a Starbaby, cruising the universe high above the fray so as not to think about earthlings. I yelled back over the music.

"My father wears *diapers*!"

Starbaby—

The poor guy didn't know what to make of that. I didn't, either. But I kept experiencing the feeling that if I kept moving, time would never catch up with me, that it would slow right down to zero, and I'd never fall out of my exalted position among the stars, earthward into a pair of absorbent adult products to shit along with the common —old—man.

I've never been much good at keepin' a secret
Now it's easy for me to say—

The policeman made me do all those things I thought were only done back in Mayberry by Barney Fife when he stopped a bad driver, things like standing on one foot to see if I can do it. I also had to tip my head back, close my eyes, and touch my nose. But it didn't upset me. I knew I'd pass. Piece o' cake. I even did it dancing to the music—

> *That I'm head over heels shook up*
> *About the way that you fool with me—*

He insisted that I turn the music off. I turned it down instead. Then he asked what seemed to be the problem. I answered easily.

"It *seems* like my father was a tough, highly respected administrator of a major medical facility here in the city," I began. Mr. Cop was surprisingly interested, so I continued. "And it *seems* that he began humbly, like all of us, drooling and diapered. Now—he's come full circle, you know," I said. He was still so interested that I let it all pour out. I couldn't stop it, in fact.

"Allison told me that she needed absorbent products, a nice big box of them, and I said that my father would never shit on himself and she said he already does and I said he knows better and she said it's not a question of knowing he doesn't know and I said I can't take that where's my gun I'm gonna end it all at 55 and she ignored that and said I have to embrace it sooner or later and when I heard the word "embrace," I ran out to the car and took off and got lost, and when I came to this intersection for the seventh time with the oldies station blaring on the radio, on came *Starbaby*, by The Guess Who, but I wasn't really sure who, and all of a sudden, identity didn't seem as important as this moment, as being head over heels in love with my parents' kind of insanity, and maybe *that's what it means to embrace something!*" I cried. My radio was still playing.

Starbaby—

All I remember from that point on is the cop sitting in his car checking my identity—Guess Who?—from my license, and me leaning into his window singing at the top of my lungs right into his face. But he was a pretty cool guy and pretended it wasn't bothering him. After calling Mel at work to let her know, he escorted me home. By the time we got to the house, Mel had rushed home to meet us, and the harvest was in.

The policeman even complimented Phin on his dress.

PART THREE

I admit that the temper tantrum I threw about having to go back home after some recuperation at The Villa was out of place. Dr. White said I should rest after all, and that's what a villa is for. I wasn't myself after what Mel called my "Starbaby episode." It just made me mad, that's all. I know she was thinking of my well-being, even though she was about to explode into three people. I made her drop the word "episode." After that, she just called me her 'Starbaby.'"

When we arrived back home, she walked me to the front door. That confused me. We never use the front door when we're just casually coming and going.

"Honey, where're you going? Where are you going" I demanded. I waited at the side of the house, not budging.

"Tom, please come in zis way," she said. It took all of her persuading to get me to do a simple task like using the goddam front door. She finally gave up and lied.

"Jo has polished zee kitchen floor, so we cannot go in zat way—we must come in zee front," she said.

I sighed loudly. Then I stomped so belligerently around to the front that I didn't even catch Mel in her lie —Jo stopped polishing floors after her hip mishap. We walked up the front steps, and as we arrived at the door, it swung open on its own.

"Surprise!"

There was a crowd in my house. It was yelling. At me. Everything seemed out of place and in place at the same time. Mel grinned and turned to me.

"Happy birthday, my Tom!" She threw her arms around me and pulled me into a crowd that parted like the Red Sea. Balloons and glittery things like banners proclaimed that "50 HAPPENS." Someone put a plastic top hat on my head that I didn't know until later said "Chronologically Gifted" across the front of it. Deb blared vinyl records of ABBA. She laughed mischievously, and I gave her the biggest hug I'd never given her. Everyone broke out into applause, and Deb turned the music down for everyone to sing "Happy Birthday," even though it wasn't anywhere near cake time. I got all weepy. I thought my crying ruined the moment, but all it did was add to the festivities.

After the birthday song, people began wandering all over and patting me on the back and hugging me. On the dining room table was a little decorative fountain along with the birthday cake. It was a huge sheet cake created in the shape of a gun with the phrase "50's a Bang!" pouring like smoke out of the barrel. I'd never seen smoke made out of pure frosting before. People kept laughing and asking Deb why she had the cake made in the form of a pistol. She met my eyes with a grin and skillfully avoided answering.

Out in the back, manning both the grill and his beer, was Jack. He was sweating and smiling and flipping burgers, wearing a white chef's hat and apparel. Written on the front of his apron in big purple letters was "Carpe diem, baby." He looked up and saluted me with his greasy spatula. The woman dumping ice into the nearby cooler stood up. She was pretty and had blazing red hair. It was Jenna. I remembered her. I waved to them both.

Out on the deck was a huge, long table with a royal spread on it that Jo had made. Or more accurately, Jo had directed while Stephen, Jamie, Deb, and Phineas did all the cooking. They included every imaginable way to cook our corn à la French: breads, pâtés, veggie dishes, roasted corn with a remoulade side sauce, even a corn soufflé. People were at the table two and three times for helpings. I was so proud of our corn. I was so proud of Jo and Phineas.

I remember the whole affair coming at me like a dream, really. The minute I was done talking to one person, another would appear and slap me on the back or hug me. There were old friends, new friends, friends of friends, relatives of friends, and friends of relatives. I remember Lil talking to Andre's boyfriend. She kept saying "Wonderful!" so cheerfully, and when Allison got Dad up to dance, you couldn't even see that he was wearing adult diapers right there under his trousers.

Stephen and Jamie, who was almost as large with child as Mel, were there along with a young couple with a baby. I don't recall ever meeting them. Must have been their friends. Whenever a young couple arrived, they put their baby on the floor to crawl around. Pretty soon, my living room was a baby mosh pit. The kids who were big enough to run around were doing just that. Anyone older

282

was drinking. ABBA was going strong. People danced. It was The Romper Room for all ages, and for the first time in a long time, everything in the world was right.

When I was finally left alone, I looked around at the huge pile of presents in the corner—it was for me. The whole event was for me. And next to the pile was Mel, and next to Mel was her sister Nick, and next to Nick was Marla! My ex was sitting and chatting and laughing with the woman who had replaced her. Paranoia overwhelmed me for a moment, and I was sure there was a vast female conspiracy going on. I approached just as Mel's sister said something like "Incontinence just becomes part of the experience." All the women laughed at that. That made me want to walk away again, but the spectacle of Marla holding a baby prevented me from turning and running away: My ex *did* have a baby.

Her hair was long and she had lost weight. She was wearing a nice skirt made of some shiny material. I'd never seen her like that. She was carrying the baby in a brightly colored piece of long cloth draped over her shoulder and tied around her. I guess if Dr. White hadn't put me on that prescription tranquilizer, I would have said, "Hello, Marla, nice to see you," or something like that before simply reaching out and pulling on the cloth to see the kid inside.

I stood gaping. I'm sure it wasn't my most attractive moment, but she was the most beautiful baby in the world. Imported all the way from the East. Tibet? I forgot to ask. It didn't matter.

"Hello, Tom," Marla said. She smiled.

"Wow" was all that came out of me.

"Happy Birthday," she added.

"Thank you. Um. So. How did—?" I stammered.

She explained graciously. She had bravely navigated the labyrinth of international adoption after our split and didn't tell a soul. Except for her lover, who was also the baby's adopted parent at this point, I learned, and who happened to be sitting right next to her. She introduced me.

"Tom, this is my partner, Kathryn," she said.

I sure was happy to have taken that tranquilizer. I could feel it working at that moment. An inner buzz of controlled contentment numbed the wild jab of that introduction.

"Kathryn, nice to meet you," I said. "Congratulations." I then turned to Marla and hugged her. I whispered in her ear.

"I wish you all the best, Marlie." She knows I mean it when I say Marl*ie*. "Stephen knew already, didn't he?" I guessed. "He told me about your travels, but not about the adoption."

"I swore him and Jamie to secrecy until I got everything under control. Forgive them," she said. I would. "Kathryn and I had originally gone to that part of the world because we're interested in Eastern philosophy. I ended up taking a class—" I let her tell the story. When she was done, they both smiled at me meditatively.

"May I?" I asked. I put my arms out to take the baby. That sweet bundle looked right up at me when I held her. I know they say babies can't see yet when they're that small, but I know that somehow she saw me standing there admiring her. All of a sudden, she let rip the biggest little smile on the planet. I became racked with emotion. It hit me that everyone was having such a good time on my birthday. I realized that making them happy was the most honoring responsibility a person could have, and I really wanted to fulfill it for them, like a great big "Thank you—Love, Tom." Then I realized that the opposite is true, too, that they were the reason I was alive, the reason I haven't yet taken that gun to my head. But as soon as I smiled back at the little lady, Mel let out a raging howl.

Everyone stopped and looked. The children were terrified. Marla took the baby back, and I ran to Mel.

"Wait, honey," I whispered, "we're at a party." I know that was the wrong thing to say just then. She was already going down. I grabbed my phone and called for an ambulance, but at the same time, Jo lunged forward, lifted her cane in the air and yelled.

"Stand back, *enfants—je suis une* meedwife!"

At that, everyone backed away as if she were wielding magic power and not her cane. The women sprang into action, better organized than any military unit. As if having rehearsed, the mosh pit was cleared to make a home birthing chamber. Towels were brought in, Mel was made comfortable on the floor. Babies and older children and men and anyone not part of the squad were ushered out through the sliding glass doors. I remember catching a glimpse of Jack smiling and beckoning everyone with his spatula to come out just before the curtain was drawn.

Under Jo's direction, candles and incense were lit. Jamie was suddenly there with our shower curtain to place under Mel along with every blanket, pillow, and cushion we own, and Jo's midwifing kit—housed in one of the beat-up suitcases she'd arrived with but never opened—I'd always wondered what was in there—was brought down. Jo barked at me to fill all four of the hot water bottles with hot water. I wasn't going to argue.

Phineas and I helped Jo ease down onto some pillows and into position in front of Mel. I was shocked to find out that I was assigned the role of "doula." According to that Lamaze-y course we'd taken, I was supposed to be in the role of "coach" but it didn't seem like the right moment to be arguing terminology with Jo. The women backed off into a circle around us, and I felt on stage as Jo gave me a crash course.

"Doula help zee woman, Toma; meedwife attend zee *bébés*." I've always liked the French way Jo pronounces my name. It took on an extra resonance at that moment, so I easily did whatever she showed me, like kneeling down next to Mel, stroking her hair, and describing pleasant and encouraging things for her to concentrate on. Jo nodded in approval.

"Sweet peectures, Toma," she kept saying. It had seemed easy in our classes, but in the real moment, it was hard to do with Mel groaning and yelling out intermittently. At some moments it was terrifying, and even though I love Phineas, his making periodic announcements like "Knaves! More torches here!" every time Jo or Mel needed something just wasn't very reassuring. But he did finally settle into his role as assistant to Jo and as the only other male allowed in the room. He seemed to know exactly what he was doing. Jo must have prepped him.

The circle around us was silent and almost prayer-like. Mel said later that it was her "ring of support." During a calm moment, Mel whispered that she could "feel zeir energy," and it gave her strength. It gave me the creeps, especially when I noticed that someone had grabbed both purple teddies from upstairs and brought them into the circle. They were propped up like participants, their heads bent unnaturally forward from being stuffed up against the ceiling. But for the most part, I was engaged so completely with stroking Mel and coming up with "sweet pictures" to describe, pictures like running water and gliding dolphins, that I was able to ignore them pretty well.

Now, that dolphin thing was an inspired piece of luck. I don't know where I got it, but Mel liked it, and it made her smile when she wasn't screaming. I kept it going like an extended metaphor for birth.

"You can do it, honey!" I'd say. "Our twins are just happy-go-lucky dolphins who can easily slide all the way down the birth canal." I know that dolphins probably live in open waters, not canals, but the image of their soft, smooth, wet skin enabling them to glide effortlessly was just right at that moment. I even made dolphin noises. "I'm communicating with the babies via sonar," I said. I put my head to her belly, when she was facing forward, anyway. "They're saying they can't wait to slide down that warm slippery slope like a water park ride." I wished I hadn't said "warm." Despite all the eye-rolling from the women, Mel squeezed my hand.

I noticed at one point that the ambulance folks had arrived. They were kneeling down among the women in the circle as if they were relatives or close friends of the family, smiling and waiting there for my twins. I could tell that even they thought my dolphin noises were kind of funny and that Jo's terrific midwifery was wowing 'em.

I can't really say how long that all went on because all of a sudden my daughter's head popped out, just like that. And it did seem to really pop. Jo guided the rest of her entrance into this world, then did it all again for my next daughter. After that, there was no circle anymore, just women—and Phineas and I—swarming around while Jo performed the most amazing post-birthing techniques. She was massaging Mel and ordering the EMTs around. They did whatever she said. I noticed Phineas dutifully placing the ceramic bowl of placenta in the fridge. I have no idea what Jo did with it after that. Our corn was already harvested. I didn't ask.

Mel and I were finally baby-holding. It was miraculous. All the women were around us, baby-touching. After a while, we realized that we'd forgot all about the guests outside. Zoe accompanied me as I went with my two tiny twin girls in my arms to the sliding glass doors. She pulled back the curtain.

Everyone stopped and looked up, one by one. The guests closest to the house put down their paper plates or beer and started to draw up into a semicircle around the glass. It only took a few seconds for the others to follow. A few of the men, headed up by my son, were pacing empathetically, and one was smoking nervously as if it were his wife who was giving birth and not Mel—he finally stomped out his butt and looked up. The semicircle drew in tight. There was a hush and a moment of awe. All at once, everyone burst into applause, and Zoe barely had time to squeeze by me to slide the door open for them before they all heaved forward and poured inside like water through a floodgate.

From there, everything flowed like liquid via the happiness that babies bring. I'm starting to believe that there should be a mandatory birth at every funeral—loss would turn to hope before people's very eyes. Phineas was so happy that his face was tear-streamed the entire afternoon.

"His delights were dolphin-like, lords—she is delivered!" he kept repeating.

The EMTs strongly suggested that they take Mel and the babies in for all that follow-up her OBGYN ordered. Jo couldn't have cared less. She was not insulted at all. Her job was done. As I was holding our babies and Mel's hand and trying to keep up with the EMTs as they wheeled my wife horizontally out the front door, I peeked backward out the sliding doors to the deck.

Phineas was there with her. They were sitting on the love seat. Jo was leaning forward with one hand on her cane. In the other, she held her pipe to her mouth. Her head was tilted skyward just a bit. She puffed as she stared out over the horizon, and as the smoke trailed off in the breeze, she was done with just another everyday miracle.

.   .   .

The closest anyone can be to his parents is during "sandwich" time, I now realize. It's true. It's as if, when parents bring kids into the world, the kids are unruly and start right in looking forward, wanting to grow up and away from the parents, driving them crazy in the process. And even though the parents are cleaning the kids' backsides and feeding them, the little ingrates don't appreciate it until much later when the tables turn and they have to do the same for their parents. Then the parents start to drive the kids mad, and the kids are forced back toward the parents, where they start to accumulate some wisdom and realize that they, too, one day, may end up in adult diapers and need their own kids' help. We simultaneously get wiser but weaker—kinder, perhaps, but madder—and isn't that just about as humbling as it gets? Sandwich time may have a purpose after all.

These days, I go over to Phin's place regularly to check on him. I often find him in his dark cellar smoking his pipe. Once recently, I let myself in, went down to the basement, and sat at the bottom of his stairs. He didn't seem to see me at first. When he finally looked up, he spoke calmly.

"The play is marred," he said. "It goes not forward."

I didn't know what to say. I didn't want to respond at all, but I said, "Phin, please come up. Mel and Jo made a nice dinner—come over and join us." When I moved to take him gently by the arm, I was shocked by his explosion. He yanked away and began yelling things. Angry things.

"Toad-spotted traitor!" he cried. "The most infectious pestilence upon thee!" and "Thy lips rot off!" and those are just the ones I can remember. The more I tried to calm him down, the more he kept insisting, "A plague o' both your houses!" *Both* my houses. That hurt, but there was no time to be insulted. I had to finally admit that he'd been going downhill.

I bolted up the stairs and outside to get away from him so I could grab my phone and call 911, even though I didn't like the idea of calling 911 on him. I really was thinking more about his own safety—I was hoping they could give him something to calm him. From the basement window, I heard things being flung. They were crashing, and who knows where that lit pipe landed? I was desperate, so when I realized that my phone was not in my pocket, I ditched the idea of calling 911. Instead, I dug into my mental depths to pull up my high-school and college Shakespeare. I kneeled down on the concrete, leaned into the broken cellar window, and addressed him urgently.

"Who can control his fate, my liege?"

A sudden silence. Then, some shuffling footsteps. He came into the light at the window and peered up at me with his blue, blue eyes.

"One sees more devils than vast hell can hold," he said. I waited for a moment before answering.

"You are moved, Prince," I said. "Let us depart, I pray you, lest your displeasure should enlarge itself to wrathful terms." I was on a roll, so I concluded with, "You flow to great distraction. Come, my lord." He slowly came up the stairs and out into the sunlight. I led him over to our house and made sure he got a nice, hot dinner.

. .

Sometimes I drive all the way out to The Villa, even when we have no plans to stay there, to pick up Ol' Greg and take him out for a beer. He likes that. So do I. We never bring up the Viking find at all. Occasionally, I do think about how crazy things can get when you're not watching yourself. Like how a guy can, in a moment of crisis, let himself take direction for his life by "reading" under what feels like one thousand noon suns a "map" created by a mystical X-wielding Viking-turned-interior-designer. Because that's how people are supposed to navigate their lives, right? By the idea that pirates, or Vikings, or some goddamn Martians, or ancient maritime merchants, or anyone for that matter would leave a buried chest of valuables anywhere, and that two hopeful guys would find it hundreds of years later just to feel like fate put their little lives on the map of the broader world. It's all about perspective.

Someday, Stephen and the twins will inherit our find. Since Dr. Willows thought it was so interesting, I guess I could try to pawn it to him or to anyone with an intellectual investment in the various Ages of Exploration, but for now, I'm leaving it in my safe deposit box for future generations to decide what direction they'll take with it. Or from it.

Recently, I was helping Allison lift Dad into the medi-van. He uses a walker these days, but on bad days, he needs the wheelchair. As he sat, levitating slowly upward, he looked at me with the saddest embarrassment I've ever seen, and when the lift stopped, we were eye-to-eye. I peered into the mirror of his face, and strangely, I felt myself lifted as well.

"Daniel," he started—sometimes he calls me "Daniel" by mistake—"I feel stupid."

I paused for a moment.

"Stop calling my dad 'stupid,'" I said. The sadness in his eyes faded right away. I guess I said the right thing for once. I took his hand. We stayed like that for quite a while, and as we did, Allison waited off to the side, quietly and patiently. I'd forgotten she was even there. Then Dad spoke again, out of the blue, as he does lately.

"I'll call you," he said. It was an ironic statement, to be sure.

This morning, I decided to take a screwdriver to the chair lift and purposely throw it into a loop. That's why I'm sitting here on it, riding up and down, typing on my laptop, and enjoying a salt bagel with cream cheese with my coffee. It tastes so good.

Oop! I'm going up.

Mel is scooting around getting the last of the twins' things ready so that we can go to The Villa for the weekend. She said she doesn't mind when I feel the need to sit off to the side and work on my memoir. She knows I've been trying to get back to it. Apparently, she's been reading it since the first page. I wish I'd known that. She called it "delightful" and said I should try to publish it like famous people do with their memoirs, people like Dario Faux (Fo? Phoe?), but I don't know who he is.

Goin' doooown.

Oh. Mel just passed by on her way upstairs to grab beach towels, so I asked her. She said the guy's name was "Dario Fo" and it's spelled "F-O" and that he was a famous Italian director much loved in Paris. She said his memoir was delightful, too.

I've put together a poem dedicated to Dad that I'd like to include here. It's fashioned out of lines I've pulled from the plays of Shakespeare. Mel, if you get to this part, please don't laugh at me—it's inspired by none other than Phineas, of course, who taught me that nothing is ever as it seems:

> For do but stand upon the foaming shore,
> while we in your motion turn.
> If everyone knows us, and we know none,
> 'tis time, I think, to trudge, pack, and be gone.

Till then fair hope must hinder life's decay,
as time comes stealing on by night and day.
We know what we are—not what we may be.
Alas, our frailty is the cause, not we.

But hear me this: One time will owe another;
therefore, let us fly while we may fly.
For emulation hath a thousand suns—
like the sequel, I.

Is there comfort in madness? Probably there is. Perhaps that's why, after 80+ years on this crazed planet, the brain hurls itself headlong into it. Because it's comfortable. No need to keep a lid on it anymore because that's exhausting. So is it madness, then, if it's always been there?

Oh! Goooooin' up ...

Perhaps it's just the release we all crave. Maybe it's each person's final swan song, our last little bit of real humanity, slowly unfolding along with our depravity, like a flower. I remember a line from a song of my youth that talked about that. Flowers blooming like madness. Because that's exactly what madness does. Bloom.

Is it crazy to traverse the world with a fancy title like "Merchant Marine," sailing on a huge chunk of iron ripped from the earth in order to move goods and command the high seas, living free of responsibility? Or is it crazier to wander your own property, deeply enjoying the warmth of a sunny day, free of pants? Do footballs turn into chickens and fly away at the end zone? Is there really a galaxy out there with a thousand suns? Even if there isn't, or is, why do we buy it when it's written in a poem, or a book, or shown on a screen? Why do we embrace anything at all?

Goin' dooooown ...

The other night I had a dream that I was all dressed up, feeling pretty good, and Mel was decked out and beautiful as always. We were sitting in a large theater enjoying that stomping show. After a moment, I realized that the performers were all very elderly, even though they were great dancers. And stompers. They began making the strangest eye contact with me, and even though the theater was dark and there were hundreds of people in the audience, I remember thinking, "How can they even see me out here?" They also seemed to be moving as a well-oiled group toward the front of the stage. It was a big group.

Then suddenly, they were tossing away their garbage can tops and sticks and crates. They came bounding off the stage and were stampeding through the aisles toward me like a flood, pointing at me and yelling, "There he is! Get 'im!" I turned and ran, jumping over seats. There were no other audience members around all of a sudden—even Mel had disappeared. I stumbled out into an aisle, through the foyer, gasping for breath, and when I tripped out into the street, I hailed a cab and jumped in, shaking and traumatized.

I slammed the door and locked it just in time. In the next second, the elderly stompers were all around. They fell on the cab and blocked out the light. They started rocking the whole vehicle as if they were going to overturn it. I was screaming, "What're ya, *crazy*?" but then, I noticed the driver just sitting there, unruffled. He finally turned around to ask me, "Where to?" It was Jack.

Gooooin' up ...

During the Inquisition, individuals were given the choice between abjuring their beliefs and being burned at the stake. Ha! That's a no-brainer: Abjure! Abjure!

Lately, I've been zooming out mentally to satellite height to get the whole picture. I put my crosshairs on the problem and realized that when you zoom out, the thing you're looking at becomes the small dot in the middle of a bigger picture—the micro only makes sense within the macro. It has a place there. *Not sane* has a place somewhere, but we never zoom out far enough to locate it. I used to think, for example, that yoga and meditating and those kinds of things were BS, but I saw someone I thought was Miss Gilling on the streets of London, and even though she wasn't *my* Miss Gilling, I know I experienced her, and it was good.

Goin' dooown ...

There's that Norman Mailer quotation my undergrad American Lit professor had on the board on the very first day of class, the one about madness being "no more than the acceleration of thought." I remember thinking at the time that Norm was wrong, that it's a slowing down of the mind, but now I'm not sure: *If I only had a brain.*

A scarecrow sang that, remember.

Last night Daniel and I were floating again, but for the first time, we weren't in the water on that sand ridge or in a field. We weren't even on earth. We were out in space, wearing those astronaut helmets that are like dark mirrors, big, and rounded over the front of the head. I was staring, fascinated, into his helmet to watch myself in that cumbersome suit trying to communicate with him, to move around without gravity. As I did, his tether became detached from the mother ship. As I watched him slip

296

beyond my reach, all I could see was me, reflected back at myself on the front of his big helmet. I was thrashing about uselessly and in agony as he floated calmly backward, out and away into deep space.

Maybe life is the acceleration, and at the end, it intensifies just before release into nothing more than weightlessness, untethered, and compared to the here and now, the floating only seems like heaven.

Goin' up.

I'm really enjoying peeking out the landing window at the top of each lap to watch Mel help Joelle and Danielle put their beach toys into the hatchback. They've got that small children's canoe and matching oars we bought them, and they love using it down at the lake's beaches. As I watch my little girls with their mom out on the driveway, it occurs to me suddenly that the Vikings were not the merchant marines of their time—they were just plunderers.

But I'm not upset by that. In fact, I embrace it.

Acknowledgments

I am indebted first and foremost to my developmental editor, Catherine Adams of Inkslinger Editing, Inc. for reading my mind so brazenly; to Wyn Cooper, my copyeditor, for his attention to detail; to Angela Jernejcic for her gargantuan talent, insight, concept, and cover art; to Carol Ruzicka for bringing Tom's whims so playfully to life; to Andy Keane for his designful ideas and web support; to Katrina Kastberg for her elegant French; to Sidney Brown and Erin Ryan for tirelessly tracking the Star Baby; to David Hou for his legal advice and experience in the writer's life; to Kinney Group Creative, Inc. for doing what they do so superbly; to Keith Jackson and Martin Edic for their invaluable advice; to Paul Bloser and Michael Flanagan for sharing their experience; and to the memory of writer Susan Eckert, for her erudition, great reads, and simple friendship.

And of course, to Carole P. Bloser, Mary P. Flanagan, Jessie D. Peters, and Phyllis Pittman Kitt for propping up my life when it was sagging most.

About the Author

Phyllis Peters is an author and educator who holds degrees in music, literature, and education. Daughter of a writer of wry wit and phenomenal sensitivity, she has always been in love with the word. Her fiction and nonfiction have appeared in magazines, online publications, and literary journals such as *The Pinch*, *The Ampersand Review*, and *Munich Found*. Formally a reading teacher, she has also variously embodied the spirit of musician, waitress, filmmaker, rape crisis advocate, wanderer, and ingrate.